CHASING CYPRESS

By the Author

Changing Majors

Catching Feelings

Chasing Cypress

Visit us at www.boldstrokesbooks.com

CHASING CYPRESS

by

Ana Hartnett Reichardt

2023

CHASING CYPRESS
© 2023 By Ana Hartnett Reichardt. All Rights Reserved.

ISBN 13: 978-1-63679-323-8

This Trade Paperback Original Is Published By
Bold Strokes Books, Inc.
P.O. Box 249
Valley Falls, NY 12185

First Edition: February 2023

Credits
Editor: Barbara Ann Wright
Production Design: Stacia Seaman
Cover Design by Jeanine Henning

Acknowledgments

The vast agriculture industry and the different pockets of ideologies and methods within it have always fascinated me. I received a degree in fruit and vegetable production from Auburn University and was exposed to so many different characters with varying ideas about what the industry should look like. Agriculture seems to reflect the worst of us and sometimes the best of us. There is enough space in the industry for two people to want the exact same outcome while having opposite ideologies. This spawned the idea for my characters Maggie and Olivia.

That being said, I want to thank all of my horticulture professors for putting up with me. I promise I slacked off the least in your classes.

As always, a huge thanks to Rad and Sandy for the investment you make in us as authors. Your continued support is invaluable to me, and I truly can't thank you enough. None of us would be here without you.

Thank you to my editor, Barbara Ann Wright. Without you, my books would be letter smoothies that make no sense. But really, you make the editing process fun, and I always look forward to your hilarious comments. Most of all, you take the time to make me a better writer. Thank you.

This was not an easy book to write. As my deadline crept closer, life threw some obstacles in my way to make it just a little more difficult. When I'm down to the wire and need support the most, my wife, Sarah, is always there to keep me on track. Thank you for the endless support and patience. I love you.

One of my favorite things about being an author is the gorgeous sapphic writing community I gained access to when I started. Morgan, Kris, and Rivs, you already know what you mean to me. I can't imagine being on this journey without you. And a huge thanks to the veteran authors who have been so generous with their experience. Georgia Beers, Melissa Brayden, and Aurora Rey, thank you for taking the time to extend a hand to a newbie like me.

To my readers, you are what makes writing so special. Thank you.

This one is for my dad

CHAPTER ONE

L uis and I peek over our shoulders to make sure we're still alone in row thirty-one of the Granny Smiths as my brother, Aiden, does an impeccable impression of our father. He narrows his eyes at an imaginary apple and takes a bite of air, chewing thoughtfully, then nods. "That right there tastes like hard work and determination. What this family was built on," he says, matching almost perfectly our father's timbre and cadence. My laughter shakes loose all the tension in my shoulders after a long day of harvesting our orchard.

Luis chokes on his beer between eruptions of laughter and thumps his chest with a fist. "Every time," he coughs. "You get me every time with that impression. Spot on, man."

"Ready for Uncle Ward's?" Aiden asks.

Luis wipes the remnants of beer from his mustache. "Save it for next season. I'm heading back to camp. Don't forget to say bye before you guys leave for school tomorrow." I know he'd hang out with us longer, but I've heard his stomach growl twice, and he told us the chef is cooking lamb potpie for the pick crew tonight.

My brother and I reluctantly say good night to Luis, one of our best friends and—while he's here—an assistant manager on the orchard. He's been coming from Mexico every harvest since he was eighteen. He's twenty-three now and is one of the millions of migrant workers who come to the States for all kinds of harvests every year. Not many folks realize the entire livelihood of our country depends on migrant work. Without this influx of people, there would be no food on anyone's table. It's really that simple.

The same crew comes back every year, sometimes with new

faces replacing older folks who retire. We're able to retain the same group because we treat them how every employee should be treated. We provide free housing on our property, a chef to prepare meals, and an average pay of thirty dollars an hour. We treat our crew well, but it's the least they deserve. What we provide should be industry standard. Unfortunately, the abuse of migrant workers is a dark stain on agriculture in America. My family's role in this system is something I think a lot about. One day, I hope to help change these policies. It's one of the many things about the industry that needs fixing.

Luis disappears through the rows of apple trees. "I'm gonna miss him," I say.

Aiden chuckles and sips his beer. "We say the same thing every year."

"He's seriously the best. Can you please marry him? I want him to be my brother."

It's impossible to know how many times Aiden and I have sat together on the hood of our tractor, right in this very spot on the western face of our orchard. Up from the woods where we built our childhood kingdoms, fell out of trees, and in our later years, kissed pretty girls. As of recently, pretty boys for Aiden. I shift my weight an inch away from the butt-numbing hump in Paula's hood, closer to my little brother. Aiden named our tractor Paula when he was ten and going through an intense Paula Abdul phase.

He sighs. "Honestly, it makes me want to shit my pants just thinking about it." He's not talking about Luis; Aiden would marry him in a millisecond. He's talking about the fact that he hasn't come out to our father yet.

He scrunches his nose at the August stars, his number-four buzz cut refusing the breeze's attempt to play with it. His misty eyes match the deep brown of a healthy wetted soil, mineral flakes and all, the same as our dad's. This used to bother me because I inherited the brassy auburn hair and bird-shit-green eyes of our mom, who left us when Aiden was five and I was seven to "follow her heart" to Nashville. She hoped to break into the music scene, but as it turns out, no one there seemed to appreciate her playing as much as I do. *Did.* Now she's bartending and trying to figure out what to do with her life.

It hurts to think of her that way, struggling. But maybe she shouldn't have bailed.

"I know it's scary, but he won't care, Aid. I promise." I pat the pockets of my dusty Carhartts. "Can I borrow your knife? Left mine in the back barn when I was grabbing more beer."

He sighs and slides his new Benchmade from his pocket. "Fine, but be careful. I literally just got it, and it's still so perfect." I wedge his pretty knife under the cap of my beer as his hands hang suspended in the air. "Careful," he begs.

The bottle cap pops, and I fumble to snatch it before it falls off the hood to the ground. I shove it in my pocket and take a sip. The twinge in my neck prickles my nerves, so I crack it—four satisfying pops, two on each side—and hand Aiden his knife. "No one buys a knife like that just to keep it pretty," I say.

He shivers. "It's gross when you crack your neck like that. Gives me the creeps."

I shrug as he opens his own beer and grins, but after a few sips, he stares at the stars as if they can give him the courage to come out to our dad. I drape an arm over his shoulders and tug him into me.

"Aiden, listen to me. Dad won't care that you're gay. He literally could not have cared less when he found me kissing Sarah Freeman. He shrugged. The man *shrugged* and told me to lock the door next time." The memory of getting caught with the daughter of our church's outreach director makes me push a grin against the lip of my bottle. That first kiss was summertime-sweet from the Georgia Belles we devoured in the orchard. Her hands were sticky from the ripe peaches and stuck in my hair when she tried to run her fingers through it. We were thirteen doing what curious friends did on hot summer days. The memory shoots a pang through my chest. Sarah and I never stopped once we started. We were inseparable all through middle and high school.

Until she left.

"Sarah Freeman. Now that's a name I haven't heard in a minute," Aiden says.

"Yeah. No one really stays here, you know." I used to miss her. We were never officially together, always more friends than lovers. But friend or lover, it doesn't matter. They're both going to leave East Sparrow at some point. I love our town and our farm, but a part of me is jealous of them, Aiden and Sarah. They get to embark on life-changing travels and adventures while I'm here. *Always* here. I clear my throat.

"Anyway, I know we go to church and all, but he doesn't care about that stuff. He loves us and wants us to be happy. Sarah Freemans, boys, whatever."

He fingers the disintegrating Sweetwater label. "But it's different. I'm his son. I'm a farmer and—"

My chuckle cuts off his nonsense. "Okay, *farmer* is a stretch."

"Shut up, Maggie. I work hard, too."

"Look, Dad is the best person I know. He helped Mom go to Nashville because he wants the people he loves to be happy, not to be some macho farmer dude who represses his sexuality." I take another sip and listen to the crickets chirp while Aiden sits in silence. "You don't even want to be a farmer," I say softly, not sure if he's admitted this to himself yet. I feel for him. Not wanting to stay in the family business must feel like a whole other form of coming out. He has a big conversation ahead of him.

He groans and stares at me. "Don't you see how that makes this one thousand times worse? I'm his son. I'm supposed carry on the family business and—"

"What are you even saying?" I yank the bottle out of his hands and take two quick sips. "Sexists don't get beer."

He tugs it back and continues to pluck at the soggy label. "Come on. I didn't mean it like that. In, like, the general worldview, I'd be expected to be that person for the family. But I'm not, and I don't want to be."

The only reason he can even say those words is because he knows *I'm* that person. He knows he doesn't have to worry about carrying on our family farm, our family business, or our family legacy because I'm going to do it. I'm rooted to this place like our father and the two generations before him, but Aiden inherited our mom's traveling feet, and he's itching to run. He's only going to Alder University because it's free, thanks to generations of legacy and donations from our family.

Then he'll be free.

I'm not free. I flick the thought away like it's a thirsty mosquito. Even if lately, they've been sucking my blood and leaving itchy lingering welts, those thoughts don't matter. They don't matter because what I truly want is to take over our family business. Everything else is just college fever dreams and frivolity, a distraction from the real end goal.

Aiden shifts, and I return my focus to him. "I think we all knew you weren't going to be a farmer when you crashed Paula into that row of Pink Ladies the first time Dad let you drive. Besides, that's what I'm here for. It's what I want to do with my life." I'm the one who will hold this all together after my father retires.

I drop my head and watch a puddle of moonlight shimmer and pool in a small dent on the tractor's frame. Right above the tire. *My* small dent, not Aiden's. My stomach still drops when I think about my own collision with the end post of a new trellis system my dad, Uncle Ward, and I had just finished installing when I was sixteen. I'd rather throw myself into a volcano than ever disappoint my father like that again. He patted my shoulder and told me that every real farmer dents a tractor at some point, as if he was welcoming me to an elite inner circle. When my lips broke their tension and I felt my jaw relax, he tightened his grip and ducked his head, making sure we had eye contact. *First and last time. Am I understood?*

Yes, sir.

As loving as my father is, the farm and his family are two different things to him. If I want to take over when he retires, I better be damn sure my résumé is the strongest in the pile. I know I'm on the right trajectory, but I need to stay focused and committed, or he may make an outside hire. My father doesn't mince his words, and he told me this before I left for my freshman year.

No more mistakes like that stupid dent. No more bloodthirsty thoughts trying to distract me.

I shake off the memory and think about Aiden. I don't hold his adventurous spirit against him, but it's hard not to judge him for wanting to leave this piece of earth where generations of our family grew food, community, and love. Hyde Hill Farm is the second largest apple orchard in Georgia, not to mention the pie-perfect blueberries and peaches my dad planted after he and my mom got married. They were her favorites. This place is magic from its crops to its soul-shaking beauty. How could he—how could our mom—turn their backs on it? Turn their backs on me and my dad?

Maybe I do know.

The crackle of my dad's choppy voice on the walkie-talkie breaks the silence between us. "Y'all come get cleaned up. Uncle Ward popped burgers on the grill," he says.

I hop off the hood and snatch the walkie from the seat in a hurry. "Yes, sir."

Aiden climbs into the pick bin hooked to the back of the tractor. I wait for him to crouch into a safe position before I crank the engine and drive us through the peaches, past the Honeycrisps, and back to our house, admiring the falling night.

I adore the dark. Up here in the rolling hills of East Sparrow and the inky black of a country night, the stars are neck-achingly intoxicating, and the moon hangs fat and low. I park Paula in the back barn, and we walk to our house, an old one-story farmhouse that my dad renovated after my mom left. Now it looks like it could be on HGTV with its clean white exterior and oak shutters. Our house is beautiful, but it's the amber light glowing in the windows that I love the most.

The smell of burgers on the grill hits me at the same time as Aiden's shoulder as he walks past. "Come on," he says as he climbs the steps to the front porch and disappears through the door.

I shuffle my boots in the gravel and take one more moment before I follow him into the warmth.

❖

My dad pulls the bottle of Buffalo Trace from the liquor cabinet and pours two glasses, neat. Aiden and I exchange a quick grin as he dries the last dish and I slide the leftovers into the fridge. My dad has been drinking a fancy bottle of E.H. Taylor lately, but he wouldn't waste that on Uncle Ward. Not because he's selfish but because "He can't even appreciate the difference," my dad whispers as he grabs the glasses and strolls into the dining room with us on his heels.

Uncle Ward accepts the bourbon, dipping his head in thanks, and pulls a deck of cards from the old Western Cartridge Company ammunition box where we keep our poker chips and game supplies. My dad sits and scratches the graying whiskers on his square jaw. More gray permeates his jet-black hair every year, leaving him more distinguished looking than the last. He'll shave in the morning. As opposed to Ward, my dad likes to keep clean and neat.

Wax flows over the lips of countless candles and down the old wine and whiskey bottles that serve as holders. The candles provide the majority of our illumination in the dining room because Dad is sensitive to "fake light" once the sun goes down. If it's too bright, he rubs his temples and complains about it being "loud in here." But Aiden and I love it. It doesn't get much cozier than candle glow in an old farmhouse.

"Wyatt, you ready to get your ass kicked?" Uncle Ward asks, emphasizing his banter with a crisp shuffle and bridge, the glint in his eye hinting at something feral.

My dad takes a slow sip and closes his eyes. He's good at enjoying every little moment. Says that working as hard as we do makes everything a little sweeter: days off, cheap whiskey, a hot shower. "Whatever you say, Ward."

He's older than Ward by four years, and my grandparents died young, so when my dad inherited Hyde Hill Farm, he also inherited the responsibility of looking out for Ward. But my uncle isn't helpless. He's strong and handy with mechanics; there's not much around here he can't fix. But his biggest flex is his love for the farm and his love for us: me, Aiden, and my dad. He never married or had kids, and I think he sees us as his own. After my mom left, my dad let him build a small cabin on the edge of the property. And when I graduate from Alder, I'll build my cabin, too.

Aiden sits across from my dad, and I sit across from Uncle Ward, who deals. My brother's beard isn't as aggressive as Ward's or my dad's, but he still shaves, leaving his eternally pink cheeks bare. The kid always looks as if he just hopped out of a hot shower.

We've been playing Spades for as long as I can remember, and early on, my dad and I had to split as partners because we won every game. Now, he's stuck with Aiden, and I'm stuck with Uncle Ward. Aiden bids two. I've got the queen of spades and nothing else.

"Nil," I say. I try to maintain a poker face as I stare at our walnut table. It's full of nicks, scratches, and its fair share of mysterious dents. This table has been here since my great-grandfather, Walter Hyde, established Hyde Hill Farm in 1919, after he got home from the war. It's basically a museum piece, but you wouldn't guess it from how we treat it. Good thing we at least wax it, or it'd be dust at this point.

Uncle Ward sets down his glass a little too hard and wipes his whiskery lips with the back of his hand. His salt-and-pepper bangs hang heavy with grease above his bushy eyebrows. The thing about my uncle is it feels like he's always a sip away, or a bad day away, from completely losing it. I can see it in the glint in his eye, an ember just waiting for something to burn. I can see it in the pink shine of his cheeks. He's never done anything too wild, beyond some drunken nights or sketchy mechanical work, but there's always something looming in his energy. "Attagirl," he says.

I wink, trying not to think about why that phrase hits me in the gut like an underripe apple. I'm always fighting for respect, trying to prove my worth, but that fighting makes me feel as childish as Uncle Ward's words. It's a vicious cycle.

"Seven," my dad says.

"Jesus, Wyatt. Whatcha got over there? A fat stack of spades?"

My dad shrugs and sips his bourbon. "Reckon you're about to find out. What's your bid, Ward? Let's get this show on the road."

"Well, shit. If you're seven, and junior is two, I guess I'll take three and make it interesting."

We play to five hundred points and receive a thorough beatdown from my dad and Aiden. Not to be petty, but Uncle Ward burned five times. *Five times.* Not sure how we're supposed to win when he overbids fifty percent of his hands. I bite my lip to avoid saying this out loud, but the need to place blame square on his deserving shoulders nags me.

Uncle Ward gathers the cards and tucks them away in the box.

"Play that ace sooner next time, kiddo," he says, eyes narrowed as if he's dropping some epic knowledge on me. That does it. The *kiddo.*

"Well, dang, Uncle Ward. Hard to win when you overbid every hand," I say in exasperation, and Uncle Ward cocks his head, as if he still doesn't understand why we lost. "But you're right, that ace"—I shake my head and blow a piece of hair out of my face—"that ace sank us."

My father drops a hand on my shoulder as he passes behind my chair. "Being a sore loser may be your worst look, yet, Maggie. Your weakest, at least," he says in an even voice. His disapproval guts me. Filets me right open like a rainbow trout. I'm forever stuck in his crosshairs of boss and father, and it's safer to err on the side of interviewing with my future boss. I'm the only one in my family under this kind of pressure. Aiden and Uncle Ward don't have to constantly worry like me. Everything I do is part of the interview for my future job here. I straighten under his palm and try to change my sore attitude. I can be a little competitive.

Uncle Ward considers me with hesitation, seemingly lost in this interaction. I'm being a jerk. A childish ass. I sigh. "You're right, Uncle Ward. I should've played the ace off the rip and drained their spades. We'll get 'em next time. Good game, guys."

He smiles and fist bumps me across the table. "Damn straight, we will."

After cards, we retire to the porch, Dad and Ward with whiskey and Aiden and I with beer. Our dad doesn't care if we drink beer, but he only lets us have the hard stuff on special occasions until we turn twenty-one. I've already convinced him to let me use his allocation at Hendry's Liquor to buy a bottle of Weller Antique for my birthday in December.

"Well, y'all ready for school on Monday?" Uncle Ward asks as he rocks slowly in his chair, hands folded over his ever-growing beer belly.

Aiden chuckles and leans into my shoulder. "He makes it sound like we're going to middle school," he says.

Uncle Ward shakes his head. "It feels like just yesterday I was driving y'all, with your little lunch boxes and backpacks, to the little schoolyard, with your little bitty friends all running around like ants." He wiggles his fingers at us.

I hate when he makes me sound so juvenile in front of my dad, but the man is misty-eyed, so I let him get away with it.

My dad stops rocking and raises his glass. "And now Maggie's starting her junior year and Aiden his sophomore year. Here's to Alder University."

We all lift a glass and toast to what will hopefully be a great year.

"And one more thing," my dad says. "Y'all aren't allowed back here every weekend. I don't care that it's harvest. I didn't have kids to cut back on hiring other employees. Ward and I have been working the orchard our whole lives, and while you two are exceptional workers—"

"At least one of us is," I whisper to Aiden. He jabs me hard in the ribs, and to my mild horror, I yelp.

My dad clears his throat, and we both straighten, my cheeks hot from the shame of acting so immature. It's a hard balance to strike.

"As I was saying, your uncle and I have plenty of help and will not be requiring your assistance. Of course, you can come visit but sparingly. College is a special time in your lives, and I don't want y'all wasting it here. Any questions?"

"No, sir," we reply in unison. I appreciate what he's saying, but I also can't help but read between the lines, even if there's nothing there. What I hear is we are unnecessary to the functioning of this farm. We're *replaceable*.

"Good."

Though I want to be on the orchard as much as possible to build my experience and continue to prove that I'm the next leader of this business—and irreplaceable—I'm relieved to be banned from here for a while. I'm twenty. I want to get at least a bit of mayhem under my belt before I settle back into Hyde Hill Farm. Forever.

❖

I lie awake in my childhood bed the Saturday night before the drive to Alder. As much as I hem and haw about not wanting to miss our harvest and not wanting to leave my dad and Uncle Ward to handle everything themselves, the truth is that I adore Alder University. Not just the college or the campus or the fact that the main agriculture building is named Hyde Hall after my grandfather; the thing I love most is its complete otherness from East Sparrow. Even if it is just down the road, Alder is a big bright world of other people and different experiences. A world that I'll lose after I graduate. And though I would never admit this to Aiden or my father, I'm scared I'll be lonely. Scared I'll miss out on whatever life has to offer if I work on the farm.

But I can't have it all.

Ugh, stop being so childish. I kick the quilt off my feet and sigh. I love our farm, and I will love my life here. It's what I want. I just wish I had someone other than Dad and Ward to share my life with. That's it. That's gotta be it. I want a partner.

My phone lights up with a text from Tessa. She's been my roommate and best friend since the first day of freshman year, when she laughed at my muddy Blundstones and asked if I was expecting to wrestle pigs on my first day of class. I love her because she is so completely different than I am and because she's an amazing friend. I love her even though she's leaving after graduation for San Francisco. Almost as far away as possible. Another one here and gone.

Tessa: *Hey, farm girl. I'm excited to see you tomorrow. Bring apples.*

Me: *Hey, weird girl. We're fresh out. Condolences.*

Tessa: *If you were out of apples, would you combust? Surely, you wouldn't be able to maintain your human form without the fruit of your wood and leaf overlords.*

I grin and slide the brightness level of my phone to low, my eyes sore from the sharp light. *If you didn't have Ashley, would you melt into a pile of complicated sad girl? Surely, you wouldn't be able to maintain your human form without your much cooler better half.*

Hey, Maggie?

Yes?

Go fuck yourself.

My chest rumbles with chuckles as the dots on my phone bubble up and down.

Tessa: *I can't wait to see you, tomorrow. Drive safe.*

Me: *All forty-five minutes, I promise.*

Tessa will be my most painful loss when we graduate. Sorry, Aiden.

CHAPTER TWO

M y stomach tightens as I shift my old Ranger into second and crawl up the steep drive to Alder University. With every foot of elevation gained, the anticipation of the year lights the kindling inside me. The path flattens into the mouth of the university, crowned by the admissions building, the first building erected on campus and arguably the most beautiful with a now-defunct clock tower that reaches toward the sky like a cypress. We turn left to continue into the belly of campus.

I park in the small lot of the lower quad where Aiden lives in Grayson Hall. He hops off the cracked leather seat and snags his bag from the bed of the truck.

"See you for dinner?" I ask.

He pokes his head back through the window. "Yep. Text me when you want to go."

He turns toward the dorm, hitching his duffel up his broad shoulders. I wish he would have come out to our dad over the summer, but he's on his own journey. Nothing I can do about it but try to support him the best I can.

"Aiden," I call.

He whips around. "Yeah?"

"This year is going to the best yet. For both of us. I love you."

He half-smiles and nods. "Love you, Mags. See ya later."

I shift into gear, loop around the back of the student center to the main parking deck, and ditch my truck. Because we've kept our same rooms since freshman year, we don't have to move out and back in every summer. I grab the only bag I brought home and walk toward the upper quad and Magnolia Hall, my dorm. I chose Magnolia as my dorm preference on my paperwork freshman year because it was the only dorm named for a tree instead of a person. Best decision I ever made. Magnolia brought me Tessa, and Tessa brought us Ashley our sophomore year.

I pass through the lower quad and take the steps two at a time to the upper quad. Excitement burns in my chest when I reach the front door of Magnolia and swipe myself in. I glide up the stairs to the second floor and burst through the door of room 223.

Tessa and Ashley pull away from their make-out session in the middle of our dorm room.

"*Argh.* Come on. On day one? Day *one*? We have established rules, and they are meant to be adhered to," I whine, but I don't actually care. Nothing could dampen how thrilled I am to be back with my best friends. My bag slides off my shoulder onto my bed, which I am then tackled onto by Tessa and Ashley.

"Maggatron! You're an hour early. You can't blame us for what you walk into," Tessa says as she rolls off me and smooths her faded tie-dye crop top. It fails to cover her giant tattoo of the Chariot, her favorite tarot card. The color-blasted stallion stampedes out her waistband, up her hip, and into her shirt. She shakes her long brown curls and stretches her arms above her head. I avert my eyes, knowing from experience it's a toss-up if she'll accidentally flash me or not. A sight I have seen way too many times for my liking. She's beautiful and all. But to me, she's just…Tessa.

Ashley rolls off my other side and chuckles, her magnolia tattoo flexing as she shakes out her wrists. "We missed you, Maggie. And I promise, now that you're officially here, all previously agreed upon rules will be adhered to for the rest of the school year."

I fight the smile I feel stretching my lips and try to maintain my tough guy farce, crossed arms and all. "Including…"

Ashley pushes herself into a sitting position. "Including locking the door when things get steamy," she says.

"And no more making out in your bed," Tessa adds.

I wiggle out from between them. "*Ugh.* You guys are gross."

"Well, you were early," Tessa says again as she whips her hair into a topknot and grabs her wire-frame glasses from her desk. I will never be as hip as these girls. I love them.

"I missed you guys," I admit.

"We missed you more," Ashley says. She slides off my bed and unzips my duffel, taking a quick peek inside. "Even if you didn't bring us delicious fresh-picked apples."

I cross the room and fall onto Tessa's bed, taking pleasure in ruffling her mandala-sun blanket. "Come off it," I say. "All you guys ever eat are hot Cheetos."

"Because hot Cheetos fucking rock," Tessa says.

"What is she even good for if she doesn't bring us apples?" Ashley asks.

"Honestly, I have no idea," I say through a chuckle, but the thought lingers in my brain as Tessa crawls on the floor and searches under her bed. I swing my dangling legs out of her way.

"I think we all need to pick a card for the new semester," Tessa says when she emerges, her thick stack of tarot cards in hand.

"Good call," Ashley says. She tries to find the contraband "energy work" candle that Tessa hides in the wormhole of her desk drawer. Tessa claims it's for doing readings, but I know she likes to use it for mood lighting when Ashley comes over, which is a lot. Even though Ashley has a great house, she's at our dorm all the time. They mostly just go to her place to hook up, and even then, they often opt for the dorm room. After multiple walk-ins last year, I made them each sign a contract I created for our benefit: *The Ethics of Sex in a Shared Space, a Contract.* I've seen less of their bare butts since then.

Ashley finds the stubby candle and drops it in the pink Himalayan salt holder before lighting it and placing it on the ground in front of Tessa, who sits cross-legged on the carpet in the middle of the floor, pressing the deck to her chest. I used to make fun of her for being into crystals and tarot, but now, I get it. It's her form of meditation and setting intentions. No matter what cards we pull from that deck, the end result will be three friends sitting together and sharing their thoughts and feelings about the year to come.

"Come sit," she says, eyes closed, fingers pinning the cards to her tie-dye. Ashley and I join her on the carpet and stay quiet as she pulls the deck from her heart and runs her fingers over the edges of every card, shuffling here and there. Finally, she pulls a single card from the middle of the stack.

Tessa studies the full-figured woman with a crown of stars. "The Empress," she says.

Ashely grabs the card and traces the curves of the goddess-like woman. "Aw. Your year will be so full of abundance and warmth. You are clearly an empress. How do you feel about it?"

"I think the deck is telling me to lean into my femininity. Good things come when I'm loving and patient and strong." Tessa squeezes Ashley's knee. "Like abundance and warmth."

I smile at them over the small glow of the candle. It took me a while to act normal in these situations with Tessa, then with Tessa and Ashley. Since my mom left, I've gotten so many stupid comments and looks of pity from people thinking that because my family consists of three men and no women, I am anemic in tenderness. As if a man is incapable of running a loving household. My family is plenty warm. Even so, tarot readings, thoughts and feelings all the time, and low to minimal physical boundaries are something I had to get used to. And I really only share that part of myself with Tessa and Ashley.

They got to me when I was a freshman, before Tessa had all these plans to move away to California. All these plans to rip herself out of my life. I know, it's dramatic to be so torn up about it. Everyone disperses all over the world after graduation. But because I know I'm staying where I've always been, it feels like everyone is leaving me.

Ashley pulls the King of Pentacles.

"That's good, right?" I ask.

Tessa nods and squeezes Ashley's shoulder. "Maybe this is the year for Alder Queer Fellowship. You gotta channel all your badass leadership skills and release your inner king."

Ashley is an officer of AQF, an organization that she helped form as a freshman. Getting recognized by the university is at the top of their agenda, along with securing basic protections for the LGBTQ+ population of Alder. She lets her head fall back and chuckles. "About damn time. Let's all keep our fingers crossed. Plus, it'd be nice to put that on my résumé when I'm hunting for jobs in Cali."

I snap my attention to her. "Wait. What? You're going, too? I thought…"

Ashley grimaces and pats my ankle. "What did you think?"

What *did* I think? Ashley and Tessa are in love. They're partners. Why would it not occur to me that she would go with Tessa to California? Maybe I was hoping the connections she's made professionally through AQF would root her here or somewhere close, like Atlanta, where she's from. I glance at our forest-green walls covered in Tessa's Tibetan prayer flags and Grateful Dead bears and my prints of trunk dissections and plant anatomy. A tsunami of sadness crashes over me. It's all slipping through my fingers so fast. Soon enough, I'll be alone.

Again.

"Margaret," Tessa says.

I clear my throat. "Damnit, Tessa. My name's not Margaret." She knows my name's not Margaret. She just says it either to piss me off or to get my attention. My name is Maggie. I bring my Social Security card to my first day of class, in case I get a stubborn professor who doesn't believe me. But I'm only in ag classes at this point, and all of the professors know me or my dad or knew my grandpa. They know my name. Half of it's on the building.

"Margaret is in her feelings," she whispers to Ashley.

"I'm not gonna miss you at all," I say.

Ashley nods and whispers back to Tessa, "Aw. Margaret is sad that I'm joining you in California."

"I hate you both."

"Your feelings are valid, and we will miss you, too. But we have two whole years left. And who knows? California is the plan right now, but two years is a long time. Things could change," Tessa says.

Ashley hands me the deck. I stare daggers at both of them for a beat longer, then turn my attention to the cards. I don't believe these cards hold any power, but just in case, I take my time with them and try to touch every card, like Tessa. I close my eyes and ask the deck what the new school year will bring into my life. My fingers stop at the edge of a card that pokes out from the rest. I pluck it and flip it.

"Two of Cups," I say.

Tessa and Ashley exchange a look, and I'm pretty sure I catch a wink in there.

Ashley considers me, her blue eyes sparkling. "Junior year is going to be a very good year for you, Mags," she says. The corners of Tessa's lips are pinned to her cheeks in a goofy smile.

"Let me guess. This year will bring me an abundance of friendship, straight As, and all the money in the world?"

They both shake their heads. "Even better," Ashley says.

"This year will bring you love," Tessa says.

The card depicts two chalices with a pair of matching roses. I guess it's pretty obvious it signifies love and relationships, but I'm not feeling very hopeful for either. How can I, when I can't even keep a friend in North Georgia?

"Well, I guess we'll see about that," I say with all the melancholy of Eeyore.

Tessa rolls her eyes. "You know, you being so stubborn about staying in East Sparrow is the same exact thing as everyone else being stubborn about their own dreams, whether those lead them to California or Europe or Atlanta. No one is leaving you, Maggie. They're just following themselves. So buck up, and let's see what happens. Okay?"

I hold her brown eyes and nod. She's completely right.

"You know," Ashley chimes in, "I really think your deck may be magic." She takes the Two of Cups from my hands and lays it on her open palm as if to weigh it, then hands it back to me to put away with the others.

"Everything has a little magic," Tessa says with a wink, and Ashley looks at her like she's her real-life empress.

I clear my throat and push to my feet. I'd like very much to have a break from their sickeningly perfect romance, but who am I kidding? I want to be around them all the time. Even if they are a painful underscore of my lack of romantic options. "I'm going to meet Aiden at the dining hall for dinner. Want to join?"

"I wanna see Aiden. Of course we want to join," Tessa says.

"Hell, yeah. Let's go."

When we arrive at the dining hall, a buzz of excitement reverberates against the stone walls. The hall isn't full, just vibing with the palpable energy of the handful of students who are scattered about its tables. We spot Aiden and his roommate, Scott, four tables down and join them after we buy dinner.

"Baby Brother Aiden. Or should I say Prince Hyde?" Tessa says as we approach their table. She messes up his neatly styled hair. "And Scott, hello to you, too."

Aiden drops his fork with a sigh and rockets his hands to his hair in an attempt to smooth it, not that it can go too far out of place in its current crop. "Come on, Tessa. Why do you always have to mess with me? Hey, Ash."

Tessa lowers herself on the bench next to him. "Because I don't have a little brother, so there's all these pent-up interactions I never got to have with said little brother, and now, you get to receive all of my older-sister attention."

Ashley laughs. "Lucky you," she says to Aiden.

He finishes smoothing his hair and groans.

"How was your summer, Scott?" I ask. He is to Aiden as Tessa is to me. They were suitemates as freshmen and decided to be roommates this year. My heart swells knowing that my brother has someone like him. Scott is the only person he has come out to besides me, Ashley, and Tessa, and he could not have been more loving and supportive.

Scott briefly closes his eyes, and a warm grin stretches over his lips. "It was one of the best. We spent most of the days out on the lake swimming, tubing, and fishing. And my older brother came home to visit for two weeks. It was awesome."

"Sounds like a great summer," I say.

"So, Aid," Tessa starts, "did you, uh, you know..." She dips her head in what I know is an attempt to ask if he came out to our dad with her eyes, but he stares at her in confusion. "You know. Did you tell your dad about this..." She leans over the table, and like a magnet, Ashley bends to meet her lips in a quick kiss.

Aiden rolls his eyes. Which is progress. Last year, he would have tugged on Tessa's arm to get her to stop and search over his shoulder for the gay police. Progress.

"Not yet," he admits.

"No rush, Aid. You'll get there when you get there," Ashley says.

"She's right. There's no rush," Scott says.

❖

As soon as we say good-bye and walk out into the night, Tessa whips around to face me and Ashley. "Holy shit, y'all. They're together," she says.

Ashley and I look at each other in confusion. "Excuse me?" I say.

"You guys couldn't see it because you were across the table, but when Scott said it was okay to take his time, he squeezed Aiden's knee. And fucking *lingered*."

"Oh, wow. Yeah, they're totally together. Guys don't platonically squeeze other guys' knees. I mean, they should be able to, but they don't," Ashley says.

I shake my head. I know Aiden is gay, but Scott? He hasn't pinged my gaydar at all. "That doesn't mean anything. Scott doesn't strike me as gay." Everything I know of him from last year screams youth minister with trophy wife. *Oh wait.* Youth minister with trophy wife does sound pretty gay.

They both cross their arms and stare. "Oh yeah, Mags? And do you want to stand here, God as our witness, and describe to us what a queer man should look like?" Tessa asks.

I stare at them. "This feels like a trap."

Ashley sighs and loops her arm through mine to pull me toward Magnolia Hall, Tessa following a step behind. "Of course it's a trap. We don't know about Scott, but we'll see. It'd be nice if Aiden had someone to explore with," she says.

I laugh. "He's done plenty of exploring."

"They're hot together," Tessa says from behind us.

I gag at the thought of Aiden in any way that even hints at sexual. But I would love them together, too, if that's what Tessa means. Scott has this calm, sweet demeanor that balances out Aiden's hyper personality, but for some reason, in my most selfish of hearts, I feel annoyed. I feel annoyed that Aiden gets to be whisked away on this adventure of love and not have to stress about where it will take him. He doesn't have the constant knowledge encapsulating him in concrete that he has to go home after graduation, and whoever he is with has to sign off on it.

He's free. And maybe has found someone.

Everyone but me.

CHAPTER THREE

M onday's alarm finds me on the wrong side of the bed. For a girl who grew up waking at dawn on the farm, early mornings don't normally bother me, but this seven fifteen is feeling a whole lot like four fifteen. I slide out of bed in an exhausted blob and pile myself into the shower, hoping the water will help to wake me. Today is the first day of class, and I have an excited knot tightening in my gut. Maybe there will be someone who captures my attention. Though, all of my classes are higher-level agriculture courses, and the odds of a new face in the crowd is low. Like, next-to-zero low.

I dress in my go-to outfit; a flannel, my nice pair of brown Blundstones—which aren't caked in mud, thank you very much—and fitted jeans with my pocketknife clipped discreetly inside the waistband. As I'm grabbing my bag to leave, I pinch Tessa's blanketed toes.

"*Psst*, Tessa. It's quarter to eight. You slept through your alarms."

For how intense her major is, Tessa never seems harried or worried about classes, much less getting to them in time. Some people don't have to try that hard. And for Tessa, microbiology just makes sense in her brain. It's her passion. She already set up her microscope and laid out her box of fresh slides for the semester, always collecting a bit of lake water or soil or culturing the bacteria from our doorknob. She lets me use her microscope occasionally but only under her intense supervision. I like to look at plant cells when she's feeling generous.

She groans. "Mm-hmm. Okay, okay. You don't have to yell."

"I'm literally whispering." I give her toes one more squeeze and leave.

The day is bright, and campus is brimming with excited students walking to their first classes of the semester. Freshmen stick out like city folks on a horse with their campus maps spread in front of their faces and their crisp Alder U T-shirts. I blame it on my harsh wake-up this morning, but they're striking a nerve. Everyone is just visiting. They come from Knoxville, Nashville, Asheville, gawk at the drip-castle buildings and mountains, snag a diploma, then disappear to whichever "ville" they came from.

But I didn't come from a "ville." I'm a townie from East Sparrow, and Alder University is my backyard. My great-grandfather was the first of our family to attend college here, and my grandfather helped to establish the agriculture department. I buy a coffee on my way to class and sip it as I stand in front of Hyde Hall. I try to let go of my bad attitude with every sip and, instead, enjoy the sight of my family's legacy. The front lawn is small but neatly planted with native bushes and trees and is bisected by wide stairs leading to the double-doored mouth of the building. Flowers pop in bright yellow and pink in front of the gray stone building. It's gorgeous. I can't help the pride that straightens my posture when I look at Hyde Hall.

As I pull open the door, someone runs into my backpack, jabbing the tip of my water bottle into my ribs. "Watch where you're going," I mumble, gripping the tender spot on my back. I turn, still holding the door half-open, to find a girl I've never seen before. Or at least, I think I've never seen her before, but there's something about her that gives me the sense that I know her. That I've *known* her.

She takes a quick step back and touches her fingertips to her forehead, a delicate blush peeking out the neckline of her purple shirt. "I'm so sorry. I thought you were moving a little faster than you were, and I looked down for a second, and now, here I am, rambling the lamest of apologies."

I pull my eyes from tracking the blush as it slides up her neck and into her cheeks like a slow flow of lava. I step inside the building and nod for her to follow so we can clear the doorway. She considers me with watery blue eyes. Blue eyes that I want to soak in. The kind of blue that may drown me. The sleepy downward pull of them matches the sinking curve of her mouth. The angles allude to something earthy and soulful, the same way Uncle Ward's eyes hint at something untamed and wild. I stay quiet, caught off guard by how affected I am by this person.

She pushes some blond hair out of her face with a ring-clad hand. So many rings; fat rings, skinny rings, gold rings, rings with gemstones. This girl doesn't seem to belong here. I peg her as English Lit or some major like that, full of ethereal things that I can't wrap my hands around the way I can the trunk of a tree or the handle of pruning shears.

"Anyway, sorry for the little collision."

Right. The collision. Her gaze wanders to the brick wall that holds the portraits of all the deans and department heads over the years. Alder is *really* into portraits. Maybe, one day, I'll add to the small ranks of women's portraits on these walls, continuing the Hyde legacy but in a slightly different way.

She nods toward the wall. "A little unnerving, right? Always a bunch of old guys welcoming you into every building on campus."

I should speak at some point. "And the spittoon." My words coast from my mouth in a vast breath, as if I lost my ability to pump oxygen when I met this girl, and I just started breathing again. I clear my throat, praying my larynx doesn't fail me. "I mean, there's probably *not* a bunch of spittoons welcoming you into the other buildings on campus." She quirks a brow, and I continue to babble because I am clearly brilliant at talking to beautiful women. "Other buildings, which I assume you frequent because you don't look familiar to me." *Shit. Pure shit.*

She stays quiet, brow still raised and the corner of her mouth tugging up in a half grin. Probably because she thinks I'm ridiculous. *I don't even know what I'm trying to say at this point.*

"Um…" I point over her shoulder to the notoriously disgusting water fountain in the foyer. "It's not a real spittoon."

She follows my point and finds the defunct hunk of metal, its basin plastered with a layer of black gunk, like the floor of a swamp, formed by years of ag students using it for their dip spit. The janitorial crew threw in the towel a couple years ago and refused to continue cleaning it. Instead, they hung a sign above the fountain that reads, *this is not a spittoon*, and wiped their hands of it. The sign is just ironic at this point.

"Oh," she says. "So there are actually zero spittoons." Her eyes crinkle, and she chuckles under her breath. At me, I'm sure.

I exhale and smile, relaxing into the interaction. "Well, when you say it like that, it's way less exciting."

She nods and captures a bit of lip under her teeth, and a speck of her baby pink lipstick clings to the white of her enamel.

I want to know this girl. "I'm Maggie Hyde."

Her eyes dart back to the wall of portraits, surely finding my grandfather's and his nameplate, *Wesley Hyde*. Her lips part, and she directs her pouty eyes back at me. I catch her look me up and down and feel an instant tug in my gut, a tug that pulls me a step closer. She holds out her hand. "All right, Maggie Hyde. I'm Olivia Cypress."

I take her hand and hold her gaze, soaking in every moment of being connected to Olivia Cypress. Her shirt hits right above her waistband, allowing a sliver of creamy skin to peek at me, and I do my best to not drop her gaze, even though the tightness of her jeans hints at the curves begging to overflow them.

"Your name," I start but lose the nerve to finish telling her how beautiful it is. How lucky she is to be named after such a spectacular tree.

She tilts her head a degree and grins, the upward turn of her lip pointing to an elegant beauty mark above the corner of her mouth. "*Your* name," she counters, and makes a show of looking me up and down. "Maggie *Hyde…*"

I nod, wondering if she's going to continue with her thought or leave me hanging, like I just did to her.

She sighs. "Well, I should really get to class. Nice to meet you, Maggie."

The abrupt end to our conversation disappoints me, but I suppose she's right. Class is about to begin. "Nice to meet you." She walks down the hall, throwing a smile over her shoulder as she disappears into the flow of students, and I kick myself for not asking her number.

It takes forever for my feet to come back to life and carry me to Dr. Young's class. His classroom is the same as it always has been: plants lazily trailing down walls, hazy sunlight flooding through the grimy stacked windows, and the scent of his millionth cup of coffee mixed with wet earth. With plants respiring and cuttings rooting in makeshift greenhouses, the classrooms in the ag building are always humid. It's a welcome, familiar warmth.

He looks up from the whiteboard and smiles his goofy smile when I walk in. "Maggie. How's your dad doing? How's harvest?"

I reciprocate his fist bump and take a sip of my coffee. Dr. Young was in class with my father back in the day and, as my dad tells it, had a giant platonic crush on him. Following him around labs, through the greenhouses, trying to partner with him for everything. His fondness for my father has only grown over the years with everything my dad has done for the Ag Department, like his father before him. "Hey, Dr. Young. He's doing well. He and Ward made us promise not to come home to help with harvest, so you'll have to give him a call and get the scoop yourself because as of last Saturday, I'm unemployed until summer."

He nods with enthusiasm and pushes his gold, wire-frame glasses up his bumpy nose. It's funny how his glasses are the same as Tessa's, yet on him, they only accentuate his older age. "He's a good one, your father."

I smile. "Yes, sir."

"All right. Go on and take your seat, and we'll get this show on the road."

I turn toward the rest of the class and find an empty chair at one of the lab tables near the back of the room. As I'm walking to my seat, I hear someone smother a coughed *suck-up*. I find the owner of the muffled cough one table over. It's Olivia, her down-turned eyes crinkled in a smile. When she catches my gaze, she offers a playful wink, which stirs the coffee in my stomach into an acidic vortex. I slide into my chair, shaking my head, but return her wink with a smile and a wave. Olivia Cypress is in my Sustainable Tree Fruit Production class. *Interesting.*

Laura, whom I've shared almost every class with since freshman year, plops down next to me. We exchange a few pleasantries about our summer and settle back into our comfortable companionship. We don't often hang out outside of class, but she has been a welcome constant in my life at Alder since day one. Her dream is to help establish community gardens in under-resourced neighborhoods. I wish her luck and hope that she succeeds, but I don't think gardening will do much to fix food inaccessibility. Unfortunately, it's baked into our society, thanks to the terrible consequences of redlining. And passing the buck from the government, to the farmers, to the under-resourced communities doesn't seem fair to me. Rich communities aren't tasked with growing their food in neighborhood gardens, and vulnerable communities shouldn't be either.

Everyone should have access to fresh food.

The only way for Laura to cut to the root of food deserts is to get into policy and try to repair that damage. But Laura's never asked my opinion, and maybe gardens would be a relief for those communities. But they sure aren't the cure.

Dr. Young finishes with his computer and snags a clipboard from his desk. "Welcome, everyone. It would appear I know all of you, except for…" His squints at the clipboard. "Ms. Cypress?"

Olivia doesn't flinch at all the eyes turning toward her. She stands, raises her hand, and smiles. "Yes, sir. That's me."

Dr. Young gives her a quick once-over. She stands tall—for her short stature—with a bright smile under the scrutiny of a bunch of strangers in their dirty boots and Dickies. She stands out in the best way, but she stands out.

"It looks like you are auditing this class, is that correct?"

She nods. "Yes, sir."

"Do you have your textbooks and required course materials?"

"I"—Olivia plops her green backpack on the table and shuffles through folders and stray papers—"I swear I packed them this morning." She gives up, crushing the loose papers in her bag with the irrelevant binders and folders. "Must have left them on my desk. Sorry, Dr. Young."

My cheeks burn for her and the stark contradiction of her calm confidence and chaotic school habits. To me, Olivia Cypress appears to be one big contradiction.

Dr. Young swallows, his eyes seemingly searching hers for some sign of belonging. Just like I am. He clears his throat in the most obtrusive and dominating way. "And you feel confident you'll be able to participate during labs and keep up with the other students? This is a high-level horticulture course that has prerequisites. Though I assume someone gave you an all clear if you made it to my roll call." He taps the old clipboard.

She takes a moment to compose herself before she responds. "Yes, Dr. Young. I understand. I spoke with Dr. Petrova at the end of last semester, and we came up with a summer study plan to prepare me for this course," she says without a tremble in her voice or a fidget in her hands. She has completely recovered from her textbook blunder and is now the definition of poised. Except…didn't I make her ramble when she ran into me?

Dr. Young looks displeased but tosses the clipboard on his desk in defeat. "Well, then. Welcome, Olivia." She nods and takes her seat. I glance at her from the side of my eye and catch her take a breath as she flips open a blank notebook. "All right, class," Dr. Young continues. "This course is listed as Sustainable Tree Fruit Production, but we are going to be learning about high-yield farming and how to scale production."

Most of the class nods along, but Olivia stills, peers over her shoulder, and catches me watching her. *What the hell?* she mouths, eyes wide, as if the class topic change horrifies her. My cheeks burn from being caught watching, but I give her a measly shrug in response.

I know why Dr. Young is changing the course. This room is filled with students like me, and we don't need to learn how to grow one organic peach tree in our nana's backyard. We need to learn how to run a farm in order to make a living and feed our communities. While Olivia is annoyed, I'm excited. Hopefully, this course will arm me with tools to grow the family business when I graduate.

It's hard to care that my new quasi-friend won't be learning how to do whatever it is she's here to do when there are people to feed. Communities to sustain. I assume that she doesn't get it. That her interest doesn't break the border of her own property. When her head cocks to the side, and she narrows her eyes at me, I swallow hard and drop my gaze to my hands.

"Excuse me, Dr. Young," Olivia says, hand raised. I am, again, completely mortified for her.

Dr. Young's irritation is thinly veiled as he pushes his glasses up his nose and sighs. "Yes?"

She closes her notebook and taps her eraser against her chin before she responds. "I understand the needs of the class may be different than mine, but couldn't one argue that sustainable production is the crux of scaling output? What does it matter if you hit higher yields while stripping your soil of nutrients required to grow your crop?"

Holy shit. My cheeks are on fire, and I wring my hands in discomfort. Olivia is one of the boldest people I have ever met. Dr. Young lets his head drop back as he laughs at her, the boys in our class chuckling along. While I want to side with him, I also have the strong urge to dump his coffee down his shirt and turn a pot of soil over his head. How dare he laugh at a student like that? How dare he laugh at *her* like that?

"It's called fertilizer, Ms. Cypress. Try to keep up," he says.

Her brows meet in a vee as she digests his curt response. "Actually—"

"Actually, Olivia, as much as we all have the utmost interest in whatever it is you have to say, it's time to begin class." He bends to make a note on his roll call and snaps the tip of his pencil. "Aw heck, Maggie, can you give me a hand, please?" Dr. Young holds up his pencil and fingers the leadless tip. "They got rid of my broken sharpener but never brought me a replacement."

My cheeks warm under the gazes of my fellow students. Of course I'm proud of my family's legacy, but dang, Dr. Young doesn't have to constantly paste the label of teacher's pet on me. I'm still trying to look good in front of the new girl. The new girl who just got completely roasted by the guy. "Yes, sir." I walk to the front of our class and try to imitate Olivia's confidence by standing tall and moving with determination, but the only reason I'm feeling self-conscious is because of her. She's an outsider in my domain—a super attractive outsider—and I can feel her eyes on me.

Dr. Young hands me his pencil, and I pull out my Blue Ridge Zancudo, my trusty pocketknife that was two hundred dollars cheaper than Aiden's. It's tough enough to cut through stubborn bark but delicate enough to slice perfectly along vascular cambium for whip grafts. It gets the job done without me having to worry about keeping it nice and pretty. The best knife isn't always the most expensive.

With a couple angled swipes down the tip of his pencil, I shave it back to a nice point, then drop to my knees and scoop the shavings, like a good little teacher's pet. Olivia raises a dark blond brow and stares me down as I walk back to my seat. She puts me on edge. Puts me on a stage of bright lights, and she's in the audience, arms crossed, judging me. I can't even sort out if I like her attention.

Our first class consists of going over the syllabus for the semester and general chatting about everyone's summer and updates on their farms. When Dr. Young ends class early, Olivia sidles up to my table, eyes scanning my notebook, my bag, my hands. "You just carry around that knife, chomping at the bit for any opportunity to whip it out, don't you?" She flips her hair over one shoulder, baring soft-looking skin and the hollow of her neck. "I knew many wannabe country boys in high school who did the exact same thing."

I know she's teasing me, but her joke only solidifies my assumption that she indeed does not belong here. I slide my notebook in my bag and take my time zipping it before I turn to face her. She looks at me with a cool challenge in her eyes. I think this girl may be flirting with me, so I take a chance and rib her back. It's been a while since I've had fun banter with someone.

"If that's why you think I carry a pocketknife, you may be a little out of your league in this class." I suck in the corner of my lip to keep from chuckling and breaking character. Though I would miss seeing Olivia around, I kind of mean what I said. *Why is she here?*

She drops a hand on my shoulder, and my tooth sinks painfully into my lip as I try to stay steady under her touch.

"Margaret—"

"Maggie. My name is Maggie."

"*Maggie.* I am not going to take over a family farm, like most of our class seems to be planning on. My last name isn't written in stone on this building. But I think you'll find me quite motivated to get what I want out of these classes because just like you, I care."

"What do you care about?"

Her fingers slip to my bicep, and I instinctively flex under her grip. She grins at my self-conscious pop of muscle and squeezes. "That's the vaguest question that has ever been posed to me."

"You just said—"

"Kidding. I'm kidding, Maggie," she says and releases me.

I close my eyes and shake my head, taking myself back through the last minute of our conversation. "Wait, *classes*? Plural? You mean, you're in more than one ag class?"

She nods, and before I can pose one of my million follow-up questions, she asks, "Do you have a class right now?"

"I…what?"

"Class. Do you have class right now, or are you free?"

My blood runs thick and hot in my veins. I feel it push through every inch of my body as Olivia looks at me, speaks to me, stands within three feet of me. I've never felt so unsure of myself around somebody. Have never felt so off-balance. I struggle to stabilize and swallow a dry gulp of nerves, hoping to find some sort of homeostasis with her soon.

"No," I finally say.

She scrunches her nose, drawing my eyes to the pale freckles that kiss the top of it. Only a handful. Five, maybe. "It wasn't a yes or no question. No, you don't have a class? Or no, you're not free?"

"No, class. Yes, free." I'm not free. I'm stuck in the prison of my own awkwardness. It's hot in here. I tug at my collar, horrified to feel how warm and damp my skin is.

"Grab a quick breakfast with me?"

My mouth dries as I stare into those eyes. Everything about her vibe is earthy and watery, except for that blazing passion that is beginning to show itself. "Sure," I manage to say out of the deep end of my attraction to her.

She chuckles and squeezes my elbow. "Wow, Maggie. Don't sound *too* excited about it."

"I didn't—"

"I'm kidding. Come on."

She tugs me through the mostly empty classroom by my sleeve, and I offer Dr. Young a quick wave as I follow in the wake of her subtle, earthy scent. It's not a specific scent but one that encompasses. It's nerve-racking and exciting to have someone crash into my life with enough force and flare to make me curious for what the next day will bring. Hell, what the next hour will bring. For a girl whose life is basically spoken for, a little spice, a little Olivia, sharpens the colors in my world.

❖

We sit at one of the long oak tables with our trays of eggs and toast. Well, no eggs for Olivia. Her plate looks sad with only a banana and toast with maple syrup. *Weird.* "Your hair is, like, this super intricate shade of reddish, brownish, goldish," she says.

I consider her food choices as I take a sip of orange juice. "Everyone says it's auburn."

"Yes. Auburn, sure. But, like, at the same time, so much more than auburn." She points her fork at me. "I see different reds and—" She reels back her hand, knocking her water bottle into a threatening wobble. I stare at it, thinking it will steady itself, but Olivia tries to grab it and punches it over. Water floods the table, and I jump off the bench before it can cascade into my lap.

"Shit," I mutter as I reach for the useless little napkins on our trays.

Olivia swings her legs over the bench. "I am so sorry. I'm not normally so clumsy." She shakes her head. "Well, that's a lie. I'm actually pretty clumsy. I'll be right back with some towels."

She disappears, and I'm left in a wave of shock. Not so much about the spilled water—that's not a big deal—but the way I feel like I have to be on my toes around Olivia makes me feel hot and cold. Like, being friends with her could be exciting, or it could be scary. Either way, it's clear it will be messy.

Olivia returns and wipes a rag over the lake she created on our table. "Didn't want to waste any more paper, but you'd think I was asking for the nuclear codes trying to get this bad boy." She holds up the saturated rag. "These must be kitchen-crew gold."

I shrug.

Once all has been dried and Olivia returns the rag, she sits and looks at me, waiting until she catches my eye to speak. "I'm sorry about that. I really don't mean to be such a mess." She waves a hand over the table, maintaining a safe distance from any liquid. "These mishaps are attracted to me. They kind of find me. Like a magnet."

"They...find you?" This is strange. What I'm hearing Olivia say is that she isn't careful, and careful is a choice. Being grounded is a choice.

"They find me." She shrugs, the shoulder of her shirt slipping an inch, making me not care so much about her calamities. "Anyway, about your hair. Auburn, red, or gold, who cares? You're beautiful."

Her attention on my physical features makes me forget how to drink from a cup, and I dribble pulpy orange juice down my chin, feeling a little clumsy myself. I snatch my napkin and wipe my chin dry, clearing my throat. "Why toast and maple syrup? They have pancakes, you know?" I don't mean for it to sound judgmental. I'm just trying to steer her gaze away from my own clumsiness. Away from the very obvious fact that she caused it.

She cuts the soggy toast and looks at me as if she was waiting for this moment. "I'm vegan. Pancakes, at least dining hall pancakes, have eggs, milk, and butter. That's a hard no for me."

"Oh." I don't know any vegans, but from what I can tell, she matches the stereotype in my head perfectly. "Why? If you don't mind me asking. You're the first vegan I've met."

She drops her utensils and stares. "The meat and dairy industries are literally pure evil, Maggie. Cows are intelligent, sentient beings who form bonds and interact with social complexity." Her chest rises and falls as if she's giving a nation-saving speech. "I mean, it's incredible the cruelty that we turn a blind eye to just because cows and pigs don't happen to be the animals we choose to keep inside our homes." She shakes her head. "We continually rape dairy cows to keep them pregnant and steal their calves, killing the males and entering the females into the same torturous existence. That's where your butter and cheese come from." My body stiffens at her gruesome depictions as she eyes my buttered toast. "Not to mention, beef production is ruining the earth. Not only from the methane and emissions of the whole production supply chain but the deforestation, as well."

Her words trigger every defense mechanism in my brain, but I keep my mouth shut. I know from growing up with Uncle Ward that there's no changing folk's minds on something they care about. After one too many political arguments with my uncle, my dad finally told me to let it go, that I'm only beating my head against a wall for no reason because Uncle Ward finds his identity in his right-wing political views, and when someone puts that kind of identity into something, they aren't about to be swayed.

I may be liberal, but I also have a reasonable head on my shoulders, and it annoys me when rich Democrats have no concept of what issues we face as small-town folks and what it takes to feed our nation. Our *entire* nation, not just the people who can shop at Whole Paychecks. It's easy for Olivia to spout all of this vegan idealism because she's well-off, I assume, and goes to a fancy college and has access to fresh food. But what if someone lives in a food desert? Are they going to feed their family a vegan diet to save the cows? No. Are they going to feed their family a vegan diet to save the world? No.

People save themselves. It's in our blood. Like every other organism on our planet. It's nature.

After taking another bite of toast, she narrows her eyes as if studying every feature of my face. "You've got this whole femme-farm-girl look down to a T. Like, I totally believe that you could take any of the guys in our class and do all the hard farm work"—she swings her bent arm back and forth in what I assume is her impersonation of hard work or maybe a march—"but then, I get the vibe that I could take you." She winks.

That does it; I'm right back on the Olivia train. My scrambled eggs roil in the cauldron of my belly, and my freckles burn on my cheeks like little stovetop burners. There is no way I am reading this wrong. Olivia is clearly flirting with me, and I'm loving it. One day, we'll talk about food accessibility and veganism, but right now, I'm focused on the challenge in her eyes.

"I, um, yeah…" I sputter.

"Yeah, what?"

I harvest some confidence, pass a hand over my being, and attempt some of Olivia's signature humor. "Only girls are *taking* this."

She bites her smile as she watches me make a fool of myself. "That's quite forward, Maggie. I was talking about fighting. Not about taking you to bed."

I drop my hand on the table and sink into myself with embarrassment. What the hell am I doing? I apparently don't know the steps to this dance, but she has me so riled—

Her hand covers mine, and she ducks to look at me while I try to hide my burning cheeks. "I'm just kidding." She continues to work through her toast, licking a spot of maple syrup from her bottom lip. Who is this person, and why is she in my class, and how is she so magnetic? "Good to know, though," she adds.

I ignore the flames licking my cheeks and how her words slither over my skin, tickling me to my toes. "Why are you in my class if you're not a horticulture major?"

She takes a moment to adjust to my one-eighty. "*Your* class? Should I be calling you Dr. Hyde?"

Every time I take a step away from her, she pulls me right back flush against her. "You can call me anything you want."

"Well, Marg—"

"Except for that."

She grins, and I can tell she loves this, knowing pretty much exactly who I am while she remains a mystery girl who is crashing my class. While she pushes around the food on her plate, I wonder if her lip would still taste sweet from the syrup.

"I'm auditing Economic Entomology and of course, our not very sustainable Sustainable Tree Fruit Production class." She shakes her head and continues. "I'm a finance major. But I want to learn more about sustainable farming. I want to be able to grow most of my own food, and since I'm vegan, it shouldn't be too hard to accomplish one day. Plus, my other bigger dreams. I want my senior year work thesis to be agriculture related, and hopefully, somewhere cool." She takes a sip from her Nalgene, plastered with countless stickers of the places I assume she's been. "Somewhere international. I'd love to be abroad for a semester."

Figures. She's itching to get out of this place like everyone else. Not only that, but she's a garden-variety hobby gardener who is crashing my education with all of her judgments and impossible ideals. Of course she's disappointed with Dr. Young changing the content of our class.

"So this is just for fun? These classes require a lot, you know." *A lot of what? Think, Maggie.* "There's loads of chemistry, microbiology, and…bugs. In Economic Entomology, you have to dissect a cockroach." I pump my head back and forth like I dropped some huge bomb of knowledge and changed her mind about taking these courses.

She wipes her hands and pushes away her plate. "Let's see." She counts on her fingers. "I took microbiology last year, I aced Chem One as a freshman, and I'm basically a math whiz. What was the last thing you said?"

"Bugs."

She points at me. "Bugs, yes. The last offensive thing you insinuated I wouldn't be able to handle. I'm from the South. I don't know if there's any better prerequisite to dealing with bugs than that."

I swallow. "I didn't mean to—"

"No? You weren't trying to belittle my intelligence? Just trying to chase me away from the College of Agriculture? Why, because I'm not going to inherit a fully functional and profitable farm that I didn't have to help establish?"

My cheeks burn, and I push my plate out of the way, too. "I work hard for the orchard," I say. "I earned my position."

Her smile drips with sarcasm as she shakes her head. "You fell into agriculture. All you had to do was say yes and be willing. Why can't you accept that I care about the same thing as you and just as much as you care about it? We may have a different knowledge base, but I took summer classes—a full summer semester that I had to pay for myself—so I could find the availability in my schedule to attend upper-level horticulture classes that I won't even receive credit for. So no, this isn't *just for fun*. I plan to change the world." She shrugs as if her plan to change the world is as simple as her plan to grab an iced coffee after class.

I chuckle, and though I instantly regret being such a condescending ass, I double down. "You plan to change the world, huh? What, with your organic backyard garden?"

She raises a brow that makes me shift on the bench. "Yes. I do. But if you would have been a little more curious about me and a lot less of a dickface, you would have listened when I said I also have *bigger* dreams than my garden. I plan to create a crop-adaptable guidebook that will help farmers streamline the process of going organic while maintaining or beating their previous profit margins. And I want to turn the whole world vegan, obviously."

Now, I really laugh at her. I mean a full, chest-heaving belly laugh. She stares at me as if I may be the most repulsive creature she has ever had the displeasure of crossing paths with. I don't even care at this point. I'm basically Dr. Young. Reckon I shot myself in the foot a long time ago, and the more Olivia talks about her granola dreams, the more I realize I wouldn't want to date her anyway.

I wipe the laughter from my eyes. "You know 'organic' is a load of crap, right? It's just a giant marketing scam so people have to pay more for the same food while farmers have to jump through stupid hoops and pay stupid marketing people for a stupid little green circle that says 'organic.'"

She presses both palms against the table. "It is not a load of crap. Are you serious? Being certified organic is one of the best things you can do for your farm and the environment."

I shake my head. "No, being certified organic doesn't mean anything besides you can't spray certain pesticides or fungicides that are synthetically made. Have you heard of Rotenone?"

She shakes her head.

"It was used as an organic pesticide. Everyone thought it'd be harmless since it's derived from plants, but now it's banned and only used to kill fish because it's believed to be a risk factor for Parkinson's. Organic pesticides and herbicides can be just as dangerous while often being less effective, meaning they have to be sprayed more than conventional products. But, hey, it's labeled 'organic.' So who cares?"

She scoffs, and I grip the edge of the table, leaning closer toward her.

"And why does everyone assume that farmers who aren't certified organic are just dumping pesticides into waterways and poisoning consumers? These things are so delicate and intricate and far from black and white. Or organic versus nonorganic. We use Integrated Pest Management, for crying out loud. We care," I say.

We stare at each other in gridlock. Olivia's gaze is electric, as if there could be a man-of-war hiding in the depths of her ocean eyes. I begin to wonder how loud we've been talking and if the whole dining hall is listening to me fight with this beautiful, frustrating stranger. I release my death grip on the edge of the table. Enough is enough. I can practically feel my father's disappointment in my juvenile outburst. My loss of control.

"I gotta go," I say.

"Really? Just like that? We were having such a pleasant discussion."

Yes. Just like that. This entire conversation is annoying me, and I need to get some fresh air before I explode even more. I pick up my tray and stand. "I have class."

She stares at me as I step over the bench, my mind racing with so many more points I want to make in this argument before I leave. I close my eyes, drop my head back, and sigh. One more. One more, then I'll drop Olivia from my orbit and continue with my life as it was.

"I'm not saying that some organic farms aren't great and some conventional farms aren't terrible. I know both are true. But organic farms can have horrible practices and get away with it because that label shields them. They can spray as much as they want as long as it's an organic product. I think there should be a different way of labeling farming practices."

What I don't expect to see when I open my eyes is Olivia grinning. Not smirking or mocking me, like I did to her, oh, I don't know, *a million times*, but full-on grinning. The coursing currents in her eyes have quelled, and she waits a moment before responding.

"It was lovely to meet you," she says.

I blink. "You, too?"

"Especially in such an *organic* way." She grabs her backpack and tray. "See you on Wednesday, Margaret."

I watch her hips sway as she walks away.

"It's Maggie," I say to no one.

CHAPTER FOUR

S he's one of those people who you meet, and it's like, they instantly solve the Rubik's Cube of your entire personality, but you're still a confused mess about who they are and what they want from you. Also, she thinks she knows everything about horticulture and the world. And let me tell you, she doesn't." I groan.

Tessa, Ashley, and Aiden stare at me and nod, all of their mouths partially full. The basement of Magnolia is empty. Because it's only the first week of classes, there's not much work or studying to be done, so we brought our dinner back to the dorm to have a quiet catch-up.

Ashley swallows first and runs a hand through her platinum locks. "So what you're saying is, this chick is hot, and she's crawled under your skin?"

"She's the bane of—" The nearest wall-mounted candle flickers and extinguishes, leaving us in an even cozier, dimly lit basement.

"That just happened twice in Grayson. They need to change out all these old electric candles. Time for some recessed lighting, am I right?" Aiden says.

Everyone ignores him.

"She's scorching hot, apparently," Tessa says.

I sigh and push my chair onto its back legs, my feet perched on the edge of the table. "That is so far from relevant," I say.

"Is it, though?" Aiden chimes in. "How I see it, you wouldn't have gone through all the effort to have breakfast with her and yell at her about organic farming if she didn't have some kind of hook in you already."

"Your kin is absolutely right," Tessa says. "You supposedly hate this girl, and yet, she's the only thing you've talked about all night."

"I don't *hate* her. I don't hate her at all." I sigh and let my front chair legs hit the ground. "Olivia is one of the most magnetic women I've ever met. She has these sleepy eyes that can turn electric in a second."

"But…" Aiden says.

"Look, her eagerness about veganism and organic farming is one thing. But if I'm being honest about my attraction to her, and why it's a terrible idea to even be thinking about her in that way, what bothers me the most is she seems flighty, you know?"

"Flighty as in, not totally present?" Ashley asks.

"Well, yeah, she's super clumsy. But I mean, she seems like the kind of girl who will just travel around forever and not settle into one place or one life. Like, she'd be the person who sleeps in some farmer's barn in Ireland for a month to 'gain the experience.' She has to do a work internship for a semester next year, and she wants to do it somewhere international. And that is the farthest thing from what I'm looking for in someone. I don't know. She's kinda hippie."

"Kind of hippie, huh? And that's a bad thing? Your roommates are queer tarot-reading stoners, and you like us fine," Tessa says.

I take a bite of cheesy pizza and pluck at the stringy mozzarella stretching from my mouth. I chew enough to speak. "First of all, I only have one roommate."

Ashley throws a dry crust at my chest. "Rude."

I wipe the crumby debris form my shirt. "And second, that's my point exactly. Y'all are too cool and adventurous to stay in Georgia. You gotta run all the way across the country to California." I point at them. "So you know, everyone in San Francisco is cool. You're going to be small fish in a big pond. But here"—I press a finger against the table—"here, you'll always be the coolest, biggest fish."

Tessa breaks into laughter, and Aiden shakes his head in embarrassment.

Ashley narrows her eyes. "Hold up. Can you backtrack a little? Did you say her name is Olivia?"

"Yeah. Olivia Cypress." Ashley and Tessa exchange a knowing look. "Oh, dear God. What? Do you know her or something?" I ask, afraid of the answer.

"Yeah, I know Olivia. She's one of my best friends outside of you guys. I should have known that's who you were talking about, but she didn't say which classes she was auditing," Ashley says, a huge grin spreading over her lips. "And I'm pretty baked. This is excellent. You have nothing to worry about with her. She's an awesome person."

"Oh, yeah. I love Olivia. She has this super chill vibe, but she's deep, too," Tessa says, nodding.

"What? How did…why haven't I met her before?" I ask at the same time I notice the red haze in Ashley's eyes. And Tessa's…

"Hmm." Ashley taps her nails against her teeth and looks at Tessa, trying to bite back her giggles. "I guess when we hang out, it's mostly here in Magnolia, and I'm focused on you guys. I met her in my accounting class, and we had finance together after that. We hit it off. But after one kiss, we knew there was no romance between us. Just an awesome friendship."

"You've kissed her?" I ask, my fingers pressing into my temple. I don't know why I'm so shocked or why this bothers me so much. Probably because *I* want to kiss her, and I wish I'd met her sooner.

Whoa. If my automatic thought is that I want to kiss Olivia Cypress and I wish I'd met her earlier, I'm in trouble. Also, the fact that Ashley has a whole best friend who I've never heard of is mind blowing.

"Well, yeah. Are you okay, Mags?"

"I can't believe she's, like, your best friend. And I've never heard of her," I say.

"You probably have heard of her. It just didn't stand out like it will now because you didn't have a crush on her. Also, she's been at almost every party I've had, so y'all have definitely crossed paths."

I blow out a deep breath. *How did I not notice her?* "I wish I'd known."

Aiden leans over to Tessa and Ashley and stage whispers, "Holy shit, Maggie has a huge crush on this Olivia chick."

"Not as big as your crush on Scott," I say.

"Shut up, Maggie."

"Where is Scott, anyway?" Tessa asks.

Aiden stands, wiping the pizza grease from his hands in his dirty napkin. "He's at some dumb church sing-along thing."

My family is religious, and we have always gone to church on Sundays. I'm not trying to piss off the big guy when we have trees planted in this earth, but we all drew our own lines there, just Mass. None of us care for the frills. "Why are you running away so fast, then? Your boyfriend is otherwise occupied," I say.

He drops his bag in the chair and stares me down. Then gives a similar, less heated stare to Ashley and Tessa. "Look, y'all are my friends, and I get that this is playful banter, but"—he scans the room and drops his voice—"I'm not out yet. And maybe y'all can look back and remember what it's like. Scott is terrified, okay? We're figuring it out, but it's so goddamn stressful. Can we pump the brakes on the Scott and Aiden jokes, please?"

We look around the table, finding the guilt in each other's faces. It's easy to be so cavalier when you're already passed that phase of queerness, and it's too easy to make fun of Aiden for literally everything.

We mumble our apologies, and Ashley wraps him in a bear hug. "Sometimes we forget what this time in our lives was like," she says.

"Or maybe we all blocked it from our memories," Tessa says.

Aiden throws his arms around Ashley and pulls her in tighter. When I catch his eyes watering, my heart completely breaks for him and the stress he's under. I love him fiercely. I stand at the same time as Tessa, and we pile ourselves onto the group hug, giggles emanating from the core. We send Aiden and Ashley on their way, and Tessa and I head upstairs to bed.

"How are your classes looking so far?" I ask.

Tessa pulls back her covers and crawls into her old twin bed. She's the kind of girl who makes this dorm room feel small. Her being, personality, and potential are immense, and to watch her roll around on that tiny plastic mattress makes no sense in my brain, but I try to burn the scene in my memory for when she's famously successful and living in a mansion in California. She once slept in this small room with me.

"Pretty solid. My Organic Chemistry TA is so hot, Maggie. She's got this eyebrow piercing that is fire, and she wears that white lab coat like it's her job. I mean, it is her job. But damn, that girl is one sexy scientist." I'm a little struck as I crawl into bed and Tessa talks about this other girl. This other girl who isn't Ashley. "I swear to God she's flirting with me, too," she says.

My mind trips on the conversation, and I have no idea how to respond. I stay quiet while I try to think of an appropriate response. "Um, I don't mean to be a jerk, but you already have a pretty bomb girlfriend, and I've never heard you talk about other women like this before."

Tessa perches next to me on my mattress. Her hands fidget in her lap, and she exudes an unsteady energy that is uncharacteristic. She normally emanates the calmness of still lake water.

"Are you okay? Did you guys break up or something?"

She draws in a deep breath and looks at me. "I'm sorry. I know I'm acting strange and am probably giving off some weird vibes. This is just harder to tell you than I was expecting, which is so dumb because it definitely shouldn't be."

My heart rate picks up, and my brain turns over every possible thing she could be talking about. But I can't come up with a single one she would be stressed to tell me. She's already told me she wants to move across the country, she's out, and she and Ashley haven't broken up. And I don't think she's pregnant. I pull her hyper hand into my lap.

"Tessa. You can't tell me anything worse than the fact that you'll abandon me in two years. Lay it on me."

She sighs and squeezes my hand. "I hate how much attention I've put on this by semi-freaking out about telling you because it isn't a big deal. It's honestly super chill, but I guess coming out is always a little unnerving."

"Coming out? What are—"

"Ashley and I are non-monogamous. We can sleep with other people within a set parameter of boundaries that we've agreed upon. And my hot TA, Jocelyn, is within those parameters, so technically, I have a shot with her."

I take my time to absorb this information before I respond. Non-monogamy is something I have zero experience with or exposure to, and I know the words you hear after coming out—no matter what form—are weighty. They matter.

"Wow. Thanks for sharing that with me." I squeeze her hand while I struggle to come up with more words. I don't want to berate her with questions or reiterate why any healthy relationship she wants to have is perfect and beautiful because she's in it. She knows all of these things, and it's patronizing.

"I am so in love with Ashley. I know what we have, and I don't want others to cheapen it because of their own narrow views on love and traditional relationships. It's our business, and I don't feel the need to tell the whole world about it, just those who it pertains to and our close friends."

"Yeah. I get it. I felt that way when I came out. Just because I won't be in a relationship that matches societal norms doesn't mean it won't be amazing and special. If not more special. It sounds like you and Ashley are trusting and honoring each other. I'm really happy for you guys."

"Thanks, Mags. I love you."

"I love you, too."

She drops my hand. "Because I love you, I'm going to be blunt."

"Okay." My concern draws out the single word.

"You're being a complete dumbass about Olivia. So she's vegan and cares about the world? *You* care about the world. So she wears fun crop tops and rings and forgot her materials on her first day of class? That doesn't mean she's going to abandon everyone and everything. If you weren't such a defensive shithead, you'd see that she's the complete opposite of that. You've known the girl all of one day, and I can vouch for her. Olivia is dope."

"That was a little harsh." I know she's right. I can feel this armor forming over myself when I talk to Olivia or about Olivia. I can feel myself looking for every little reason to hate her and every bit of evidence that she may like me.

It's not that I'm not self-aware. She reminds me of my mom. All the bright and shining beauty of Olivia reminds me of what I loved most about her—the fire and the passion and the fun—but those are the things that stole her away from us. The passion for music led her to Nashville, the fire for life led her to a life without kids, and the fun... well, I don't know if she has much fun anymore.

"It's the truth. I know you, and I know you're drawing all these similarities between Olivia and your mom. It's not fair. Stop it."

"I know. I know, okay?"

"Okay."

❖

I'm early to Dr. Young's class on Wednesday, and after he talks my ear off about my father and the benefits of planting more cold-hardy cultivars, I sink into the same seat I took on Monday. Only a few other students have arrived when I pull out my phone and text my dad. *Dr. Young fangirls over you so hard.*

My dad is typically slow to respond, but he pings me back within a couple minutes. *Harold is a good guy. Be nice to him. And stop texting in class.*

Me: *He's fine, I guess.*

Dad: *Tell him the harvest party will be on November first this year, and we'd love to have him and his family join us for the festivities.*

Me: *Okay, but it's your fault if class is delayed by half an hour because he won't shut up about you.*

Dad: *Enough, Maggie.*

Me: *Yes, sir. I'll tell him now.*

Dad: *Thank you. I love you.*

Me: *Love you.*

I walk between the lab tables to the front of the classroom where Dr. Young scribbles some notes on high-volume propagation on the whiteboard, the curve of his letters sloppy and sharp at the same time.

"Excuse me, Dr. Young?"

He turns, and his face lights up. "Maggie, yes? What can I do for you?"

When I open my mouth to invite him to our harvest party, Olivia walks through the door in all of her ethereal glory. She smiles as she brushes past me, and I turn to watch as she walks straight to my table and pulls out the chair next to mine.

"Maggie?" Dr. Young asks.

"Yes. Sorry." I got wildly distracted by the wildly attractive girl who chose the seat right next to mine. "My father wanted me to make sure you know our harvest party will be on November first this year, and he hopes that you and your family will be able to come."

He pushes his glasses up his nose and breaks into a giant smile. "Oh, of course. Tell him we wouldn't miss it for the world. Our kids love coming to Hyde Hill Farm. I'll text Melanie right now to tell her to mark our calendar."

"Okay. Great. I'll let my dad know."

Dr. Young nods and pulls his phone from his front pocket. I take a fortifying breath and walk back to my table. Olivia scribbles something in her notebook, her hair falling over her bowed head, and her ring-clad fist moving over the paper in a determined slide. I pull out my chair quietly, not wanting to disturb her, hoping somehow, she won't notice me sitting next to her the entire class period.

She drops her pencil and runs a hand through her hair, stretching over the back of her chair. I don't mean to look, but when her crop top rides up even more, her exposed skin lassoes my gaze. I snap my attention to the front of the class when she straightens and adjusts her shirt.

I clear my throat and remember Tessa's advice. Her scolding, really.

"Hi," I say, eyes still glued to Dr. Young's loopy chicken scratch.

"Good morning, Maggie."

I can smell her morning shower—peaceful and earthy—and I swear to God, I can feel the heat of it, too. Can feel her looking at me. I hear her quiet breaths.

"After how our breakfast went on Monday, I wouldn't have thought you'd want to sit next to me," I say, finally facing her. Students file in, and when Laura sees her seat has been taken, she shrugs and continues to the back of the room.

Olivia half grins and half smirks as she nods. "What can I say? I'm a sucker for ill-mannered women."

I swallow her words, and they sink deep into me, filling me with a warm pressure. "I'm sorry for getting heated. I swear, I'm normally very polite; p's and q's, manners, respect. I guess I wasn't expecting to be talking about…" I tamp the urge to hurl myself right back into the pit of this argument. "The world of organic farming. Reckon I feel pretty passionately about it." My hands feel damp, and no amount of rubbing them on my jeans is helping. But I try, regardless.

Olivia's knee knocks against mine under the table, and I focus on her. A long gold chain hangs from her neck, a green crystal dangling from the end of it, right above her breasts. Her lips are a touch redder today, like the darkest shade of a Pink Lady apple. Just as sweet, I'd bet. As if her knee pressing into mine wasn't doing enough to my nervous system, she grabs my forearm. My forearm that lies in my lap.

Her fingertips ignite the nerve endings in my thigh like sparklers. "Do you want to be my friend?"

"Yes." One thousand percent. Where do I sign?

She squeezes my arm and leans back. "Great. I think we could learn a lot from each other."

While I'm not exactly sure what I could learn from Olivia Cypress, I keep my mouth shut and nod along because I do know a couple of things: it feels like the drop on a roller coaster when she touches me, and I'm dying to know how it feels to touch her.

"Why are you a finance major?"

She turns to me, eyes widening with her lips. "You are very direct. I feel like this is my friendship interview."

I stare at her, not sure how to respond. I want to know the answer.

"Well, I may come off as a little scattered, but something about numbers and spreadsheets makes sense to me. It's my biggest strength. And though I run into the backs of pretty strangers and spill water at breakfast dates, I never miss a single digit in a data set. When I'm working or playing music, everything else melts away."

Her gaze is beyond me, probably in that sweet place of music or finance. It's warming to listen to her talk about her passions. "Maybe I can be too blunt sometimes. I'm curious is all. I want to know more about you, and I'm glad I asked."

Her gaze skips from my right to my left eye. "Me, too."

Dr. Young walks to the front of the class, ending our conversation for now. "All right, happy Wednesday, everyone. While you get settled, I have a couple of announcements to make before today's lesson. We will be doing a partnered project on scalability in tree fruit production. This should cover all aspects of scaling production on an orchard. We're talking everything from soil management to finances, to storage, to transportation. You will choose an orchard to study and utilize data from, then come up with an actionable plan to increase production by thirty-five percent. I know that's a big jump, so this plan can span years. Doesn't matter, as long as it's attainable. Attainability, folks. That's the key."

I missed everything he said after partnered project.

"If you work on a farm, you are welcome and encouraged to use it for your project. Especially if you plan to be there long-term. There are no hard rules on formatting, but I want a written proposal, as if you were pitching to investors, and a presentation to match. This will be due"—he hunches over his desk calendar and traces the dates—"the Wednesday before finals. Plenty of time. I'll give you a couple minutes to partner up and exchange information. I believe we have an even number."

A rumble of chatter and chair legs dragging across the floor takes over the room. Olivia and I turn toward each other and smile. I jump in before I chicken out, or before Laura can ask me. "Will you be my partner?"

"Only if we use an organic farm as our model." Right when I'm about to protest, she winks. "Just kidding. I'd love to be your partner. Do you want to use Hyde Hill, or do you want to branch out?"

I consider her question. "Yeah. I'd like to use our farm if you don't have any objection. I have access to all the numbers, which will make our lives easier, and if we do a good job, maybe this project will be something I can use one day." Maybe it will earn me some points with my dad.

"Sounds perfect." She pulls her phone from her back pocket. "What's your number?"

I recite it and promptly feel a buzz in my own pocket.

"That's me," she says.

"That's you."

"How do you feel about getting together this week to hammer out details? We can choose the parts we want to work on and go from there. Maybe weekly meetups?"

This girl just crash-landed into my life, and I hope she stays. "Yeah. That'd be nice."

She quirks her brow and scans my face. "That's quite the change of tune from Monday, Margaret."

I groan and swing my knee away from hers. "My name's not Margaret."

"There she is."

Chapter Five

I didn't know that going to church was no longer "cool" until I became Tessa's roommate. Being from a small farming community like East Sparrow, it hadn't crossed my mind that people didn't want to go to Mass or that anyone was strongly opposed to the Catholic church in general. Tessa has explained to me thousands of times why I shouldn't go anymore, but here I am with Aiden, kneeling during Communion like we do every Sunday. We're Hydes. It's in our blood. And it's in the university's blood; Catholicism laid every stone in this place.

I'm not ignorant to the hypocrisy of it all, but I'm here for me. I believe in God, and I find myself in these pews, and no one—Tessa, priest, parishioners, or Pope—can take that from me.

Aiden has a small coughing fit, and heads whip around to find the source. Just like working on the farm, he's only here until he doesn't have to be anymore. I don't know if he's only here for me, but I want to tell him to stop wasting his time. I don't care if he goes to church or not.

"Sorry," he mouths.

I shake my head and try to focus on my prayer and reflection, but Olivia keeps popping into my thoughts. She texted me yesterday to make plans to meet for our project. We only exchanged a few messages, but I swear to God—*sorry, God*—everything we say to each other is charged somehow. Maybe I haven't had the most experience since Sarah, but a sack of potatoes could tell that Olivia is interested in me.

And aside from the giant orange *Hazard* sign flashing in my head, I'm interested in her, too. I know Tessa is right; I'm being too harsh a judge. But when Olivia shows up unprepared to the first day of a class she supposedly cares enough about to audit, it gives me pause. I'm looking for a rock, sturdy and dependable.

Not a vagabond heartbreaker. Not Olivia.

"Mass has ended. Go in peace to love and serve the Lord," Father Kyle announces.

That was a complete blur.

❖

"We should go to Nan's soon," Tessa says as she lounges on her bed with Ashley.

I love Nan's. It's the perfect dive bar to escape to when I need a break from the university. It also helps that they have the best fries in the world, and Ashley's cousin, Sam, is the bartender. He is *very* generous with his friends-and-family discount and looks the other way for a select few underaged folks.

"I'm always down for Nan's," I say.

"For sure. Sam has been bugging me to get down there soon, anyway," Ashley says.

My phone buzzes. It's Olivia: *Just got here. Someone let me in. What's your room number again?*

Cool. I'm 223.

"Olivia's here," I announce.

"Does she know we're friends?" Ashley asks.

I shake my head. "It hasn't come up."

"This will be fun. Worlds colliding and all," Tessa says as Olivia knocks on our door.

I pass a hand through my hair and hope it looks all right. Regret rushes through me as I reach for the doorknob. *I should have worn something different.* Why am I in my Carhartts and a flannel? Even if the pants do fit me nicely, they're old work pants. I could've worn jeans like a normal person, or even sweats would have—

"Hi." Olivia's eyes are bright, and her cheeks are slightly pink. Her smile is warm and begs me to gaze at her beauty mark, which in turn, begs me to look at her lips. Her eyes roam my body, and her smile morphs into a smirk. A sexy smirk. I guess she likes my old canvas pants.

"Hey. Come on in."

Olivia brushes by me and drops her bag. "What...how? Hi!"

"Surprise." Ashely hugs her and grabs the green stone at the end of Olivia's chain. "When did you get this jade?"

"When I was visiting Riley in Asheville over the summer. How do you—"

"Tessa and Maggie have been roommates since freshman year," Ashley says.

Olivia looks at both of us, head tilted as if she's analyzing something. "Right. Hi, Tessa." She waves.

"Good to see you, Liv."

Olivia spins and looks at everyone again. "This is..."

"Weird," I supply. "It's weird. But here we are. Should we head to the basement to get some work done?" I grab my sustainable production notebook from my desk.

She snags her bag from Tessa's rug and nods. "Yeah. I suppose that's what I'm here for, even if now all I want to do is hang out with you guys." She turns to Ashely. "You've been holding out on me, girl."

Ashley shrugs. "It honestly never crossed my mind until Maggie came home from her first day of classes with her feathers all ruffled by this 'Olivia girl.'"

Olivia breaks into uncontrollable laughter. When she catches her breath, she says, "Maggie's going to like me. She just doesn't know it yet."

Tessa muffles a cough of laughter. She knows it. I know it. Surely, Olivia knows it.

I put my hand on her shoulder and still at the feel of her. "All right. This has been interesting. We should get to work, though."

As I follow Olivia out the door, I hold up a middle finger for Tessa.

"Rude," she calls as the door falls shut behind us.

Olivia and I walk the quiet hallway to the stairwell, my mind screaming at me to say something. Literally anything.

"Tessa—"

"I loved your room. What little I got to see of it, anyway. Those prints of the trees and the little pothos that trails down your desk. You really love plants, don't you?"

I hold open the door for Olivia and follow her down the stairs. "Is there anything else worth loving?"

She shrugs. "People."

"Well, yeah. People, plants, and animals. What else is there? Everything else is just metal and plastic. Plants, though. Plants are life."

Olivia pulls out a chair and motions for me to join her.

"Are you trying to seduce me, Ms. Hyde? Because your Carhartts are one thing, but this poetic little number about plants is a whole other level." She waves a hand over me, and I completely drop through the floor, through the foundation, through the layers of soil, all the way to the molten core of the earth.

I sit next to her, our shoulders barely touching. "Aren't you?" I ask.

"Aren't I...what?" Her words are slow and tentative, but her eyes are wide with anticipation, as if she knows exactly *what*.

I swallow. This is too fast, too dangerous. I literally know nothing about this girl besides the fact that she's a farm-loving finance major who is friends with Ashley. And the most important part: she won't even *be here* next year.

I pivot. "Aren't you excited for Laura's twenty-first birthday?" I ask. Her entire face falls, and all the sharpness in her eyes dulls. Her disappointment hits me in the chest like a meat tenderizer, but I continue. "We're all going out to Nan's the weekend after next to celebrate."

She nods. "Sure. Sounds cool."

"Ashley and Tessa were talking about trying to make it there soon. We could all go together," I suggest.

A small sparkle returns to her eyes. "I'd like that. Apparently, you're best friends with my best friend, so I guess we should probably all hang out together."

"Yeah, I know. So weird. When I came home from the first day of classes all agitated by a certain someone"—I nudge her shoulder—"Ashley told me she knew you, and that you are, indeed, the worst."

"Shut up." She shoves me away and unzips her bag, pulling out the green spiral notebook she uses in our sustainable production class, the plastic cover graffitied in national park stickers like her Nalgene. "Hey. Do you have any notes from class on Friday? For the life of me, I have no idea where I put mine."

"They're not in there?" I eye her notebook.

"They would be, but I didn't bring it to class that day, so I used a piece of paper, which I obviously lost."

I have some hesitation giving Olivia my notes because the girl clearly has a penchant for losing things, and I *really* want to keep my notes on increasing production in orchards. Obviously. And we're continuing the same lesson tomorrow, so I need them to refer to in class.

She must sense my hesitation because she pinches my elbow and says, "I'll bring them to class. Don't worry."

"Okay. Yeah, that's cool." I hand her my notebook, and she slides it into her bag.

"Awesome. Thank you. Okay. I was thinking we should divide and conquer during the information-gathering phase, then join back up and figure out how to pull it all together. How do you feel about that?"

My shoulders fall in disappointment. "No more meetups?"

She drops her pencil and stares. "You are giving me very confusing signals. Or maybe, they're not confusing at all, and *you're* just confused?" I open my mouth to protest, but she holds up a hand to stop me. "Don't answer. It doesn't matter. You and I can hang out whenever we want, but in terms of this project, and for the sake of efficiency, you collect your farm's data, and I'll work on how to find the funding. Do you know if y'all owe on the farm?"

"We don't." My response is automatic and defensive, but the truth is that I have no idea if we owe on the farm. Just because it has been in our family for four generations doesn't mean my dad or grandad hasn't taken out a loan on it to cover some kind of cost. "Actually, I don't know if we owe on it. I'm sorry."

She scribbles a note. "Don't be sorry. I like that." Her hand drags across the paper, the delicate veins shifting and trailing over her bones like vines on tree trunks.

"You like what, exactly?"

She stops writing and looks at me. "I like that you can admit you don't know something instead of rambling on with worthless guesses. My mom always says there's strength in admitting what you don't know and weakness in pretending you do."

"Your mom sounds like a smart woman."

"She is. She's an aerospace engineer who works with mostly men, so she's around her fair share of that kind of thing."

This is my window to find out more about Olivia. I want to know everything. I angle my body toward her. "And your dad?"

"Also an aerospace engineer but in Florida. My mom and I live in Huntsville."

"Does he have to commute?"

She furrows her brows. "Commute? No. He doesn't just work in Florida. He lives there, too. He and my mom got divorced a long time ago." She sighs and plucks at a thread on her sweater. "My mom got the job he wanted, and that was it. He couldn't handle being second best, even though they were college sweethearts. He made up some bullshit about unreconcilable differences, but the truth is that he couldn't handle the fact that his wife is a better engineer. Men are the worst."

I jump to defend my dad. "No, they aren't. Sounds like your dad is the worst, but I'm the only woman in my family, and we're as close as they come. My dad is probably the most loving person I know." I think about how complex our relationship is and feel the need to add, "I mean, he's tough on me but in a business way. He doesn't mess around when it comes to that stuff, but he's still loving."

She drops her pen and studies me. It's hard not to squirm under her scrutiny. "Aren't you kind of a shoo-in for taking over the family business, though?"

"If you're asking if I have a huge head start and am the favorite candidate, then the answer is, yes, I'm definitely the shoo-in. But I feel like I'm paying for it."

Her eyes widen as if she's thought of something epic. "With gold bars and blood? What dirty secrets do the Hydes have?"

"You are too much." I chuckle and pick up her hot-pink pen. Click it a few times. "My dad has this goofy side," I begin to explain, but when Olivia's hand gently covers mine, I realize I'm clicking her pen in rapid-fire. She gives a soft smile and lets her hand linger for a beat longer before pulling it away.

"Your dad has a goofy side…"

I pile my hands into my lap and nod. "Yeah. You should see him with Tessa and Ashley. He turns into this giant goober-y goofball thing."

Olivia giggles. "Goober-y goofball thing, huh? Sounds fun."

"Well, that's the thing. I feel like everyone else gets to have this familiar and intimate relationship with my dad—Tessa, Ashley, Aiden, my uncle—because they don't have to worry about impressing him. Taking over the farm is the only thing I want, and my father may be a goober sometimes, but most of the time, he's a hardass." This is the first time I've ever expressed this out loud. Before I assigned words to them, these constant feelings of being scrutinized and held at a distance cleaved together like a thick rubber band around my chest. A relentless pressure.

She stays quiet and watches me.

"I'm aware of every time I'm even a miniscule disappointment to him, and though I do everything in my power to be all he wants me to be, I can tell he enjoys being around other people more. I think it's because they don't care as much about the farm as I do. I'm work in my father's eyes, and they're leisure." I shake my head and pick at my cuticles.

"Sounds like an impossible balance to strike in your relationship. Doesn't he allow a little gray area for you guys? You know, a little grace for his daughter?" she asks quietly.

"Yeah. Sometimes." I'm hit with guilt, talking about my father this way to someone I've just met. Not even Tessa knows how I feel about this, but something about Olivia makes me want her to know. Makes me want to bare myself to her. "My dad is a great guy. I hope you know I'm not trying to say he's not."

"I know," she whispers.

"I showed up late once." I hold up my pointer finger. "One time ever. I was at our neighbor's house for a sleepover when I was sixteen and overslept. I was twenty minutes late for work. He gripped my shoulder and stared into my eyes. Then he told me he couldn't care less if a Hyde ran the farm or not. He told me to never forget that, and I never have."

"What about your mom? Does she feel the same way as your dad?"

"No. She doesn't care about us or the farm. She left when I was seven and my brother, Aiden, was five."

Her hand finds my knee under the table. "I'm so sorry. Where'd she go?"

"She wanted to be a singer in Nashville, but she never made it work. She stayed there, though, so I reckon her career wasn't the only thing pulling her away from us." Her fingers dig into the canvas of my pants. It feels good, sure, but also misplaced. "You're reacting differently to my parents' divorce than I did to yours. I feel like people see it differently because it was my mom who stepped out instead of my dad."

She shakes her head. "What? I'm not reacting any—"

I cover her hand with mine. It's soft, not calloused from grafting and pruning and harvesting. It feels good, if not a little foreign. "I think you're going to leave a bruise of your handprint."

She pulls back, and a slow blush creeps up her neck.

"It's okay. I'm used to people having big reactions to it. Especially when I was younger, I could see how the older women in my town treated me differently. The pity was etched in their faces. For me, my mom leaving hurt and was an adjustment, sure. But if I were to lose my dad…" I blink back the wetness in my eyes that has amassed just from saying those words out loud. "Well, I'd be completely crushed." Losing my dad is my biggest fear. My biggest fear that is guaranteed to come true unless he loses me first. "Anyway, it always bothers me when men are depicted as helpless when it comes to raising their own children. Or like they're incapable of the warmth of a woman." I wave a dismissive hand. "It's all bullshit."

Olivia pushes her notebook away and crosses her legs, angling her chair toward me, her pale ankle on display before it dips into her sky-blue Toms. "I guess my mom's not very warm, so you may have a point there. At least you have one good one," she says, then waves her hands in front of her face. "I didn't actually mean that. My parents are good people who love me, and I love them. But I hate being home." She pushes her pen against her lips while she gathers her thoughts. "It doesn't even feel like home. It's a drain to be there, and home should be a radiator."

"A radiator?"

She smiles. "Yeah. A radiator, something that gives warmth. People and places, they're either radiators or drains. You're a radiator." She pokes me softly in the shoulder and clears her throat. "Anyway, when my mom bought me my first car, I was out of there." She throws a thumb over her shoulder. "Visiting my friend Riley in Asheville, checking out the waterfalls in Georgia, even driving all the way to Austin to see my favorite band one time. It's how I fell in love with traveling."

She stares into my eyes, and I do my best to smile and hide the disappointment I feel. Loving to travel and explore new places is normally a trait that would attract someone to Olivia, but how could that possibly work with what will inevitably be my life? I will never choose something different than living in East Sparrow, so why would she choose something different than traveling?

I am so wrapped in my thoughts that I completely miss her reaching for my face and startle when her fingertips brush a strand of hair behind my ear. "You were just so far away," she says.

"Sorry. I'm back now." I trip over her slightly parted lips and fall into her eyes. They pull me under like quicksand.

"You don't have to be back. You can keep looking at me that way for as long as you'd like."

I chuckle and shake my head, wondering what she saw in my expression. Longing for something that I can't have? I may be assuming too much about her. Maybe a home and a family could be her priority over seeing the world or living in cool cities. "What's your ten-year plan?"

She chuckles and presses the back of her hand to her lips as if the question is nauseating. "My ten-year plan?" She cocks her head, and I study her studying me. "I can barely keep up with my one-week plan. Why would I have one of those?"

"Why *wouldn't* you have one? They're super motivating and a useful tool for helping you make decisions now that will affect your future." Her eyebrows knit together as she watches me. "Do you know where you'll be in ten years?"

"I'll be honest, that sounds incredibly limiting. I'm here to build a launchpad with my finance degree and the skills I acquire over these four years." She cuts a horizontal line through the air. "I'm building a foundation. But I'm not going to shrug and build myself a log cabin right now. What if something I can't foresee pulls me to the beach, and I need a beach house instead? What if I take in twenty foster dogs and need twenty acres of land? This is the time to be as open to every opportunity as possible. Why would I narrow my options with a limiting mindset like that?" She shrugs, her shoulder barely skimming the bottom of her ear. "I have literally no idea where I'll be in ten years. Hopefully, somewhere cool like Portugal or New Zealand. Nepal is where I want to visit the most." She pauses. "That bothers you, doesn't it?"

"No." It shouldn't, at least. But I'd be lying if I said I'm jiggling my foot for any other reason than the fact that everything she said is the opposite of what I wanted her to say and exactly what I wish I had in my life. Uncertainty, a blank page, and adventure.

She drops her voice. "You think you have everything figured out. You think you know exactly what your life will look like in your thirties, but the truth is, you have just as little a clue as I do. Life is fickle, Maggie. Things change, and ten years is a long time."

I play with the end of my shirt, trying to fold the thick rectangular tail of it in half. She's wrong there. Unlike me, Olivia doesn't have a true passion. She may show up to a couple of agriculture classes and call it saving the world, but I have a physical, attainable, true dream, and I'm already halfway there. If I can stay focused, the finish line will be around the corner. That's my number-one priority. Once I have that, maybe I can mess around a little bit and try to obtain priority number two—a partner. "There is no world in which I'm not working on Hyde Hill Farm and living in East Sparrow in ten years," I say.

She shrugs, the little beauty mark above the corner of her mouth twitching. "Sounds claustrophobic."

Why does the one girl at Alder who makes my palms sweat and my heart heave against my chest have to be the most ill-suited person for me? "Yeah, well. It's not for everyone."

"Doesn't have to be for you, either."

I snap my head up. Is she trying to upset me? Her face is blank, but her eyes hold my gaze with an unflinching intensity. "It's the only thing I want," I say.

"The only thing?"

As much as I want to know her, and for her to know me, I can't go there. I can share my feelings about my complicated relationship with my dad, sure. But to give a home to the discontent I feel about my future plans by prescribing words to it...I can't. "Yes. The only thing."

"Right." She sighs and pulls her notebook back in front of her. "I guess we should finish this meeting so we can pass the assignment and remain in accordance with your ten-year plan, Mags."

"That would be ideal."

What would be ideal is if Olivia could understand that I'm not available for the kind of life she wants. And if magically, she'd want to settle in East Sparrow with me, that would be ideal, too. I watch her flip to a clean page.

Then she wouldn't be Olivia Cypress, and I wouldn't care what her life plan is.

❖

The next Monday, I manage to avoid too much small talk with Dr. Young and take my usual seat, anxious to see Olivia and get my notes back. I wouldn't consider our last exchange a fight, but it definitely wasn't filled with butterflies and rainbows. We managed to get our cart back on track and worked through the initial planning phase of our project. I think both of us were relieved that it didn't take too much effort, and we didn't have to be around each other much longer than another twenty minutes.

It isn't hard for me to imagine that she feels the same way about me as I do about her. She likes me. Maybe has a crush on me, but I am the opposite of what would fit into her non-ten-year plan. One of our plans is significantly more flexible than the other and... *Jesus, it's not like I'm proposing to the girl.* I may be putting too much stock in my crush. So what if Olivia isn't my person? I still enjoy her company and am thankful to have a new friend. And that's that.

"All right, class. Today, we'll be continuing our conversation about increasing production and therefore talking about postharvest management and ways to scale storage, transportation, and shelf life. This should be very relevant to your projects," Dr. Young announces. I glance at the door. No sign of Olivia. I really want to add to my notes from Friday, but I pull out a different notebook instead.

Another ten minutes passes, and my annoyance grows. She *promised* she'd give me back my notes for today. I slip my phone into my lap and text, *All good? I see you're not in class today.*

I scribble some lecture notes as the minutes tick by until my phone buzzes. *All good. Just skipping.*

Just skipping? So her word means nothing? I fumble around the little keyboard on my phone. *You said you'd give me my notes back. I really wanted to have them for today.* Irritation prickles me, but more so, the disappointment I feel in her makes me ache. All of the reasons why I shouldn't date her aren't hard and fast; they wouldn't actually keep me from her. But letting me down? That is an absolute deal breaker.

Oh my God. Your notes! I'm so sorry, Maggie. I can come drop them off. Dr. Young will hate me even more for showing up in the middle of class, but who cares?

I read the text and feel more irritated. I don't even care about the notes anymore. It's the principle of it. Even if there was no ill intent, she's still prone to all of these mishaps, to letting people down, because she's too scattered to truly care. Too scattered to really be there for people. I don't want that in a partner.

Don't worry about it, I say.

Maggie, I'm really sorry. I promise this kind of thing will never happen again between us.

I feel a little guilty for being so harsh, but I like her, and she let me down. Also, so much for being motivated and passionate about agriculture. I don't respond. Have nothing to say. Olivia is the type of girl to bail on a whim. And I'm not.

CHAPTER SIX

The next two weeks pass in an uneventful blur. Even though I had the perfect excuse of gathering data for our project, I haven't gone home to the orchard like I promised I wouldn't. Aiden has been sneaking around with Scott; Ashley and Tessa are still enviably perfect as ever; and Olivia and I are just friends and project partners with a growing space between us. I think I thoroughly turned her off from any possibility of actually liking me by acting so distant these past couple of weeks and being so obstinate about my ten-year plan.

Doesn't matter anyway, since things between us would never work, as she made evident by bailing on me. Once we finished delegating our responsibilities for the project, there hasn't been much need to get together, so we skipped last week's meeting but agreed to touch base after Laura's birthday outing tonight.

"I am so excited to meet this girl," Aiden says as he bounces on the edge of my bed with Scott.

I turn away from the mirror, a little lost when I have to dress for something other than work or class. It's always some variation of the same outfit. I have my boots, my nice pair of dark fitted jeans, and my quintessential flannel. I am painfully aware of how many flannel stereotypes I fall into being not only a farmer but a lesbian farmer. I'm wearing my green flannel, which I have dubbed my fancy flannel because Tessa told me once that it makes the green in my eyes pop. I run a hand through my hair, which is also highlighted by my fancy flannel. Sometimes, I think it's not so bad that I inherited my mom's looks.

"I'm not sure why she has to meet us here," I say, trying to maintain some boundaries when it comes to Olivia.

"Because you invited her two weeks ago, and she's our friend. We're going to all hang out, and we're going to all have a good time. Got it?" Ashley asks.

I nod, allowing some muffled sound of discontent to slip from my throat.

"Did you just growl at me?" Ashley asks, a hand pressed to her chest in feigned horror.

"Did I?" I shrug and turn away. She knows I'm kidding.

"Y'all are really going to let her wear that?" Aiden points the butt of his beer bottle at my general being, and I fling the pen from my desk at him.

"What?" I hold out my arms. "It's a dive bar, not the Oscars."

"It's the same damn thing you wear every day, Maggie. You just brushed your hair."

Tessa stands in front of me. "He's—"

"A jerk face," I say.

"Well, yeah. But he's also right. Can we at least..." Her hands work to unbutton my flannel, revealing my black tank top, which is strictly an undergarment. I don't have big boobs, but the swell of my chest takes me a little off guard when I look at myself. "There. Now you look like you're about to go out."

"Knock, knock." Olivia breezes through our open door and completely takes my breath away. I swallow a dry, grinding gulp and bat away Tessa's hands. Olivia wears a skintight white tank top that disappears into her flowing green skirt. Pale yellow and purple flowers skitter over the green fabric and look like they're blowing in the wind every time she moves. Her jade stone pops against the crisp white of her top, but I can't pull my eyes away from her bare shoulders. Her bare chest.

I've done well at tamping my attraction to her. Two weeks passed without me losing my breath from the sight of her—at least, not more than a couple of times—and she has the nerve to waltz right in here, looking like that and making my knees wobble. *Shit.*

"You made it. Guys, this is my friend Olivia." Ashley lays a hand on her shoulder. "Olivia, this is Maggie's little brother, Aiden, and his…" She pauses a moment, seemingly not knowing how to introduce Scott.

"My roommate, Scott," Aiden supplies.

"Nice to meet you both. Maggie has told me all about you, Aiden."

Olivia scans the boys, no doubt taking in their closeness, how they naturally bend toward one another like a plant to the sun. *What is that called again?* Why am I blanking on this simple term? I've only written it a thousand times over my college career.

"Phototropism."

Everyone stares at me, eyebrows raised.

Olivia grins. "No, my name is Olivia. Remember? We have a class together? We're working on that project together? You don't like me very much…"

I take a step toward her without a single idea about what I'm doing. My hands rise and fall to my sides. "I don't *not* like you." I feel everyone's eyes on me, and it only pushes me deeper into *what the hell am I doing* land. She bites the corner of her lip as she watches me flail. It's that look she's giving me. It's her soft shoulders, her flowery skirt, and the jade bouncing over the tops of her breasts with every move she makes that is pushing me, making me slip into the warmth of her. Notes be damned.

"Phototropism," I say, doubling down. "A plant's growth response to light." I point at Olivia, look at my finger in brief horror, then say, "Cypress trees love the sun. Positive phototropism."

Aiden leans into Scott, eyes wide. "How many times is she going to say phototropism?"

My whole face heats as if licked by a solar flare. *What is happening to me?* I shove my traitor hands in my pockets and sway on the balls of my feet.

"Okay." Tessa slides out of bed and rubs her hands together. "That's your horticultural fun fact of the evening, folks. Thanks, Mags." She squeezes my shoulder. "Y'all ready to roll?"

Tessa is my hero.

"Yep. I'll drive," Ashley says.

Everyone stands and makes sure they have their phones, keys, and wallets.

"I'll drive, too," I offer.

"Perfect. Let's head out. Whose birthday is it again?" Tessa asks as she walks out the door.

"Our classmate, Laura. It's her twenty-first," Olivia says.

"Good luck, Laura," Tessa says.

❖

The boys and I take my truck and pull into the gravel lot behind the girls. I can tell from the outside that Nan's hasn't changed since last year. It never does, and it never will. Nan's is one of those things about a town that remains a constant. In Alder, you can always count on the fact that the university will stand at the top of the forest, and Nan's will stand in the small valley of the town. Each of them, if changing at all, changes at a pace so slow, it's unrecognizable from one generation to the next. My dad used to come here with his buddies, just like us, and my kids will come here with their buddies, just like us.

Aiden and Scott hop onto the gravel, boots crunching. I can smell their aftershave as I follow them, all of us braiding into the other half of our crew on the way to the entrance. I end up shoulder to shoulder with Olivia, naturally. *Phototropism.* How could I not bend toward her when she emanates all the light and warmth of the Georgia sun?

We bring up the rear, allowing a gap to form between us and the rest of the group. "I'm sorry for being so weird in the dorm before," I say, my gaze on the stars above, the wind tickling my chest through my unbuttoned shirt. The night is clear and unusually warm for late September.

She loops her arm through mine as we walk, and the contact submerges me. "You *had* to drive a truck, didn't you?" she asks, completely ignoring my apology.

"It's pretty useful on the farm, yeah."

"It's pretty attractive."

I clear my throat and tighten my arm around hers, pulling her to a stop. "You know I like you, right?"

She looks at me in amusement, the currents in her eyes working, building that electric energy of hers. "I know. You just don't *want* to like me."

I gnaw on my lip as she waits me out. "You're right. I think…" I look to the sky again. "Look, I know I've made this clear already, but you really disappointed me when you didn't bring my notes to class a couple weeks ago."

She slips her arm out of mine and frowns. "You're still upset about the notes?"

I look at her, trying to find a way to explain my feelings. "You know it's not about the physical notes. What's been bothering me so much is I told you something was important to me. You had control over that something and asked me to trust you with it. I did. And you let me down." She stays quiet, a rarity for Olivia. I'm a little taken aback that she doesn't have a cutting retort to make me feel silly for being so agitated over this. "I think I got so worked up because…because, honestly, I've never felt this way about someone before," I admit.

She nods and sighs. "I hate that I let you down. I've been trying to move past it because I'm so disappointed in myself, and it hurts to reflect on it. I know it's not about the notes." She squeezes above my elbow. "I really *really*, like you, Maggie. All I can say now is that I'm sorry, and it won't happen again. I've got you."

She drops her hand down my arm, and I catch it. "Thank you. I'm sorry for not being more up-front earlier."

She squeezes my hand. "It's okay. I think I knew how you felt." I nod and look at my feet. "You know, for things that are really important to me, I never mess up like that. And I can't emphasize enough that I won't let you down again. Okay?"

There's a sincerity in her eyes that I trust, even if deep down, I'm not completely sure I believe her. But I want to. So I choose to. "Okay."

She smiles and tugs me toward the door. "I knew you had a crush on me," she says.

I laugh, hoping I can laugh out all of my fear of her hurting me. "I never said *that*."

She flashes a mischievous look over her shoulder, her eyes narrowed in challenge. "Is that right?"

"Technically."

She holds open the door and stops me as I try to slide past her into the bar, trapping me against the doorjamb. "That's fine. I like a chase."

Her words force me to let go of my hesitation and leave me with an overwhelming need to be close to her.

She slips into the entryway, and the door closes behind us. We are instantly absorbed into Nan's. The soft red of the darkness, the old wooden booths with the cracked leather cushions, the twang of a country trio performing on the tiny makeshift stage. The stage is the only new thing. After hosting a couple of events and their performers asking for more of a legitimate space to play, the owner of Nan's had a simple ten-by-ten wooden platform built in the far corner of the pub, and naturally, the floor space in front turns into a dance floor on the weekends.

That is where we find Laura grinding all over Ryan from our sustainable production class. I can only imagine how much alcohol she's already consumed if she is trying to make a baby on the dance floor to a Jimmy Buffet song…with Ryan. He's a fine enough guy, but he's not exactly a catch. Freshman year, he had to get fifteen stiches on his left hand after smashing his knife into his own fist attempting to banana graft a pecan tree. *After* Dr. Young warned the entire class not to hold the trunk under the graft cut.

I peel my eyes from the dancing and lean into Olivia.

"Can I get you a drink?" I ask.

I spot Tessa and Ashley in a booth overlooking the dance floor and Aiden and Scott huddled in a dark corner, seemingly having an intense conversation. I think I know what they're arguing about. It's hard to be in such a public place—a place where everyone is drinking and showing major PDA—with your secret boyfriend and not be able to touch him.

"Yes, please. I'll come with you."

The bar is crowded with the usual mix of students, professors, and locals. It's weird to think of getting wasted in front of your teachers, but when your college town literally has one bar, both parties tend to look the other way. I wiggle between the backs of two burley men and flag down Sam, Ashley's cousin. He smiles when he sees me and lays down a check for one of the econ professors, then heads my way.

Laura and Ryan wiggle in next to us.

"Hey. Happy birthday," I say. "Are you having a blast?"

Laura's eyes are the color of graying meat. The kind that's been on manager discount for three days, and she doesn't seem like she can form words. Laura is no longer a part of the conscious community. Instead, the corner of her mouth twitches in an attempted smile, and she sways into Ryan, who looks like he's halfway to Laura's level of drunk.

I shoot a worried glance to Olivia, whose eyes are narrowed in concern.

"Two Buds," Ryan calls to Sam.

I catch Sam's eye and try to signal to him that they are already way overserved. He shakes his head and slams two ice waters on the bar in front of them. Ryan seems to know better than to argue with the one bartender in town and grabs the glasses.

"Let me give you guys a ride home," I say.

"No. One more dance. One more. Then home," Laura says, her words crashing into each other like an eight-car pileup.

Olivia steps in. "Okay. Chug that water and have one more dance, then Maggie and I will take you home. Deal?"

She nods and pulls Ryan back toward the stage area.

"Holy shit. She's so wasted," I say.

"Yeah. Hey." She touches my shoulder. "Was my offer okay? I didn't mean to insert myself and—"

"It's perfect. What do you want?" I nod toward the bar.

Her hand tugs softly on the tail of my shirt. "I don't know. I'll just do a beer."

I order two High Lifes, and Sam slides them in front of me. "Keep an eye on your friend," he says. "I only served her one shot. Whatever she gets into tonight, it's not on me."

I nod, even though I think, legally, it may very well be on Nan's if it's the last place she was served. They must have drunk a whole distillery's worth of booze before they showed up.

"Let's go sit with Tessa and Ashley. Then I'm making you dance with me before we drive Laura home," Olivia says.

We weave through the drunken Friday night masses until we make it to the booth. I let Olivia sit first and slide in next to her. There's sitting next to someone in a chair, and then there's sitting next to someone in a small booth in a loud bar, where you have to lean in to hear anything they say. Tessa's head is bowed into Ashley's ear as she giggles, and it appears that not much conversation is going to happen across the table. I turn to Olivia and smile, her thigh flush with mine.

I sip my beer while I think of something epic to say to the cute girl I'm with. I hold up the sweaty bottle, it's label disintegrating and torn from my nervous fingers. "Champagne of beers," I say.

Olivia smiles and shakes her head. "What?"

Instead of talking over my shoulder at her, in a bold move, I snake my arm over the back of the booth and lean in to her. Her warmth and earthy spice cuts through the stale cigarette aroma of the bar, and her hair tickles my nose. Olivia's hand finds the inside of my knee, and I know I've made a good choice.

I lean even closer, my mouth barely an inch from her ear. "Miller High Life's slogan is 'The Champagne of Beers.' It's my dad's favorite."

When I pull away, she grins as if what I said was silly. I guess she was expecting me to say something suave. I'm just trying to make conversation with the girl. This is the first time we've ever hung out without the pretense of school.

Her thumb rubs along the inseam of my jeans, and I swear it moves a little higher up my thigh every minute. She molds her body under my shoulder, along my ribs, trying to reach my ear. It feels impossibly good to be so close to her. My own body's reaction startles me. My heart races, my mouth dries, and I keep pulling at the soggy beer label.

"It's sweet that you drink your dad's favorite. You and Aiden really look up to him, don't you?"

I nod, enjoying the feeling of her eyes on me. "Yes. Even before my mom left, he was everything to us. I can only hope to be a fraction of the person he is one day."

"I'm sure your dad's great, but don't sell yourself short, Maggie. I think you're pretty special. Maybe you should aspire to be yourself."

I don't really know what she means, but her words feel sweet. I'll dissect their meaning tomorrow. Olivia's lips are only a few inches from mine, and I involuntarily lean toward them. They look soft and delicious and naturally pink tonight. Normally, they arch slightly down at the corners, like her eyes, but not when she smiles, and right now, she smiles as if she wants me to close the space between us.

"*Ow, ow*," Ashley and Tessa holler at us in unison from across the table. A greasy French fry is catapulted by one of them and *thunks* against my chest.

I point to my mouth. "Up here next time, please." I turn back to Olivia. "Why are we friends with them again?"

"It was her tattoo." She points her bottle at Ashley, who is consumed by Tessa again. "It caught my attention in our accounting class, and I was intrigued. I actually thought we'd date, but after our first kiss, it was clear there wasn't a romantic spark. Just platonic. Haven't been able to get rid of her since."

We both chuckle because Ashley is one of the best friends anyone could ask for. She's smart, talented, passionate, and successful. She's part of the most exciting movement happening on campus: the Alder Queer Fellowship. Since she helped start it freshman year, it has become a bastion of not only queer rights and protection but a safe space for anyone who feels different on this campus.

"Do you go to the meetings?" I ask.

She pops an eyebrow. "What meetings?"

"AQF."

"Oh, yeah. I try to make as many as I can. Are you going to their Fall Fest in a couple weeks? Ashley told me they teamed up with the softball and baseball team to recreate their Apple Wars from last year but, like, way bigger. Instead of just for student activities week, AQF is making it into a small festival."

I try to ignore her hand, now flush against the inside of my mid-thigh. If I focus too much on how it feels, on how it makes me want to trap her hand there with my other leg, then I may combust right here in this booth.

"Of course I'll be there. I wonder if…"

"What?"

"Ashley said they were going to use the clearing in the woods, and I can't believe it didn't occur to me until now, but they should use the orchard. The culled apples are already there, there's tons of event space, and there's no place better suited for Fall Fest than an apple orchard. Plus, I think our harvest party is the week after Fall Fest. No schedule interferences. It's perfect."

Olivia's face lights up. "Oh my God, that is the best idea I've ever heard. You have to tell her as soon as possible. I'm sure they're almost done planning, but everything they were going to have at the clearing, they can have at your orchard. If anything, it makes it all easier."

"Exactly." My mind races through all the cool things we can help AQF with for Fall Fest. We could do a pie eating contest, bobbing for apples, a golden apple hunt. I grin at the memory of the golden apple hunt, one of my father's most brilliant ideas to keep me and Aiden entertained when we were young. He spray-painted an apple gold, told us to wait in our rooms, then hid it in the orchard. It would take us all day, a grand adventure, to find the treasured golden apple.

"Maggie?"

"Hmm?"

Her lips skim the shell of my ear, and every golden apple in my thoughts is applesauce. Her hand is so close, I'm worried she can feel the effect her touch is having. She drags her lips over my ear again, this time with a warm breath that tickles my spine. I'm a mixed mess of hot and cold. Fevering.

"Dance with me."

"Dancing isn't really my—"

She pulls her hand back, leaving my thigh feeling completely naked, and I realize I will do anything for her to touch me again. "Please."

"Okay."

"Do you need another beer?" she asks.

"No. I'm good, thank you. One is my limit if I'm driving."

She smiles and throws the fry at Ashley. "Come on, y'all. We're dancing," she says.

I'm grateful for the crowded dance floor. Anonymity is the name of the game for me if I'm dancing because quite frankly, I either look like a chicken with its head cut off or the most awkward version of my middle school self. Right now, I'm bobbing my head and shuffling my feet, so I guess I'm going with awkward middle schooler tonight. The girls twirl each other around in complete joy and comfort. *How do some people dance so effortlessly?*

Tessa and Ashely dance a little closer to each other every second until Ashley's ass is basically in Tessa's hands. Olivia does a form of a moonwalk away from them and back over to me, wordlessly grabbing my hand and pulling me into the deep end, away from my safe space on the edge. I wade through sweaty people until we disappear into the thick of it. There's no Ashley, no Tessa, no Scott or Aiden. Just me and Olivia.

The band begins to play "Friends in Low Places," and the entire pub erupts in excitement. Olivia wraps her arms around my neck and sways her hips, sending all the pretty flowers on her skirt dancing. When I fail to do literally anything with my hands, she drops hers from the back of my neck and runs them down my shoulders and arms until she reaches my hands. She tugs them away from my sides and positions them right on the curve of her hips, then lassos me again. She sways, and it takes everything in me not to run my fingers up and down her frame.

When a larger gentleman stumbles backward behind her, I tighten my grip and pull her into me so she doesn't get flattened by the giant drunk guy. A small gasp escapes her lips when her chest collides with mine; I can feel it under my jaw. I don't let her go. Instead, I wrap my arms around her waist and keep her enveloped in me, her fingers tangled in the hair at the nape of my neck. All of a sudden, I feel very in control.

"Wait," she murmurs and spins in my arms. Her back against me makes me crazy for her, and she knows it. As she scans the pub, she pushes into me, her fingers interlaced with mine across her belly. My mouth skims her hair, and I soak in every inch of her. "I just saw Ryan leave, but where's Laura?"

I reluctantly let her go and do my own scan of the bar. Being sober makes me feel like it's my responsibility to look out for the birthday girl, and she was already three sheets to the wind when we got here an hour ago. *Where is she?*

CHAPTER SEVEN

Olivia and I squeeze our way off the dance floor and back to the bar. We scan the length of it, looking for Laura, but can't find her. She's not in the bathroom, either. A drip of panic forms in my chest. Ryan was too drunk to drive, and she was way too drunk to give consent if she left with him. It's not a good situation for her, and I was supposed to take her home. She hasn't responded to my texts, and I don't know what to do.

"Should we check her dorm?" I ask.

Olivia looks at me, worrying her lip. "I don't know. She's probably with Ryan."

"Shit. I don't even know where he lives."

Her eyes catch on something behind me, and her entire face brightens. "Oh, thank God." She laughs and drops her head against my shoulder.

I spin to find Laura tucked in a corner booth, demolishing a plate of nachos. A red stain of salsa stands bright against her yellow shirt, and broken chips lie scattered over the table. She looks at us and grins. I laugh as I take Olivia's hand and walk over.

We slide into the booth across from her. "Hey. Where'd Ryan go?" I ask.

She crunches on her nachos, a drip of sour cream forming at the corner of her mouth. "He took a cab home," she says.

Phew. Everyone is safe. "That's cool. Do you want to go home after you finish your nachos? I bet you've had a long day of celebration," Olivia says.

She nods and licks her refried-bean-plastered fingers. I try not to gag as I watch her add a layer of saliva to them and reach for her water.

"You're cringing," Olivia whispers.

I straighten and try to wipe my face clean of any judgment. "Sorry," I whisper back.

"Are you hungry?" she asks.

I can't help but glance at Laura's nacho explosion and chuckle. "No. I don't think so."

She laughs and squeezes my hand. "Can't blame you." Laura pushes her plate away and lets out a burp that sounds like it had a fifty percent chance of preceding vomit. Olivia reaches across me, plucks a handful of napkins from the dispenser, and hands them to Laura. "Here you go. Those nachos look good."

Laura takes the napkins and does her best to wipe her hands clean. "Can we go home?" she asks.

I nod. "Yes. Definitely."

"I'll go let the others know," Olivia says.

Once we pile Laura into my truck, I climb in the driver's seat, and Olivia takes shotgun, Laura pinned between us. The second the engine rumbles to life, Laura drops her head against the back of the seat and passes out. "Laura?" I ask, just to see if Olivia and I are alone. There's no response.

"Wow. She went hard," Olivia says, leaning forward to peek at me from behind her.

I shift into gear and turn onto the main road back to campus. "For real. They must have done some serious pregaming." A beat passes. "Thanks for coming with me. You didn't have to."

"I know. I wanted to spend more time with you. Maybe after we get Laura settled, we can do something? It's only ten," she says.

The suggestion makes my chest rumble like my old Ranger. "Yeah. I'd like that." I reach for the stereo and turn on my favorite station, classic country. It's my favorite because it doesn't swarm you with nonstop Hank Williams Jr. *Vomit.* But it plays that twangy rockabilly gold. Freddy Fender fills my truck, and we drive in peace back to the university, Laura snoring between us.

I pull into the upper quad parking lot and turn off the engine. "You ready?" I ask Olivia.

She leans over and smiles. "Yes. Let's put her to bed and go do something fun." She gently squeezes Laura's wrist and says, "Hey, Laura. It's time to wake up, okay?" Laura stirs and emits a groan of disapproval. "You're going to be way comfier in your bed. Come on, now." At the mention of her bed, Laura cracks open her eyes and swallows what sounds to be a pretty bad case of sleep mouth.

"Mm-kay," she says.

We help her down from the truck and each take an arm to walk her to Baker Hall, across the quad from Magnolia. The lamps bathe the pathway, pouring shadows into the cracks of the cobblestone. Easier to navigate the trippy stones in this light. The breeze has picked up a chill; I can see it in the tightness of Olivia's jaw, and when we stop at the steps of Baker to search for Laura's lion card, she wraps her arms around herself.

"Here." I peel off my flannel and hand it to her.

"Oh, I can't. You'll be cold." But as if her arms have a mind of their own, they snake into my shirt as she speaks. She looks a little guilty as she pulls it tight. "Thanks."

"No problem." The breeze hits me, and I do my best not to show any outward sign of being cold as Olivia looks me up and down. I feel almost naked in my tank top, the cold pointing out just how much skin I have on display.

Laura groans and pulls her head out of her purse. "I gave it to you," she says, pointing at Olivia.

Olivia jumps at the accusation "What? You have your room key right there." She points to the green carabiner of keys hanging from Laura's beltloop.

"My lion card, not my room key. In the booth. You told me to give it to you so that you could let me in," Laura says, her words hoarse and sleepy.

Olivia pats her entire body and fishes through pockets of her skirt that I didn't even know existed. "Oh my God," she says. "I don't have it." She looks from me to Laura and back to me. "I don't have it," she repeats. I could chalk this up to the same thing as her not bringing my notes to class, but it's different. She had all the best intentions to help.

"Hey," I say, squeezing her arm. "It's okay. Look where we are." I nod to the stone lettering above the awning.

"Baker."

I chuckle. Her anxiety is completely misplaced. "Exactly. We know a lot of people who live here. How about you text Bailey to let us in? It's before eleven on a Friday night."

It only takes a minute for Bailey to text back. "She's not home, but she's sending her friend, Luke, to let us in," Olivia says.

Almost at the same time she stops reading, the front door of Baker swings open, and a big guy with dark brown hair holds it for us. He's dressed in navy sweats and an Atlanta United soccer shirt, the fabric stretched across his barrel chest. "Hey. Come on in," he says.

We all shuffle into the common room, which resembles Magnolia's almost to a T. The same coat of arms hangs above the same roaring gas fireplace. The same furniture sits on the same navy and burgundy rug. "Thank you so much, Luke," I say.

He shrugs. "It's not a problem at all. We were all hanging out in the basement. Do you need help with anything else?" He eyes Laura.

"Nope. I think we're good." Olivia squeezes Laura's shoulder, and Laura sways into her. "I'll call Ash and tell her to look for your lion card before they leave, okay?"

She nods.

We say good night to Luke and, after some major persuading, convince Laura to brush her teeth and put on her pj's. Once she's tucked in and snoring, we creep out of her room and back into the night. Olivia slips her hand into mine as we glide down the steps of Baker Hall and walk back to the parking lot.

"All right. Done with the chores. Now what do you want to do?" she asks.

We skip over a root that pushes through the cobblestone. "I have to move my truck to the main parking deck." As we turn the corner into the upper quad parking lot and my truck becomes visible, I get an idea. "Do you know how to drive stick?"

We stop at the driver's side. "No," she says. I unlock it and hold the door, nodding for her to get in. "Oh no. I don't think you want me to drive." She waves in front of her face. "I'm clumsy, I don't know what I'm doing, and I'll probably destroy your clutch."

I laugh and shake my head. "Come on. The fact that you even know what a clutch is puts you way ahead of the curve. You'll be a natural. I know it."

She shakes her head. "You have to promise to not get mad at me. I'm telling you, this isn't going to go well."

I lay my hand over my heart. "I promise."

She sighs and climbs into the driver's seat. I jog around to the other side, a grin pinching my cheeks. I'm pretty much on a date with Olivia Cypress. I slide in next to her and begin my spiel. "Okay. First, start the engine by pushing in the brake and the clutch and turning the key."

She considers my directions for a moment, then asks, "Um. Which one is the brake?"

"The clutch is on the far left. You'll operate it with your left foot, then the brake and the gas are the same as a regular car. Brake on the left, gas on the right."

She nods and compresses the brake and clutch, then turns on the engine.

I hold up my hand to stop her from doing anything else as I reach for the gearshift. "Perfect. Now, don't release the"—the trucks lurches and dies—"clutch," I finish and erupt into laughter.

"I told you I'd be bad at this," she whines.

I rub her knee. "Aw, come on. Let's try again, and if you don't want to do it anymore, I'll go park in the deck, and we can do something else. Deal?"

She sighs. "Okay. Deal."

The parking lot is mostly empty, and there is space in front of us for Olivia to drive if she can get into first gear. "All right. Start the car again, and this time, don't take your foot off the clutch until I say."

Once she gets the truck started again, I reach over and shift into neutral for her. "Okay. Now that we're in neutral, you can release the clutch, and nothing will happen." She looks at me and bites her lip. "I promise."

She winces as she releases the clutch as if expecting the truck to lurch and die again. When nothing happens, she lets out a breath and grins.

"Awesome. You have to shift gears while the clutch is engaged, so press in the clutch and shift to first. Don't let it go once you're done."

She groans. "Maggie, I don't want to. It's going to jump and scare me and ruin your car."

I rub her back and lean over to look her in the eye. "Who cares if you stall out? Everyone stalls. I still stall. It happens." She nods and shifts to first.

"Okay. Now for the tricky part. Release the clutch slowly, and give it some gas at the same—"

The truck takes a dramatic jump forward, then dies, and I'm thrown into the back of the bench seat. I laugh so hard, tears gather at the corners of my eyes.

Olivia flings the door open and flees. "I am so done, Maggie. Don't you make me do that again." She stares at me from outside the truck, her arms crossed.

I take a second to catch my breath and slide into the driver's seat. "But you were such a natural," I say through a grin.

"Oh, shut up."

I pull the door shut and roll down my window. "You coming?"

"Ugh. Yes."

I pull out of the parking lot onto one of the small streets that dissects campus.

"I'm starting to think this was a ploy to make me even more impressed with the fact that you can drive a stick. And you let me wear your flannel…" she says.

I smile and sneak a peek at her before I drive into the parking deck. "I'm pulling out all the stops tonight. Need all the points I can get." I park in my usual spot and turn off the engine. A quiet darkness fills the cab, and she takes my hand again.

"What are you going to cash them in for?" she asks.

"Hmm." I scratch my chin and look at the faded, stained ceiling of my truck. "Got any oversized stuffed animals in your dorm room?"

She laughs and leans her head on my shoulder. "Nope. All I have in my dorm room is a roommate, unfortunately."

"Bummer. All I have in my dorm room is a roommate and a quasi-roommate."

She sighs and nuzzles into me. "Double bummer."

Her touch sends my brain into overdrive. We could go to Ashley's house, but she has those weird roommates I don't want to deal with. We could stay in my truck, but campus security patrols the parking lots almost nonstop at night. The fourth floor—the quiet floor—of the library is tempting, but it's bright and feels too public for whatever Olivia and I are going to do tonight. "I know where we should go."

She looks at me. "Oh yeah?"

"Yeah. That is, if you want to keep hanging out."

She leans in and kisses my cheek. I swallow, my entire face heating under the contact of her lips. "Where are we going?"

I grin. "The greenhouses."

❖

Greenhouse One is where Dr. Petrova does her research on Pierce's disease–resistant rootstock for growing *Vitis vinifera*—European wine grapes—in the Southeast. The vines are gone, though. She's starting over in the spring, and the only thing in there is turnips and chard. I'm technically allowed in the greenhouses twenty-four hours a day because I help Dr. Petrova with her research, but as we skip down the steps to the large glass buildings, I keep my eyes peeled for campus security.

Sure, the greenhouses are made of glass, but it's dark, and they're filled with so many plants that no one would know we're in there. I reach for the padlock, goose bumps covering my arms, and reconsider. "It's chilly out, huh?"

Olivia huddles next to me and nods, shifting her weight from foot to foot.

"How about we hang out in the hothouse? The name is a little extreme. It's just humid and warm."

"Oh my God. Please."

We walk to Greenhouse Three, the hothouse. The structure is the same as the other two, but this one is climate-controlled to grow plants like banana trees, orchids, and other tropical perennials. I fumble with my keys and pop open the padlock. A rush of thick warm air welcomes us into paradise. Only fragments of soft orange from the streetlights sneak in through the glass. The long, lavish banana leaves pose in the dark, giving me the sense that we've walked in on something, and everything halted at our presence.

"Wow," Olivia says, crouching to read the label, but it's too dark.

I step next to her and say, "African iris. It's almost unfair how beautiful these guys are." I gently finger one of the white and purple flowers, its petals soft and full of life. The hum of the heater shuts off, and Olivia turns to me, reaching for my cheek. Her touch is as soft as the iris.

Walking into Nan's with Olivia at my side, I knew tonight was leading to this moment. Even before her hand took a trip up my thigh and before we pressed into each other on the dance floor, I knew that tonight, I would kiss Olivia Cypress. I didn't know it would be here among some of the most beautiful plants on campus and under a blanket of warm, humid darkness. I didn't know she'd be wearing my green flannel and looking at me with the sincerest longing in her eyes. These are all just happy surprises.

Her parted lips turn up in a mischievous grin. She takes my hand and leads me to the dusty workbench. I stand in front of her as she leans against it.

"Let me…" I slip my hands under the shoulders of my flannel, taken by the smoothness of her skin, and ease it down her arms. Her breath stutters as I run my hands down the length of her, freeing my shirt. I reach behind her and lay it on the soil-covered table. "Now you won't get your skirt dirty. It's so beautiful." I pinch the fabric.

She hops onto the edge of the table and crooks her finger at me. "Come here."

I step between her legs, a hand on either knee, and press my lips against hers. She sighs and pulls me deeper into her. Her mouth is hot and wet and tastes like the champagne of kisses. And as I make out with Olivia Cypress on an old potting bench in Greenhouse Three, I begin to realize…

I am completely screwed.

CHAPTER EIGHT

Aiden walks into the dining hall looking like Godzilla took a dump on Jake Gyllenhaal, then punched him in the face; unfortunately, he is Jake in this scenario. While we were dealing with Laura and doing some "research" in the greenhouse, Aiden was dealing with his relationship. He skipped Mass on Sunday and texted me that he and Scott had agreed to take "a break." I told him to come over and tell us about it, but he wanted to be alone, and now, I can see why. My little brother has been completely destroyed by this.

"He looks like shit," I murmur as we watch him zombie his way to the coffee counter and pour himself a drip. No cream—I have never seen Aiden drink black coffee—probably to match his dark mood.

Tessa cranes her neck. "Mmm. Yeah. Little bro looks like he got stuck in the spin cycle with a brick."

"He looks like he stepped on a crack and actually broke his mother's back," Ashley adds.

"Y'all..." We turn our attention to Olivia, who sits casually next to me as if she's been sitting next to me for years. Our threesome of friends has turned into a foursome. My stomach churns with happiness and anxiety over this realization. Like it has all weekend. "He looks heartbroken."

This is a side to Olivia I don't know very well. Aiden is my brother, and I just likened him to a feces-covered Jake Gyllenhaal after losing a fight to a giant lizard, but she took one look at him and now her heart is seemingly breaking for him. Maybe it's because she didn't have to put up with him her whole life, but maybe she's super empathetic. It rounds out her independent and passionate side.

Aiden trudges over, and we all shift in our seats and change the topic as he approaches.

"It was hilarious," I spit out as he sits next to Tessa.

"What are y'all talking about?" he asks, scanning us with the most depressed expression I've ever seen.

Olivia clears her throat and hops in to save me. "We're just laughing about Laura's nacho explosion on Friday. You should've seen it, Aiden. Bless her heart, she was so drunk, she practically drooled nachos all over herself."

He winces. "Gross."

"It was even grosser in person. Trust me," I add. I feel a little guilty talking about Laura this way. We all have our drunken-nacho moments, but we needed a quick pivot.

"That's what happened with Laura, but what about you? What's the story, little bro?" Tessa asks.

He sighs, and we all stop picking at what's left of our breakfast to give him our full attention. "I kissed him at Nan's, and he was into it at first. It was super hot. I had him against a wall in the bathroom stall and—"

I hold up a hand to cut him off. "We probably don't need all the details. Let's skip to after the make-out session."

He takes a sip of his black coffee and grimaces. "Anyway, after that, his whole attitude changed. He was brooding and short with me. Then, he disappeared and texted me that he was going to spend the weekend at home, and he thought it was best we take a break from 'whatever this is.'" Aiden drops his hand on the table, making our silverware jump. "It's a fucking relationship is what it is."

I wince, and he takes a deep breath. "He must be skipping class today because I still haven't seen him," he adds.

Olivia squeezes my wrist under the table, and all of a sudden, I'm wondering what *this* is between us. Are we a fling? Are we basically together? I want the answer to be yes and no to both. She squeezes me again, and I come back to earth.

I clear my throat and look at Aiden. "This must be really hard for you. Seems like the only thing you can do is give him space and wait to see what he wants. I bet he'll come around," I say.

"I guess." He shrugs and tries to brave his coffee again. "What did y'all get up to the rest of the weekend?"

Tessa and Ashley exchange a look full of inuendo and blushing. "We spent the weekend at my house," Ashley says.

"Gross," I say.

Tessa throws her dirty napkin at me. "Get your mind out the gutter. We were just watering her plants and smoking some weed. Oh, and we binged *Game of Thrones*. We haven't made it to season four yet. No spoilers."

Aiden looks at me.

I shrug. "Not much. Got caught up on some assignments and studying. And I went to church *alone*, you heathen."

"You're religious?" Olivia asks.

I hate this question. It's full of...so much. It's a yes or no question with the purpose of putting me into a singular box of identity. Yes, I'm religious. Yes, I go to Mass. But my relationship to religion is as unique as my fingerprint and a completely different thing entirely from my faith. Asking me this question so casually tells me that Olivia probably doesn't understand that or hasn't thought about it that way. Kind of like her thoughts about organic farming. Regardless, it's not the time to dive into it.

"Yes."

She nods, and I check my phone, hoping it's time to end this conversation and head to class. "Well, we should get going. You ready?" I ask Olivia.

She tidies her area. "Ready. Hang in there, Aiden. You're clearly a catch. And soon, he's going to figure out he can't live without you."

Her soft words loosen some of the melancholy that clings to him. It makes me proud to be involved with her...in whatever vague way. Almost makes me forget about how her asking about religion made me feel the exact opposite.

We walk down the concourse to the agriculture building, the air beginning to carry an October chill. I don't know what to say. I feel a little off from Olivia asking if I'm religious. Being friends—more than friends—with her feels like I'm always waiting for the other shoe to drop. When is she going to realize I'm not what she wants? I'm not edgy or well-traveled. I'm religious, not spiritual. And when am I going to admit that she's not what I want? She can't be the rock that I need. She's a puddle evaporating in the August heat. A puddle that I am very attached to.

"I didn't mean to put you on the spot back there," she says.

I loop my thumbs through my backpack straps and watch a red-tailed hawk circle the pines. At least she's aware that she did put me on the spot. "It kind of feels like you want everything to be in a nice labeled box. Organic, vegan, religious, atheist…but just like how organic doesn't cover it, I feel like religious doesn't cover it."

She slows as she listens. I match her pace and check my phone to make sure we won't be late. "I love going to Mass, but I'm not ignorant of everything the church has done. I've negotiated my relationship with religion, and it works for me. It's important to me, and it felt like you made some assumptions about me when I said yes."

She takes a moment before she responds. "It's interesting you think I want everything boxed and labeled. I would have called you the black-and-white one. I understand what you mean, though." Her brows furrow against the morning sun. "My whole world is gray, Maggie, and I'm definitely not interested in forcing people or things into data boxes, you know, except for finance." She breaks into a grin. "Look, I didn't mean to offend you. You are entitled to your own feelings about religion. I'm just a curious person who wants to know more about you. That was something I didn't know before, and it caught my attention when you mentioned it." She knocks against my shoulder, bringing a little levity to our conversation. "That's all. I don't care that you're religious. It doesn't change how I see you, okay?"

I smile. I can't help it. Whatever Olivia and I have going on feels destined to blow up in my face, but I want to take it as far as I can with her, like a game of chicken. I'm trying to ignore the inevitable end where we crash and blow ourselves to pieces. Or at least, the end where she disappears next year for her internship.

"Sorry for being defensive. When Tessa found out I go to church, I swear her head spun around like the girl from *The Exorcist*. She would not let it go."

Olivia chuckles. "I can totally see that from her."

"Let's get together after class sometime this week and hammer out the next steps in our project," I say.

"Sounds good to me. I can't wait to get my hands on those spreadsheets."

And I can't wait to get my hands back on her.

❖

After class on Tuesday, I call my dad to ask him about hosting Fall Fest. "Hey, Dad. How's it going over there?"

"It's going as well as usual. No complaints. How's school?"

"It's great. Classes are pretty chill this semester, Tessa and Ashley are still going strong, and Aiden is doing well." The last part is a lie, but it's not my business to tell our dad that Aiden is brokenhearted over his roommate.

"That's excellent news. You have to get Tessa and Ashley to the orchard at some point. We have that spare bedroom whenever they want to take a break from Alder and come see their favorite apple farmer."

I love the fact that he is so unfazed about the big fat queer world we live in. And that he's always treated me and Aiden like adults and with respect. Some parents would make Ashley and Tessa sleep in different rooms out of principle, as if they haven't been hooking up for two years now. What's the point?

I chuckle against my phone. "They do love Uncle Ward."

"You rascal."

I pause for a moment and bask in the warmth of our banter. It's interactions like these that I crave with him. The levity. Before I change the topic, I note that I was the impetus of this one. Maybe I can set a more lighthearted tone between us in the future. "Actually, Dad, speaking of visiting—"

"Not to work."

"Not to work, I promise. You remember that club that our friends run? Alder Queer Fellowship?"

"Yes, I remember."

"They're hosting an event called Fall Fest, combining the softball team's Apple Wars with AQF's fall party. There will be the apple pitching contest, bobbing for apples, and fried pie. All the good stuff. I thought it might make sense for them to have Fall Fest at the orchard. They don't have to haul away all the culled fruit, it's the perfect autumnal setting, and we continue to build our exposure." The other end of the line remains quiet for a second longer than I'd like. "Dad?"

"I'm processing. When is it?"

"The weekend before the harvest party."

"Holy hell. In two weeks? It's a bit short notice, Mags. Not really how I like to run things."

His disappointment is a blow, but he's right. I should have been more on top of this. Asking him at the last minute makes it look like I don't value his time. "I understand."

"My answer is yes. Text me the email address of whoever runs the club, and I'll extend an offer."

I do a silent happy dance. "You're the best, Dad. This is going to be great."

"Sounds like the perfect event for us."

"Oh, and thanks for sending me those spreadsheets for our project."

He's quiet again for a beat. "Not a problem. Only use what you need. It's our private business what's on those spreadsheets, and I'm trusting you to use your best judgment on how much information you want to share. Understand?"

"Yes, sir."

After I hang up, I send him Bailey's contact information and send her and the rest of the AQF officers a quick email explaining our offer, what the orchard is like, and the amenities that would be available to AQF if they let us host their party and that my father will be reaching out with more details. An excitement builds in me after I hit send, and the first person I want to tell is Olivia. I pull up our conversation and text her: *Guess what?*

Her response is quick: *You've decided you actually like me for real this time?*

I smile and shake my head. *I thought I made that clear in the greenhouse. Can you meet up? I have the data for our farm and some other fun news to share.*

Yeah. I'm in Green Hall. Booth seven. Come meet me?

Be there in twenty.

Green Hall is where the orchestra performs. In addition to the actual orchestra hall, there are noise-proof music booths available to non-orchestra students. Some of the booths are empty, for folks who have their own instruments, and some have small pianos. I round the corner of the hall and stop in front of booth number seven. Olivia plays something on the piano, her lips moving in sync with her fingers. She looks so at home. There's something in her face that normally isn't there, a small puzzle piece of joy.

I tap on the little window, and she turns and smiles. "Hi," she says as she opens the door.

I step into the small room and drop my bag in the corner. It's warm but not unpleasantly so, and the air smells like her.

"Hi." I pull her into a quick hug and kiss the top of her head. I was hoping for a smooth greeting that says *I would like to touch your body and make out with you while maintaining a healthy and fun friendship and partnership*. But my top-of-the-head kiss feels awkward and lame. We haven't kissed or had any intimate moments since the greenhouse, and I can't help but wonder if something has changed between us. Maybe she's over it. But her text hinted at the opposite.

My cheeks are hot when she pulls out of our embrace, and I am feeling very claustrophobic in the small booth. She pats the piano bench. "Do you play?"

"My mom tried to give Aiden and me lessons when we were little. I think we broke her heart when we kept running away anytime she tried to sit us down to teach us. We wanted to be outside no matter what. They could barely get us in for supper."

She smiles and runs her fingers over the keys. "I take that as a no."

"But I loved listening to her play. After dinner on a winter night, with all the candles lit, she would play for us. My dad would sip bourbon and watch her with such adoration…" My words stop flowing, and my gut twists over the memory, one of the last I have of her in our house. Of us all together. We were mesmerized by her talent, by her beauty, by her effortless radiance.

My attention is gradually pulled back to reality when I notice Olivia playing a calm number. When I look at her, she smiles. "Are you okay, Maggie?" Her question is as gentle as the melody, as if she's trying to not wake me from my nostalgia.

I nod. "You play beautifully." Even though watching her play and the joy that it seems to bring her reminds me of my mom, I don't want to think about it right now. It makes me want to wrap my arms around her and force her to stay with me in East Sparrow forever, never leaving my side. It also makes me want to run away from her as far and as fast as I can. Before she can run away from me.

Her fingers barely look like they strike the keys as they skate along. "You're feeling things," she says, letting her hands fall into her lap. The quiet is abrupt.

"Don't stop, please." I cover her hands. What am I going to do? Literally plop them back on the piano? "I am feeling things, but they're not bad."

She considers me, the corner of her lip trapped under her teeth. She begins to play the same calm song as before. "They don't seem to be necessarily good, either." The rings on her fingers mesmerize me as they flash on a C and stretch to glow on a D.

"Do you sing?" I ask.

"Not as well as I play, but yes."

I don't ask her to, but I hope one day, I'll get to hear it. Something tells me she's better than she's letting on. She stops and spins to face me, her legs on either side of the bench. "You have news. Tell me."

I just want to lie on the floor while she plays, but that moment is over. "Yeah. I was on the phone with my dad, and he agreed to host Fall Fest. He's emailing Bailey today."

She grabs my thigh and squeezes, nearly sending me into an oblivion of hope that maybe we can recreate our moment from Friday night. "That is so fantastic. It's going to be perfect. I can obviously help in whatever way you need." Her offer makes me feel like we're a team beyond our class project. Like we were a team getting Laura home. Olivia isn't an officer of AQF, and she doesn't work on the farm. She really has no dog in this fight, yet she's offering to take this on with me.

"I'm sure we could use the help."

"I can't wait."

I clear my throat and swing my legs over the bench. "I also have the spreadsheets my dad sent me." I snag my laptop from my backpack.

"Oh, perfect."

I feel her watching as I power on the computer and wait for it to load. I smooth my hair and tuck a piece behind my ear.

"You're, like, sickeningly beautiful," she says.

She stares at me. She stares at my ear, then drops her eyes to my neck, my hands, my boots. Her gaze lights the wick of my blush all the way down my body; I can see it spread into my hands. I think I'm fine looking, but I have never felt sexier than when Olivia rakes me with her eyes. My login screen finally loads, but my fingers freeze above the keys.

"Thank you. I used to hate how I look because I look like her... my mom." I stare at my dumb pink hands. Why do I keep bringing her up? I don't want to ruin this moment, and thinking about her makes my stomach ache.

In a slow, careful move, Olivia takes my laptop and sets it in the corner between the piano and the wall, leaving my hands feeling even more awkward until she rescues them by pulling them into her lap, stoking the flames under my skin. "She must be a very beautiful woman."

I swallow. "She is. I don't want to be like her, though. I want to be like my dad, but Aiden got his darker features. Which is funny because he's more like my mom."

She strokes the back of my hand. "How is he like your mom?"

The blue in her eyes is like melting ice, and the sight stills me but not enough to stop me from scratching this itch. "He's a runner." *Like you.*

"A runner? And where has he gone?" Her hands pause.

"Nowhere, yet. But he'll be looking at us in his rearview after graduation, no doubt. Just like my mom. He'll probably rarely visit and get all swept away by whatever city he ends up in."

She worries her lip. "And you don't want that for him?"

I sigh. "He can do whatever he wants. Sure, I want him to be happy. But he has everything he could ever want on the farm. Family and friends and a great job."

"Do you have everything you could ever want on your farm?"

"Yes, I..." She stays quiet as I struggle to finish. My thinly veiled attempt to relate her to Aiden and my mom is blowing up, and I don't want to admit my own feelings about my locked-in life plan. It's the life I most desperately want, but there is one thing I'm scared to lose. To not find. "Yes, I do. The only thing I don't have is someone to share it with. No one moves to East Sparrow, and no one stays in East Sparrow." As I say the words, the horrifying reality settles on me that I only have a year and a half left to find a queer woman—which is already tricky at Alder—who is willing to live on a farm in the Georgia countryside for the rest of her life with me.

It's impossible.

"Sometimes, I think you're trying to convince yourself of something. Maybe if you loosened the reins on your ten-year plan a little, you could find what you're truly looking for."

I give a sardonic little chuckle. "I won't compromise my dreams. I've been my father's right hand since I could walk, and I refuse to let him down. Taking over the farm means everything to me, and I'm not going to risk it by bailing on him for a couple years to travel. What if he hires someone else?" To my horror, I put air quotes around "travel."

"You know, Maggie, if you could get your head out your own ass for longer than a couple minutes…" I whip my head around, completely taken aback by her affront. "That's right. If you could *get your head out your ass*, maybe you'd be able to see that you've met a girl who really likes you and wants to get to know you. She even kind of likes that you're stubborn as hell and want to miss out on everything this world has to offer that isn't East Sparrow." She shakes her head. "Just because I love to travel doesn't mean I don't want to settle down. Those two things are so far from mutually exclusive."

I have no words, but I shake my head and close my mouth when I notice its dryness. "But," I say, startling myself, "what am I supposed to do? You're leaving for an entire semester next year, Olivia. You'll be gone for half our senior year, and then what? Then you think you're just going to plop down on the farm with me? How could you ever want that? You want to be free to do whatever you want and go wherever you want. You don't want this," I say, pressing a hand to my chest.

She shakes her head, and those currents in her eyes pulse as she stares into my goddamn soul. "You have no idea what I want. And honestly, I think you have no idea what you want either."

"That's not—"

"You're scared of me because you think I'm a runner. You think everyone is so weak and that all we do is run from things, but I'm running toward something. I'm running home. To that warm place that feels so elusive until…"

She pauses for a moment and brushes her hair behind her ear, muttering, "Damnit." She sighs. "Until one day, I find what I never had, and I wake up safe and sound. Not all of us are born home like you. You think it's your ten-year plan, your last name on that building, or the trees rooted in your daddy's land, but it's here." She jabs me hard in the chest. An instant pain strikes under her finger, but I try not to flinch. "You don't need to search high and low or jump on planes and trains. You're already home. No matter where you are."

Her eyes hold a sheen of wetness as she watches me. I give in and rub where she poked me. There is so much to respond to, but I have no idea where to start. "You're not home?"

My question pushes a tear over her bottom lid, and it splashes on the bench between her thighs. Maybe I should have started somewhere else. She wipes her eye and chuckles. "Wow, your listening comprehension is spot-on."

Okay, maybe it was a sarcastic chuckle, but she saves me from having to respond to her dig. "Listen," she starts. "Like all of us, you have to chase what you want. Especially the things that you can't find in East Sparrow."

The realization that Olivia Cypress may be the one thing I want outside of my perfectly planned out little life terrifies the shit out of me. What scares me more is wanting what she represents: a break in my plans. My skin prickles, as if her words are scratching me, pushing me into that terrible little place outside my comfort zone. The place where the pistol blasts, and I'm off to the races, chasing her. I guess the only thing I can do is run.

"I want you," I say and snatch her hands before they disappear into thin air. Olivia is feeling more and more like a precious resource every day.

"What?" She shakes her head in confusion, more tears welling in her eyes, but her fingers tighten around mine.

"That's what you said, right? I have to chase what I want? That if I could get my head out my ass, I'd see there's a girl who likes me?"

She nods, a blush creeping up her neck and into her soft cheeks.

"Well, I want *you*. I'm a very lucky person, you're right. But I've never felt how I feel when I'm with you. I may be home, but you make me feel alive, like cracking open the windows on the first day of spring." I swallow and brush a tear from her cheek. "I know we've only recently met, and this is a lot to lay out there so early, but I'd like to continue down the path we're on."

She nods against the palm of my hand.

"Let's go slow. Nice and easy," I say.

She takes a deep breath and rubs her eyes. I lean into her and press my lips against her salty cheek. It only takes a second before she turns and captures my kiss. Her lips are dry but soft, like rose petals pressed in a diary. I wrap my arms around her and pull her into me, opening my mouth to her tongue. Our heated kiss only lasts for a second before she flattens a palm over the throbbing spot on my chest where she poked me and pushes me away. She runs her finger down the line of my jaw and bites her lip, taking some of the sting out of our broken kiss.

"We're supposed to go slow, remember?" she asks.

I grab her hand from my jaw and press it over my heart. "There's nothing slow about that." The grin spreading over her lips tells me she can feel my heart beat a thousand times per minute under her hand.

"Thank you for listening to me. I know I may have come across a little harsh," she says.

"You didn't." I chuckle and shake my head. "You did. But sometimes, I need to hear the ugly truth."

She clears her throat and fans her eyes. "Okay. How about we dive into those sexy spreadsheets of yours. I'm dying to see what's under the hood of Hyde Hill Farm." She grabs my laptop from the floor and hands it to me.

I pull up my email and download the Excel sheets my dad sent. There are three main spreadsheets, and Olivia points to a page titled *CPP*. "What's that?" she asks.

"Cost per plant. It breaks down the CPP for everything from the cost of rootstock and grafting to planting, pruning, spraying, and harvest." I scroll through the document and scan. "Very detailed, it seems."

"It seems? You're not familiar with these numbers? I thought you'd have them memorized at this point, Ms. Taking Over the Family Business."

I stare at the spreadsheet. It's hitting me that I have been completely excluded from the financial side of our business. My dad has done it in such a sly way that I didn't even notice. With my responsibilities around the farm growing every year, I didn't realize none of them were business-related. I have a horrifying thought that I'm the next Uncle Ward for my dad. Someone he doesn't trust with the books but who is handy to have around.

"Hey," she says, interrupting my spiral. "I'm sure he's just waiting for the right moment. And maybe this project is the perfect opportunity to show him what you can bring to the table on this side of things." I nod, and she leans in to kiss my cheek. She slides my computer into her lap and familiarizes herself with the structure of the data. "Plus, this is kind of my specialty. I'm here to help."

I take a deep breath and let her do her thing. It's nice to be partnered with someone who can actually teach me something. I love Laura, but she's not exactly experienced in agriculture or finance. "Thank you," I finally say.

She looks up and grins. "You're welcome. Is it okay if I email these to myself so I can sort through everything tonight?"

"Yeah. But, uh, don't show it around. My dad asked that we only use what we need for the project."

She arches a brow. "Sure. Of course." She taps one final button and closes my laptop. "Here."

I zip it away in my bag. "I should get going. Do you want to walk back together?"

She smiles and shakes her head. "I'm going to play a little longer. But I'm excited to see you tomorrow in class, and maybe after, we can talk more about the project."

I fish my arms through my backpack straps. "Definitely. Hopefully, we'll hear from Bailey by then, too." I lean in and give her a quick peck on the lips.

"See you later, Mags."

I leave Olivia to her music and walk back to Magnolia, my mind and heart racing. She's intoxicating and scary and warm. I pull my backpack against myself and groan. I have a terrifying feeling that falling in love with Olivia will lead me to the one place I just can't go.

And what scares me the most is that she makes me want to.

CHAPTER NINE

When I get back to the dorm, I find my crew lounging around listening to the Grateful Dead and crunching on an assortment of weird snacks. Including Scott. He and Aiden sit side by side on my bed, smiling and feeding each other Gushers as if they were bites of filet mignon.

"Scott. Welcome back," I say as I kick off my boots.

His cheeks turn a soft pink. "Hey, Maggie." He swallows and fidgets with a candy wrapper. Am I the scary big sister who intimidates her little brother's boyfriends?

"We're glad you're here," I say, not wanting to put him on the spot. I'll force the details out of Aiden later, but it seems they've figured something out that works for them. I turn to Ashley and Tessa. "I have something exciting to tell y'all."

"You and Olivia finally did it," Tessa blurts, and Ashley smacks her arm.

"What? No. Shut up, Tessa."

"What is actually going on between you guys?" Ashley asks. "No judgment. I thought I'd be able to get the tea from Olivia, but she's keeping her cards as close to her chest as you."

"Incoming," I say and pounce on Tessa's bed, squeezing my way into the small space between them that is definitely not big enough for me.

"Jesus, Mags. A little decorum, please," Tessa whines.

A warm feeling spreads through my chest as I think about Olivia. She must think there's something special between us, something worth holding in private for the time being. It feels almost protective. I want to return the favor and keep what I have with her to myself. Most of it, at least.

"We're honestly just friends right now," I say.

Aiden and Tessa cackle annoyingly, and Ashley and Scott exchange a knowing look.

"What?" I ask. "It's true."

"You are so full of shit," Aiden says. I give him a death glare that has surely lost all its effect over the years.

"Yeah, Mags. Everyone saw her taking you on a trip to *Thighland* in the booth at Nan's," Tessa says.

Ashley holds up a finger to announce she is the next speaker in this great debate. "You guys may not want to admit it yet, but you're an item."

"We are literally not together," I say. But as I say it, I wonder where we actually left things in Green Hall. When I walked out the door, I felt like I was in a relationship, but we never really detailed if we were exclusive or not. I think about Ashley and Tessa's relationship, how they're non-monogamous, and reframe my thinking of relationships versus exclusivity. Olivia and I never detailed if we are *committed* to each other yet. Committed in whatever way feels right between us.

"At Nan's, after she told me you guys were taking Laura home, I offered to give her a ride back so she didn't have to deal with it. And you know what she said?" Ashley asks.

Tessa nods like a high bobblehead with a stupid grin on her face. The truth is, I'm nervous to know exactly what Olivia and I are. Obviously, I like her and want to be with her, but it's also terrifying to shoot my shot. What if she ends up not liking me? What if she ends up running?

"What'd she say?" I ask.

"Why do you need to know if you're so confident nothing is going on?" Aiden asks, sarcasm peppering his words.

I point at him. "Who keeps inviting this kid to everything?"

Scott clears his throat. "Aiden is pretty silly," he says through a timid smile.

I stare, shocked that of all the things he could say after bailing on my brother and breaking his heart, he chooses to chime in on ribbing Aiden. Scott is a nice kid. I know this. But the bastard's on thin ice. The look on my face must reflect this because the pink in his cheeks heats to red, and he looks to Aiden for support.

Aiden pats his thigh. "Don't worry. She just hasn't gotten any in a while," Aiden says.

Tessa laughs herself into a wheezing fit while Ashley smothers a smile with her hand.

I shake my head. "I can't believe I call you jerks my friends. I've gotten along fine, for your information." I haven't since Sarah, but that's beside the point.

Scott clears his throat, seemingly finding the courage to speak again. "What did Olivia say?"

"What?" I ask, too annoyed with him to even attempt to recall what he's talking about.

He looks at Ashley. "What did she say when you offered to give her a ride home from Nan's?"

"Oh, right," Ashley says and turns to me. "She looked at the booth you were in and said, 'That's okay. I appreciate the offer, but I think I'm with Maggie now.'"

I swallow my excitement. That sounds a lot like commitment to me. "That could mean anything," I say.

"It means she wants your body," Aiden says in exasperation, his face in his palm.

Tessa clutches her chest and leans into me. "And your heart."

"You all disgust me. Except for maybe Ashley," I say.

Ashley gives me a side hug. "I am so honored." When she pulls away, she plants her pointer finger against her lips. "Wait. What were you going to tell us before we fell down the Olivia and Maggie have the hots for each other rabbit hole?"

"I feel so betrayed by you," I say. "You were supposed to be the nice one."

She shrugs. "Nice with a little spice."

"I don't think I want to tell you anymore."

"Come on. What's the big news?" Tessa asks, squeezing my knee.

"Fine. I talked to my dad earlier today, and he agreed to host AQF's Fall Fest at Hyde Hill Farm." I turn to Ashley. "If y'all would like to have it there, that is."

Her entire face tugs upward in excitement. "Yes. Oh my God, yes. A thousand times yes." She gives me a bear hug that threatens to pulverize my lungs. "I mean, it will be a group decision between the rest of the officers, but the orchard would be fucking perfect."

"I think so. All the apples are already there for the softball team, it's gorgeous in the fall, and there's tons of space for activities," I say.

"Thank you so much. I'm sure we'll have a decision after our meeting tomorrow. This is a way better option than the clearing. It's a huge perk to have it on your private property so no one can mess with us or accidentally stumble upon us when they just wanted to camp and crush beers."

"That's fair." I unwedge myself from between the lovers and push off the bed. "I'm going to grab a bite from the dining hall. Be back soon."

Scott flies to his feet. "I'll walk you out," he says. His words are unsure, as if he thinks I may cause him physical harm when I get him alone. It wouldn't be the first time I've gotten in a fight with a boy.

"Okay…"

The door closes behind us, and the awkwardness is deafening, but the ball is in his court, so I walk down the hallway as if I was alone. When I reach for the front door, Scott finally speaks.

"Maggie, wait." He shuffles his feet and wipes his hands down the front of his jeans. "I wanted to say that I know how it looked when I went home and didn't come back for class on Monday. And honestly, when I left after Nan's, I was upset. With Aiden. With myself. But I needed time and space to fully process…to fully process my queerness."

I pull my hand from the door handle and listen.

"When I got home, I was so torn up, my parents knew something was off. They were really concerned. I, uh, ended up telling them about me and Aiden."

"Holy shit. This is not what I was expecting. Are you okay?"

"It was actually really cathartic. For all of us." He gives me a soft smile, as if suggesting I should do whatever cathartic thing I need to do. "Listen, I'm in love with your brother. I know you probably don't like me very much right now, but I just wanted to tell you I know exactly what I want. I want Aiden. And I will do everything in my power to love and protect him."

My mind races as I listen to his proclamation. It weirds me out a little hearing someone be so gaga over my little brother, but mostly, it puts things into perspective for me. Scott, who I thought was meek, is so bold and fierce in his desires. Maybe I need to listen to Olivia and loosen up. Free myself from my rigid ten-year plan and fight for her, no matter where she ends up next year. No matter where *we* end up. I want Olivia Cypress to be mine.

I squeeze his shoulder. It feels odd being in this *as the older sibling, I accept you as my brother's partner* role, but here goes nothing. "That must have taken a lot of courage."

He nods.

"I know you're a good guy, and Aiden is mad for you. I'm happy you guys found each other." A grin spreads over his face, and his red cheeks begin to cool into his normal pale skin tone. I reach for the door again, then turn back. I forgot to deliver the fun line. "One more thing. If you ever hurt my brother again, I'll kill you."

His eyes dart to the metal clip of my knife that peeks out of my waistband, and his mouth cracks open, but no words come out.

"I'm kidding. Relax, man."

He nods and shakes his head in a circle. "Oh. Right."

I give his shoulder a quick squeeze. "Sorry. Didn't mean for that to sound real. Anyway, I'm going now. See you later, Scott."

He waves as I walk into the night. If that guy can chase what he wants and get it, I can chase Olivia Cypress. I pull up my texts with her. *I miss you*, I type. My thumb hovers over the send key. I take a deep breath and hit it.

❖

I wake up the next morning in a dark mood. The autumn night was chilly, and my quilt did little to keep me warm against the drafty window. I make a mental note to bring home a spare blanket from the farm after Fall Fest and pluck my phone from the nightstand. Still no response from Olivia. I rub my hands down my tired face and roll out of bed. I can hear Tessa in the shower. It's a rarity that she's up before me, but it makes sense that I'm the slow mover this morning. I was up until half past two thinking about Olivia and how she must have received my text.

I guess it was too much, too soon. Overbearing, maybe? But I could swear she gave me all the signs of wanting to take the next step together. I either completely misread her yesterday, or she's as flighty as I originally thought. The second I open up to her and do something that puts me in a vulnerable position, she completely abandons me. She has to know she's tormenting me by leaving me on "read" all night.

"Good morning," Tessa says as she emerges from the bathroom in a puff of steam.

I shuffle past her. "Morning," I mumble. I squirt some toothpaste on my brush and shove it in my mouth before she can make more conversation. I spit a foamy mess into the sink and wipe my mouth in the towel. The mirror is almost completely fogged, but I guarantee I look as terrible as I feel.

Tessa riffles through the top drawer of her dresser, pulling out her quintessential grunge-chic outfit. "What's wrong with you?"

I tug on my jeans and sigh. "Last night, I texted Olivia that I miss her, and she left me on read." I know I spent all last night doubling down on the fact that there's nothing going on between me and her, but I trust that everyone knows it's bullshit. And I trust that Tessa will skip the part where she rubs it in that she was right.

She cringes. "*Oof.* I know that feeling."

"So much for being vulnerable."

"She's a good person. I'm sure there's a reasonable explanation. Maybe her phone died, and her charger got eaten by a stray cat or something." She shrugs and drops her towel in a puddle around her feet. Tessa naked is a sight I've seen a million times. It morphed from shocking to mundane within the first two weeks of freshman year.

"Sounds likely." I fumble with the last button on my shirt only to realize I'm off by one. I sigh. "I'm not rushing to any conclusions, but you can't blame me for spinning out a little."

"No blame here," she says.

"No bra there either, I see."

She smooths her baggy Deadhead shirt and grins. "That's right. My body, my choice, bitch."

When I finally get my buttons in order, I double-check that I have everything I need for the day in my backpack. "What's up in your love life? Any progress with the hot TA?"

At the mention of her new crush, Tessa grins and does her signature slow-motion head bob. "Mmm. Yeah. Her name's Jocelyn, remember? And she is super fucking hot."

"Yeah, I know about her being hot. Hence, 'hot TA.' But have you asked her out?"

She scratches her fingers through her wet hair, pulling through knots and tangles. "She asked me out. It was really cute. We were in O-chem lab—"

"Where one naturally is with their O-chem TA."

She clears her throat. "As I was saying, we were in lab, and I was ready to be done. The sun was shining all bright, and the birds were chirping, and my lab coat and goggles felt oppressive. I waited a couple minutes before I walked up to her with a random guess about what the distillate was. She said, 'You think you can charm me into giving you the answer to the lab,' and I said, 'It's worth a shot.'"

"Tessa, you did not."

"Oh, I did. She said she wouldn't give me the answer, but she would give her number as a consolation prize."

"What? How do you have so much game, and can you please share some with me?"

She squeezes my shoulder. "Maggie, when will you realize that your toolbox is full? Line up the nail. Grab the hammer." She pretends to hit a nail into my arm. "And drive it in."

I drop my head back. "I'm trying. We'll see if I hit it head-on, or if I shank it and smash my thumb instead."

"Like I said, I'm sure there's an explanation."

"Yeah." I sigh. "Back to Jocelyn."

"Yes. Jocelyn. We've been texting, and she asked me out a couple days ago." Her grin crinkles the corners of her eyes.

"That's awesome, Tessa. Why didn't you tell me?"

Her gaze tags her shoes, then pops back to mine. "I guess I'm still getting used to sharing this with people outside my relationship."

"I get it. But I'm truly happy for you. I'm your number-one fan, right here. Did you tell her about Ashley?"

She scoffs. "Of course."

"And?"

"And she's still down. We're meeting next week."

I wrap my arms around her and pull her into me. "Promise to keep me updated?"

"I promise."

I release her and grab my bag. "I gotta run. Wish me luck with Olivia."

She chuckles as she collects her essentials. "Good luck, Mags. Catch ya later."

❖

I'm a hot mess as I sit in our sustainable production class and wait for Olivia to show up. The one day I need Dr. Young to distract me, he's late. My only other saving grace would be Laura arriving before Olivia and deciding she wants to sit next to me in her old seat, but Laura smiles and walks past me to the back of the room. She was thankful for our help on her birthday, but she must also feel a little embarrassed because she hasn't interacted with Olivia or me much since.

My stomach aches with anxiety and anticipation. Dr. Young finally shows three minutes before class is scheduled to begin and sets up in a flurry. He starts class one minute past eight, and for the two minutes after that, my head spins at one hundred miles per hour, wondering where the hell Olivia is. Probably skipping class for the hell of it. When I'm about to cast her off again, Olivia flies through the door in a harried gust.

"I'm so sorry, Dr. Young," she says as she half ducks in front of the whiteboard and weaves through the tables to me.

"That's all right, Ms. Cypress. As I was saying..."

I don't care what Dr. Young was saying. I'm aware of every atom in my body, and I have no idea what to do with any of them. I'm in fucking rigor mortis. Olivia's hair is wet, which strikes me as strange; it's normally dry. Maybe she slept in like me because she couldn't sleep like me. I'm grateful for her tardiness saving us from the would-be awkward minutes before the start of class. Not much talking we can do now with Dr. Young knee-deep in which rootstocks are best suited for high-production apple orchards. I actually want to be paying attention to this, but how can I?

Olivia's energy is tired and wired. She practically buzzes next to me as she shuffles through her bag, pulling out ChapStick and every color of folder until she finds her materials for this class. When she finally has what she needs, she shoves her bag under our table and scoots in her chair. She takes a deep breath and runs a hand through her hair before opening her notebook. Once everything is in order, she looks at me. I can feel her trying to catch my eye. I bite my lip and steel myself, then turn to meet her gaze.

"Hi," she mouths.

I give her a weak smile that hides my teeth. She scrunches her face at my hesitancy while I die inside from hers. She holds up her pointer finger and mouths, "One second."

She scribbles something in her notebook and slides it in front of me. *I'm sorry I didn't text you back last night. Is it okay if I explain?*

I peek at Dr. Young. The man is so far gone in his own world, I don't think he'd notice if his desk caught fire. Olivia's eyes are a little hazy, probably from lack of sleep, but they are also hopeful. For how disheveled she is this morning, her entire demeanor is...happy. I nod.

She gives me a half grin and takes back her notebook, taking her time with this note. While she composes what better be an epic excuse for killing me, I try to reabsorb into class. I fail, but damn, do I try. After five minutes, she pushes the notebook in front of me.

First and foremost, I missed you like a crazy fool last night.

The first line puts some of my angst at ease, but still, she knew I'd be stressed all night, and she didn't do anything about it. I chew on my lip and continue:

This is going to sound like a lame excuse—I swear this type of thing only happens to me—but I left my phone charger in the piano booth last night. I loved your text and wanted to take my time responding because I have a lot to say. I made a snack and sorted through some of the spreadsheets from your farm, and when I was ready to reply, my phone had died. Green Hall was already closed for the night, and my roommate was at the library cramming for an exam, so I couldn't use hers. I accidentally fell asleep waiting for her, and as you can see, almost didn't make it to class because I didn't have an alarm. I am so sorry!

I'm rambling.

Here's my response...

I can say with the utmost confidence that I want you, Maggie Hyde. You told me you wanted me in the piano booth and that you wanted to continue down this path. I thought so much about how to respond to you last night, not because I was confused about my feelings, but because it feels like if I step into us, it could be...it.

You are one of a kind. Consider this my jump into the deep of us. Join me?

I glance at Dr. Young, still stuck in professor world, and back at her note. It's good, right? *It is.* Then why am I terrified? This is exactly what I wanted to hear, and I want to lean over and kiss her, but at the same time, I feel cortisol in my blood. I'm stressed. I'm scared. The reality of us is sinking in; the fact that Olivia Cypress wants to be with me. This is the moment that makes everything *real*, and I'm terrified she'll break my heart. She already has too much of it. A critical mass.

I pick up my pen and tell her the truth.

I'm scared.

I can't watch her read it. Instead, I turn away and find my favorite string of pearls plant hanging from the wall in front of the window. Which reminds me, I was going to get another pothos to hang from the ceiling in our dorm. I catch my grin between my teeth. I can't wait for spring, when the whole world is my nursery, and I can propagate as many cuttings as I want. *That's* what the knife is for.

Tessa has her slides, and I have my plants.

The notebook appears back under my nose, and I take a deep breath before focusing on the new addition of three small words. *I'm scared, too.*

I nod and harvest some confidence, just enough to look at her. She smiles and dips her head in a way that feels like a question, as if she's expecting a response. My response is that I want to crawl inside that warm-looking wool sweater she's wearing and make her hold me. Make her take care of me and never leave me.

I grab my pen. *Reckon we're giving this thing a shot.*

She reads it and lets out a quiet chuckle, nowhere near loud enough to alert Dr. Young of our extracurriculars. Her hand finds mine under the table, bringing me some peace. Olivia Cypress is mine. I feel a little stronger knowing this. A little more distinguished and full. Maybe everything will go smoothly for us. Maybe it won't. But nothing will ever change in my life—for better or worse—if I don't try something different.

CHAPTER TEN

After classes on Friday, Olivia, Ashley, and I stand on the front stoop of Baker Hall, waiting for Bailey to let us in. I tug my jacket a little tighter. The Alder air has officially crisped into its autumnal chill, and the leaves have begun to turn. Tessa is on her first date with Hot TA, so I assume she'll be gone all night. I know her name is Jocelyn, but I haven't met her yet, and "Hot TA" is too good to stop using. I'm on high alert around Ashley, looking for any little outward sign of jealousy, pain, or sadness about the fact that her girlfriend—whom she's obsessed with—is on a date with another woman and not here with us.

"Thanks again, Mags. The orchard is going to make Fall Fest so special," Ashley says. Her eyes are clear and bright, matching the clean freshness of the air, and it seems like she can't help a slight grin. The girl is happy. I bite my lip in disappointment with myself. Why didn't I trust that Tessa would never do anything to hurt Ashley, and that if she's on a date with someone else, it's because she and Ashley are two grown women who love each other and have thought diligently about their decision to be non-monogamous?

My inherent bias shocks me. I expected Ashley to be off tonight, but why would she be when everything in her relationship is completely normal? I'm an idiot sometimes. I shake my head. I'm done doubting my friends. They know what they want and what's best for themselves.

"Of course. It's mutually beneficial," I say.

The door opens, and Bailey flies into Ashley with a shocking amount of force, wrapping her in a tight hug. Sometimes, I forget that Ashley and Bailey go back to before I even met Ashley. Before she met Tessa.

She lets go of Ashley and pulls Olivia in next. "I'm so glad you came, Liv. Been a while."

Bailey turns to me, a smile wide on her face. "Maggie, I can't thank you enough for making this happen for AQF. Do you do hugs? May I?" She holds out her arms, waiting for some kind of consent.

I step into her, giving her a quick side hug. "It's our pleasure. Not many students have been coming to the orchard in recent years. This will be a great marketing opportunity for us," I say.

Bailey swipes her lion card through the reader and pops open the door. "Come on in. The gang's in the basement."

We follow her into the common room of Baker, where a group of three students lounge around, waving at us as we pass. One of them is Luke, who let us in on Laura's birthday. I don't know the other two, but they look familiar to me from AQF meetings. There's the blond guy who's dating the gorgeous girl with the black hair next to him.

"Have fun down there," Luke says.

"Always do," Bailey says and winks.

He turns to the girl in their group, his face contorted in disgust. "Was that a sex joke? Did Bailey just make a gross sex joke?"

I follow Olivia into the stairwell but hear the girl say, "I honestly don't know. If it was, it was terrible. And if it wasn't, then Bails has some misplaced passion for the basement."

I chuckle to myself. Why don't we hang out more with these guys?

Bailey and Ashley prop open the door to the basement, but Olivia stops in front of me, letting the door fall closed. She turns and presses a chaste kiss on my lips before following Bailey and Ashley. The whole interaction only lasts a second but fills me with lust. The smallest things…

We turn the corner to find a group of AQF officers and affiliates sitting around the long oak study tables. I know most of the faces: Noelle, Cassie, and Robert from AQF, and Maya and Andy from the softball team. In the growing queer movement at Alder University, I'm among low-key royalty. Andy and Maya gained the softball team a ton of notoriety last year through the first Apple Wars and by taking their team to the World Series. With all the hype around our team and her already popular presence on social media, Maya is blue-checkmark famous on Instagram and TikTok, bringing in some decent money from sponsorships.

I get chills being in the same room as all these powerful queer people. I'm not an AQF officer, but I can feel it. This is the year Alder University will approve the club. It sounds like such a small thing, school approval. Especially when AQF is gaining national notoriety for its efforts to band together with other Catholic universities' LGBTQ+ communities. But it's *not* a small thing. Recognition from the school and the church is the crux of Alder Queer Fellowship.

"Everybody, I'm sure y'all recognize her from meetings and Ashley's epic house parties—still waiting for the first one of the year, Ash—but I'd like to officially introduce you to Maggie Hyde. Her family, if you couldn't tell, runs Hyde Hill Farm and has generously agreed to host our Fall Fest."

The room fills with small applause and cheers.

"The softball team is so excited to be a part of this. Thank you, Maggie. Hyde Hill will be the thing that makes this event perfect," Andy says.

My cheeks heat under the attention of all these amazing people. "It's our pleasure, really. My father is excited to host it."

"Excellent," Bailey says. "Let's jump in. Robert made us a little outline of the event, and I have the email from your dad here." She hands me a printout of my dad's message that details everything he can offer for Fall Fest. "As we're discussing all the aspects of the day, jump in and let us know if it's feasible for the orchard or if anything needs to be tweaked."

"Where will the Apple Wars take place?" Maya asks. Her eyes hold an intensity that glues my lips sealed. Olivia nudges me.

I clear my throat. "There are a couple of options, but the best place would be in front of the back barn, above the Pink Ladies." Maya doesn't break eye contact, and everyone remains quiet, as if I should continue speaking. "Um. It's nice and flat. Reckon it's about a hundred square feet. Plenty of space for pitching, and it butts up to our big wraparound porch for the spectators if there's not enough room on the grass."

Maya nods once, and it feels like I passed a final by the skin of my teeth.

"That sounds perfect. Way better than the end of the concourse," Andy says.

Bailey grins and squeezes my shoulder. "Have a seat," she says to me and Olivia. "All right, Robert. Take it away."

CHAPTER ELEVEN

Planning Fall Fest was an excellent experience. With so many passionate and talented people in the same room, shit gets done. And it gets done well. Bailey and the rest of the AQF leadership had thought of every detail for the event, leaving nothing on Hyde Hill Farm except making sure the space is clear of stray working materials and haphazardly parked tractors and ATVs. It made me proud of my friends when Bailey reported back to my dad that everything was taken care of. All we have to do is show them where the water, power, and apples are.

It's the Wednesday before Fall Fest, and as we promised, Olivia and I are taking things slowly. She's had our farm's spreadsheets for a few days now, and we both decided it was time to work on the next phase of the project: how to scale production and profits. We agree to meet at the arboretum to take a walk and hang out before we get to business. I think we both know that this part of the project could get a bit tense with it being my family's business and all. And maybe my slight aversion to taking suggestions from a non-ag vegan.

But this is Olivia. She's wicked smart, and I know she has the skills to help us. Even if we don't need it. She walks next to me, her hand in mine, face tilted to the sun. The rays tangle in her golden hair as if they were old acquaintances. She catches me staring, the sunlight illuminating every fleck of cobalt in her eyes, layered and plastered over each other in a mosaic of blue.

"You're staring," she says. The chill in the air kisses her cheeks pink.

"Sorry. I can't help it sometimes." I clear my throat and take in all the trees that surround us. We're lucky to have such an impressive arboretum. "Do you have a favorite?"

Her eyes roam over the different sizes and shapes. Deciduous, coniferous, deciduous conifers...I've stolen many cuttings from this place.

"Cedar."

"Cedar?"

"Yeah. Did you know Egyptians used the resin to mummify their dead?" She tilts her head, staring into me.

"Um, no. I didn't."

"Yeah, and"—she looks over my shoulder, and her face twists in horror, brows stitched tightly over her eyes—"oh my God." I turn to find a squirrel mauled and half-dead, its pale pink intestines falling out of its torn abdomen. It pants and waits.

"Shit." I walk over to it, Olivia following. "Looks like a hawk got to him but was interrupted."

Her fingers tremble in mine. "It's horrible." She swallows a gag. "Can we do anything?"

I drop her hand. There's no hope for the squirrel, so there's only one thing we can do. Without hesitation, I raise my boot a foot over its head and slam it down as hard as I can, not wanting to risk a botched kill. The crunch of the tiny skull and the squirt of blood and brain and bone are pretty gross and send a shiver through me, like ants marching down my spine. But it was quick and less painful for the little guy than dying slowly with its organs on the wrong side of its pelt. If it wasn't me, it would have been the hawk or time, and neither would have been kind.

"What the f...fuck," Olivia whispers against her shaking fingers. She drops her hand and stares at me. "Maggie. What the fuck?" Her voice is loud now, and her eyes dart between the squirrel goo, my mucked-up boots—my nice boots, by the way—and me. All of a sudden, I feel like I've made a giant mistake. But I didn't...

"It was suffering," I say, confused by her reaction. Her jaw drops as if she thinks I just tortured and killed an animal for fun. "You wanted me to do something, so I did it." I walk to the side of the small trail, where a patch of spiny sowthistle sits under the shade of none other than a cedar tree, and wipe the guts off the sole of my shoe. Spiny sowthistle is a strong weed with sharp-edged leaves. Good for a boot scraping.

She shakes her head. She looks…ill. As the fresh pink drains from her cheeks, a gray paleness takes its place. I walk over to steady her, but she pushes me away with an open palm. "Don't—" She cuts herself off by vomiting all over her nice suede shoes, and I'm kinda horrified. This was supposed to be a nice romantic walk before we dive into our project, but now it's ruined by blood, guts, and vomit. She spits into the dirt and wipes her mouth with the back of her hand.

This is the disconnect between us.

All I can think of when I look at her ruined shoes is that she didn't *actually* care how the squirrel felt; she cared about how the squirrel made *her* feel. She doesn't want to witness an animal die, but she's fine watching it suffer? If it were up to her, that squirrel would still be choking on its final breaths for God knows how long. And she's disgusted with *me*?

That's the missing piece for us. Some people talk about things, and some people do things. She talks. I do.

"I helped," I say, my palms upturned in exasperation.

She doubles over, hands on knees, and vomits one more time. We both wait in silence until she's finished and wipes her mouth in the sleeve of her jacket. "I want to go home."

I nod. Me, too. "Okay. Um. I guess we'll work on our project some other time?"

She runs a hand through her hair, its partner planted on her belly. The color slowly returns to her cheeks. "Sure."

We walk in silence back to her dorm, which I have never been to, a fact that hasn't hit me as strange until now. But I guess since she's friends with Ashley and Tessa, it makes sense that she'd want to come to Magnolia. As we approach the door, I struggle to come up with something to say. I won't apologize for what I did. If anything, I'm waiting for her to apologize for her reaction. This is nature, the world we live in.

We reach the front steps, and she unlaces her soiled shoes, leaving them in the grass. "I'll deal with those later," she says, her words heavy with melancholy. I remain planted as she pats her pockets, searching for her lion card. "Fuck. Are you fucking kidding me right now?" she says, checking every pocket for the third time.

"Forgot it again?" I ask. Since I've met her, Olivia has gotten locked out of her dorm no less than five times. For as smart and put together as she is, she can be pretty scatterbrained.

"What do you think?" Her face is hard and leaves me with no response. Leaves me feeling a little raw. A girl walks up, eying the two of us and our shoes.

"Need me to swipe you in?" she asks Olivia with hesitation.

"Please."

The girl swipes her lion card and holds the door open. I'm not sure if I should leave or—

"You coming?" she asks. I nod. "Can you take off your boots, please?"

I pull them off and set them next to hers. Minus the vomit and the guts, they look pretty cute together.

❖

Olivia's room takes me aback. I've hugged her, kissed her, touched her, but nothing feels so intimate as being alone in her room for the first time. It's steeped in her scent, which, even in its most concentrated form, I can't decipher. I run my hand over the top of her desk and decide to ask what shampoo she uses. The corkboard above her laptop is covered in Polaroids of road trips and people I've never met before. It's strange to see a whole other side of someone's life when my only experience with them is in a small, tucked-away part of it.

It makes me jealous in a couple of ways.

The people and the places.

"I don't," she says.

"Sorry, you don't what?"

"I don't use shampoo." She peels off her socks and tosses them in the mesh hamper in her closet. "I use baking soda to clean my hair and apple cider vinegar to condition."

"Vinegar?"

"Yes. Baking soda and vinegar." My mind throws me an image of a papier-mâché volcano erupting. Hers must do the same thing because she parts the air in front of her and says, "Separately."

"What about soap?" The fact that Olivia's intoxicating scent isn't some plastic bottle of Strawberry Burst or Moonlit Jasmine makes me even more nervous and off-balance in her room. The air hugging me, the scent, it's *her*. Her body. Her natural pheromones, and it's fucking intoxicating.

"I use bulk, unscented Castile soap." She quirks an eyebrow. "And I'll answer that last question I see written on your face. For deodorant, I use a salt stone. Why are you so curious?"

I shake my head. "Nothing. Just wondering how you always smell so good."

She pulls the towel hanging from a hook inside her closet door. "The whole world is full of noise, consumerism, and fake shit like perfume and candy-scented beauty products. I refuse to pay hand over fist to smell how some corporate asshole wants me to smell. I smell like a woman. Plus, all of those products are terrible for the world. The plastic, the manufacturing, even animal testing for some." Her eyes drop, and she shakes her head.

I know she's thinking of the Maggie Killed a Squirrel incident. I take a slow step toward her and stop when she looks up. "Do you want to—"

"Shower," she supplies, holding up her towel like it's evidence. I nod. Her shoulders drop, and her brows relax. "Listen. I know I had a big reaction when you stomped the brains out—"

"Humanely put it out of its misery," I amend.

"It was like a fucking Tarantino movie, Mags." She chuckles and wipes a hand down her face. "Anyway, I need to shower and process and reset. Then we can get to work. Cool?"

I perch on the edge of her mattress like a bird, as if putting all of my weight on it is too intimate. "Cool."

"Awesome." She waves over her side of the room. "Make yourself at home. My roommate is gone until ten." She closes the door behind her, and I hear the muffled sound of splashing water.

I shake the image of Olivia showering with all her natural products out of my head. Or rather, I try to. She'll emerge all steamy and wet and smelling only like her. My core flexes around the thought. I give my head a shake and walk to her desk, taking in all the photos.

So many places. So many faces.

How can she want just me, especially knowing what she'll be

signing up for after college? How can I not be drowned out by all...
this? I count twenty-two different people and at least six different
landscapes.

Her phone vibrates on the desktop. I'm not trying to be nosy, but
I automatically look and see a text from Ashley on the locked screen:

*I don't know what else to say, Liv. There's not, like, a text
conversation I can send you where she declares she's in love with you,
but she likes you a lot. I promise. She always mentions...*

The preview of the text ends after that. I blink and wait, as if the
rest of their conversation will somehow reveal itself on her locked
screen. I sit on her bed and rub my hands over my jeans. Is Olivia
just as insecure about us as I am? Is her version of twenty-two people
and six landscapes my watertight life plan? Or is it something else?
Something I'm doing wrong, maybe. Even after the notes we passed in
class, it feels like we're both tiptoeing around something or waiting for
some other shoe to drop.

Maybe it's this project. Maybe once we dive into the meat of it
and realize we haven't killed each other, we can relax into each other
a little bit more.

"Hey." The bathroom door cracks open, and steam rushes through,
dissipating into the room. Olivia emerges pink-skinned and wet-haired
in plaid pajama pants and a vintage Alder sweatshirt. I want to run
my hands over her warm body. Find out what her skin tastes like. She
hangs the towel on her closet door and plucks her phone from the desk,
reading what I assume is Ashley's response about me, hopefully. She
types something and places her phone facedown on the wood.

"Hey," I say, the warm steam tickling my face as she sits next to
me.

"I'm sorry, Maggie. Obviously, the squirrel thing really freaked
me out." She drums her fingers on her thighs. "I've never witnessed
anything like that before, and you executed"—she cringes at her
word choice and digs her nails deeper into her flannel and the skin
underneath—"you acted without hesitation. It...it took me aback."

I take a deep breath and cover her anxious hands with mine. It's not
that I *want* her to feel insecure about how I feel about her, but knowing
I'm not alone in my wariness gives me a little more confidence in a
weird way. Like two wrongs making a right. "We raised chickens when
I was young," I say.

She pulls her gaze out of her lap and turns her hand up, interlacing her fingers with mine. Her eyes move from mine, to my ears, to my cheeks, and mouth. Then back to my eyes. "One of my bigger mistakes was setting up a Twitter account for my Uncle Ward. You'll meet him at Fall Fest and understand why. Anyway, he stumbled across this tweet one day that he fell in love with and never shuts up about. It says, 'Everyone wants to wear Carhartt till it's time to do Carhartt shit.'"

Her lips part in a small grin. "That's actually pretty perfect," she says.

I nod. "I get why he likes it so much. I feel like it encapsulates how we feel sometimes as farmers and laborers. Kind of like the world enjoys going to the fancy restaurant or buying the farm fresh eggs at the Sunday market, but they don't want to know about how I've had to kill hundreds of chickens."

She winces.

"Humanely, I promise." She opens her mouth to speak, but I'm not finished, and I want her to listen for a second longer because I'm trying my best to tell her how I feel about…about the world and my part in it. We may not be talking about organics or veganism, but I'm doing my best to let her in right now. "And I think that's why we both have big feelings about what happened today. I want to tell you how your reaction made me feel."

She squeezes my hand and nods.

"It kind of felt like you were the Carhartt wearer, not the doer. Like you wanted this certain thing or outcome, the squirrel to not have to suffer or fresh eggs on your table—well, no eggs for you, but you get it—but you didn't want to have to witness someone doing the work for you. You just want it to magically be, and that's not how the world works."

She scrapes her teeth over her lip before she responds. "I'm not trying to argue. This feels like something we both want to dive deeper into, so I want to say that this whole conversation revolves around killing animals. I don't want your chicken or your eggs, and you're right, I definitely don't want to see you kill them."

I slow my racing thoughts and try to focus on what she's saying. *This isn't an argument.* "I totally get that. But if it's not killing animals, it's the factory that makes your soap or all the gasoline you burn on your adventures. We all live these lives of consumption, enjoy the benefits, but scoff at the ones who provide it like farmers, production workers, miners…"

She waits for me to finish, nodding. "Maggie, we were born into a world that's already so far gone and so far indoctrinated into capitalism that it's almost impossible to live a life in which you don't pollute or kill or destroy. It's woven into the societal and physical construct of our cities, our culture, our way of life. You can sit here and deconstruct my life and everything I do that is counterproductive to my ideals. Fuck. I do it, too. I travel, I wear clothes I didn't make. I eat food that had to be trucked in from across the country. But I *try*. If we all just tried a little bit, we could make a big difference, a big statement.

"This shouldn't even be on our shoulders, yet the giant corporations who are draining the world of its resources and filling it with plastic and poison frame it like, *if only you recycled our bottles* or *buy our product, it's kinda green*. I know why the organic labeling system bothers you. It's not perfect, and from what you've told me, there are some major cracks that good farmers can fall through, but it's all we have right now. You may know exactly how you farm your apples, but the consumer has no clue how something was farmed. *Organic* is the one label that lets them know at least the bare minimum was put into it.

"Kind of like how you want to show me all the ways I live an unsustainable life, but I want to show you all the ways I try to live sustainably. I'm far from perfect, just like the system of organic product labeling. But you can only start from where you are, and doing something—*anything*—to try to move the world in the right direction is worth it. Even if I fail more than I succeed. How else could I live with myself?"

As she speaks, her eyes become misty, and her hand warms in mine. She's heartbroken for the state of the world, and I think I can understand what she means about consumers trying to buy responsibly. How would they possibly know what kind of stewards of the land we are? How could they know how deeply we care about applying the bare minimum of outside force in our farming? There's no little label to tell them that we rely on Integrated Pest Management and use natural growing conditions to manipulate yield and therefore taste and sweetness. And how could they know that organic farming can be even worse than traditional?

"I think I understand what you mean," I say.

She takes a deep breath and grins. "Really? Because I feel like I went on a giant rant and may have lost my point a couple times in there."

I shake my head. "You were loud and clear to me. I don't know…I guess I felt like I could speak as an authority about farming and organic versus nonorganic food. But I do believe the blind trust folks have in the organic world is extremely detrimental." I make sure I have her eye contact and try to calm myself before I continue. "I'm not trying to ruffle your feathers when I say this stuff. The chemicals used in organic farming, no matter if they're derived from nature, can be just as dangerous as the ones used in traditional farming. On top of that, those chemicals are often less effective, and more of it needs to be used. The entire organic farming system is also less efficient, taking up not only more resources but more space and soil use, too."

I sigh. "But for as much as I think about that stuff, and for as passionately as I feel about it, I never paused to think about what the consumer thinks. Which is a pretty giant piece of the puzzle and the heart of the entire organic labeling system. There has to be a better solution out there." I shake my head and chuckle. "I hate when people are so dogmatic. I don't want to be that way." I'm a little shocked to hear myself concede. Well, *concede* is a strong word. It's not like I'm calling my father to demand that we apply to become organic. But Olivia has opened my eyes to the true function of the system. It makes sense. But it doesn't work. My brain is swirling through ideas of how to come up with a better labeling system when I notice the mist in her eyes evaporate, and her lips turn up in a grin.

She is so powerful and smart. Maybe we could work together on this one day because she's been right all along. We want the same things for the world.

"I was wrong about what I said earlier," I say.

She chews on the corner of her grin. "Oh yeah?"

I nod. "Yeah. You're a doer. And I hope I'm around to witness every little or giant change you make in the world."

She pushes a gentle kiss to my cheek. "Thank you." She clears her throat and reaches for a green folder on her desk. "It's a good thing you're so amenable right now because there were a couple of things in your dad's spreadsheets that I wanted to talk to you about." She opens the folder and pulls out the first stack of paperclipped spreadsheets and hands them to me. "I printed them out so they'd be easier for you to read."

I hold the thick stack of columns and rows and feel very far out of my league. "I'm not so helpless with spreadsheets, you know."

She laughs. "Did I speak too soon about you being amenable?"

"No." I laugh, too. "I'm just trying to convince *myself* I'm not hopeless."

"Okay. Good." She taps the stack of paper. "Your dad is a diligent man. He keeps track of every penny and has kept great data."

"Yeah, he's always been really into that stuff."

She picks at a cuticle on her thumb and clears her throat before meeting my gaze again. "That's why this is a little strange, but there are a couple of things of note in here. I highlighted the sections of concern."

"Concern?" I flip through the stack until I come across a page filled with pink highlighter and scribbled notes. My blood pressure rises as I try to absorb what's *concerning* about the lifeblood of my family, but I don't understand what any of her notes mean. My eyes are stuck on one word. Unprofitable. "Unprofitable? What's unprofitable? The entire farm?"

She grabs my hand as if she's about to deliver a blow. "No. No, not at all. Don't worry, Maggie. There's nothing happening here that isn't fixable. It's just…" She trails off and looks across the room at the window.

"Hey." She worries her lips as she looks at me, waiting for me to continue. And even though I'm shitting bricks, I try to calm my nerves and even out my voice. "I trust you. Whatever it is, we got this."

"Your dad is underwater on his peaches and blueberries. See this?" She points to the *cost per plant* for the peaches. "This number doesn't make sense when you compare it to the CPP for the apple trees. It's double."

I shake my head. "I'm sorry, what?"

"Basically, the cost of planting the peaches and blueberries is significantly inflated versus the cost of planting apple trees. I don't know exactly what your dad used to calculate these values, but I did some research, and even the highest estimates of the cost per plant for these crops is way below what he has in his records."

I blink at the paper, struggling to absorb what she is trying to tell me. "What are you saying?"

"My best guess is that he didn't have the capital to plant these, and he took out a less-than-optimal loan to cover the cost. Something with a high interest rate. Maybe adjustable. That's the only thing I can think of that would skew these numbers so greatly. He must have added the cost of the loan to this data set. And with these prices"—she points to the numbers I actually know, price per pound—"he's in the red on these. Big time."

How could my father be in the red on *anything*? He has everything under control. Always. There's no way this can be right. A simple error. Olivia must have calculated her weird finance stuff wrong or misinterpreted something. Our farm has been successful for generations. I shake my head. I told her I trust her, but I also trust my dad.

"How do those numbers affect the overall financial health of our farm?" I ask. I know my dad planted those crops because they were my mom's favorite, so it could be possible that he overextended his resources in an emotional decision. But if he knew it would tank the whole farm, he would never...

She taps the air with her pointer finger. "That's a great question. But one I can't answer, unfortunately."

"What? Why not? You have all the data and—"

"That's the thing. I don't have all the data. These numbers are a snapshot of a moment in time. They're an average. There's no way for me to see what the CPP was five years ago and if that number has grown. If it has, then I'd say with more certainty that your dad took out a bad loan, and the interest he owes is piling up. That'd be reflected in these high costs. But I don't have that information. So this is really my best guess. Emphasis on guess."

I roll out my neck and run my fingers through my hair. "He planted those for her. They were her favorite."

She strokes my back in long slow drags, her head bowed close to mine. "Sometimes, things aren't always as they appear. I could be wrong, Maggie."

I smirk. "Doubt it."

"I thought about not telling you because I can't be sure that it means what I think it means, but that felt wrong."

"I'm glad you told me. I just don't know what to do with this."

Her hand stops at the nape of my neck, and she squeezes. It makes me want to melt into her. "Ask him about it. He gave you access to this information. I'm not sure if he knew we'd connect the dots, but these numbers are pretty glaring. He wasn't hiding it."

I'm nauseous. I've always assumed the farm was rock-solid because my dad was rock-solid. He's bound to make mistakes like the rest of us, but this mistake scares me because if what he owes on that mystery loan keeps piling up, then there's no way out. At least he hasn't found one yet.

I groan and lean my head against her shoulder. "This makes me feel so unsteady." She rubs my knee and rests her head atop mine. "When my mom left, it made sense to me. I knew she was capable of it, that she was the type of person to cut and run. It sucked, but it didn't rip anything out from under me, you know?"

I feel her breath on my hair, warm, then cool. "How's that got to do with what's going on here?"

"I expected my mom to be an unstable part of my life, but I never expected to have to worry about my dad. Our farm and him...they're my foundation. It's scary to find out that there may be a crack." I sigh. "What if we have to default on the loan? Then what?" She pulls away to look at me, her eyes narrowed in concern. "Then what would anchor me?"

Olivia doesn't try to downplay how I'm feeling or tell me there's no possible way my dad will default. Instead, she listens and allows me to feel my big feelings. She allows me to be shaky and scared. She runs a thumb over my cheek, and I sway into her.

"In my limited experience on this earth, it seems that life tugs at the loose thread of your favorite sweater—the one you refuse to take off, the one that makes you feel safe—until you look down one day to find you're naked. Then you have to learn how to feel at home, just you. Alone in your skin," she says. Her fingers move to my hair, and she runs them through my roots, filling me with shivers. After this conversation, she is beginning to feel like that sweater. Someone intimate and close to me. Someone I don't want to lose. Someone I *will* lose next year. "Not to say it doesn't hurt, or it's not scary as hell. It just is," she whispers.

I watch her lips move around her words and how they pull to one side when she's finished. A half-smile. A sad smile. I'm no longer thinking about my dad or the farm. For the first time in my life, they are not my priority. She is. "How's your sweater holding up?" I ask.

She leans forward and presses her forehead to my temple. I feel the connection and warmth through my entire body. "Been naked for a minute." Her whisper cascades over my ear and down my neck. Hearing her say those words shoots a pang through my heart but also stirs something low in my belly. I stay quiet, her head against mine. "It's the strangest thing, though…"

I swallow. "What?"

"When I'm with you, I feel this warmth in my chest." She rubs under her collarbone. "Like, I don't miss that sweater because I have something that lights me from the inside. Don't get me wrong, I'm comfortable alone, but with you…" She leans her head away and stares. "With you, I feel like I'm home."

I wrap my arms around her waist and pull her against me. Our kiss is slow and hot and needy. For two independent people, we find so much in each other to want. I used to think Olivia was like my mom. I used to think that nothing could hold her down, and I wasn't interested in trying to be her paperweight. When she scoffed at my ten-year plan, I thought it was because she didn't care where she'd be in ten years. I was dead wrong. I've never met someone who cares as much as she does.

She's nothing like my mom. She's one of a kind. She's Olivia Cypress, and I think I'm falling for her.

CHAPTER TWELVE

G od, I hope this goes well," Aiden says, his head knocking against the shotgun window with every little bump I drive over.

I peek over Scott, who sits sandwiched between us as if he's our kid brother. "Why wouldn't it go well?" I throw my truck in neutral and coast down the end of County Road Nine into Holston Valley. We're almost to East Sparrow. My gut tightens with excitement. Not only do we get to host an incredible event for AQF, but Olivia will see our orchard for the first time. She'll see my hometown for the first time. The thought is quickly replaced with a nervous crunch. I haven't decided if I'm going to ask my dad about the peaches and blueberries yet, but I can't stop thinking about it.

"Yeah, no stress. Sounds like every detail is accounted for. It should go off without a hitch," Scott says.

Aiden leans forward to look at me. "Sure, but what if no one shows up? It'd be so awkward."

I shake my head. "There's no way that will happen. AQF has a huge following at this point, and the softball team alone could fill a whole event. It's going to be perfect." It *is* going to be perfect. It's the end of October, and the weather is cold but bright and sunny. The perfect fall weather for the perfect Fall Fest.

Scott, Aiden, and I left for East Sparrow right after our last class today, and the rest of the AQF crew and Maya and Andy will meet us bright and early tomorrow morning to begin setting up. I hate that Olivia isn't the one sitting next to me right now, but she insisted I take Scott and Aiden in the hope that when it's the three of us, Aiden will work up the nerve to come out to our dad. She's coming later tonight with Tessa and Ashley. We get one night at home with just the six of us.

I clear my throat and let the hot anticipation swirl in my stomach. There are three rooms; Aiden's room for him and Scott, the guest room for Tessa and Ashley, and my room…for me and Olivia. We'll share a bed. My mouth dries at the thought, and I bite at a dry spot on my lip. I'm so fucking excited, I shift in my seat. "Do you think you're going to tell Dad?" I ask.

Aiden grabs Scott's hand from his lap and pulls it over. "Reckon if Scott is brave enough to tell his super conservative folks, I can tell our super fucking awesome dad."

"You got this," Scott says through a smile.

"You definitely got this. He won't be fazed, I promise. Shoot, he probably already knows. You got pretty lax with your secrecy senior year."

"What?" Aiden scoffs. "And how is that?"

I chuckle. "Oh, I don't know, Tommy Price practically falling out your window trying to sneak out before Dad woke up. Only, Dad was already out on the tractor, and Tommy's car was parked in the Fujis, the same apples that were on the pruning schedule for that day." My chuckles turn into full-blown laughter at the memory. "Oh my God, Aid. I remember Dad being like, 'There's a truck in the Fujis. It's in my way. Tell Aiden to take care of it.' Scott, you won't believe it."

Scott bounces along happily between us and smiles, wordlessly telling me to continue. I don't sense any jealousy from him, so I mentally give him a point.

I slap the steering wheel. "Okay, so my dad and I are having our coffee, and he tells me about this truck that's in his way. As if on cue, we see Tommy fucking Price sprinting across the front yard down to the Fujis. Then we hear him peel out. And my dad says, 'I swear to God, if that kid takes out a tree, I'm going to kill Aiden.'"

"What? You never told me that story," Aiden says.

"Yes, I did. You were drunk when I told you. You probably forgot." I turn left on Robin's Egg and climb Scout Mountain, which is now referred to by everyone as Hyde Hill. "Anyway, my point is that he probably already knows, and he definitely doesn't care."

He sighs. "Whatever. Guess we're all about to find out, huh?"

We are. The mouth of our gate welcomes us home. It looks like

Uncle Ward touched up the paint on our sign, and I grin at the thought of him out there with all his paints. He tries so hard. *Hyde Hill Farm. Georgia's Best.*

I told my dad we needed a cleverer tagline, but he refused. "It's traditional. The people trust it more than something witty or clever," he said. The sign may be basic, but it catches people's attention. The lettering is crisp burgundy against the bright white background, the design my mom made of a honeycrisp tree and our tractor trails off into the upper corner. It's clean and beautiful.

My truck crunches up the gravel drive past rows and rows of trees. It's looking good. Most varietals have been picked, and my dad should be in the last leg of harvest. We pass the warehouse and storefront on the right, and our house comes into view. My whole being is instantly at ease at the sight of the farmhouse. My dad and Ward sit shoulder to shoulder on the front steps drinking High Life and chatting. My heart swells with so much affection for my home and family. Until I remember how much stress my dad must be under if Olivia is right about the data.

They wave as we drive past to the back barn. I turn off the engine, and we hop out, practically skipping to go meet Dad and Ward.

"Welcome home, y'all," Ward says as he swallows Aiden in a bear hug.

"Hi, Maggie," my dad says as he pulls me into a gentler hug. Then Uncle Ward pushes him out of the way and scoops me into a rib crusher.

"Wyatt, this one here looks new." Uncle Ward tilts his head toward Scott, who stands with his hands deep in his coat pockets and his eyes skipping from my dad to Ward to Aiden.

Aiden fixes his hair and drapes an arm over Scott's shoulders. "Keen observation, Uncle Ward." He takes a deep breath and swallows hard. *Oh shit.* He's going for it off the rip. "This is Scott. He was my suitemate last year, and we decided to room together this year." He looks at my dad and clears his throat. "Scott is also my boyfriend."

A smile spreads across my dad's face, and Uncle Ward drops a hand on his shoulder. "I knew it. I knew it, Wyatt. I told you as much. All them kids are gay. Dang, I love this family," Uncle Ward says. And I swear to God, he wipes a tiny tear from under his eye. He's happy.

"Come here, son," my dad says. Aiden steps into his arms, and my dad kisses the top of his head. "I'm so proud of you." When he releases Aiden, he shakes Scott's hand. "Welcome, Scott. You can call me Wyatt, and this here is Ward. We're happy you're here." Scott's whole face lights up as he thanks my dad for having him. I wink at Aiden.

My dad claps his hands, ending Aiden's coming out with the perfect amount of love and time spent on it, the brevity of the conversation reflecting how little he is fazed by it. "We're missing two. Where are my girls?"

I guess it's my turn. "Three. We're missing three, actually. My friend, Olivia, from my class with Dr. Young, is coming with Tessa and Ashley."

"Spill it, girl," Uncle Ward says. He takes a sip of beer and peers into my goddamn soul.

"Spill what?"

"The tea. I know you got tea, Maggie. Go on, now, spill it."

My first reaction is to deny, deny, deny. Again, as much as we've talked about our intimacy and where things are going, Olivia and I have yet to even utter the word *girlfriend* in front of each other. While I don't imagine she is in pursuit of another relationship—I'm certainly not—introducing her as my girlfriend would be a stretch and not the actual truth. I am also not naive and understand that if I deny she's my girlfriend, I will get roasted by Ward and Aiden. *Roast-ed.* And way more attention than is necessary will smother us the rest of the weekend, while Aiden and Scott get off easy.

"We're basically together, but Olivia isn't technically my girlfriend. But I hope she'll be soon. So it would be great if we could all be chill this weekend."

Uncle Ward salutes me. The man has zero chill.

"I'm excited to meet her," my dad says. I'm counting on him to keep Ward in check for me. "What are y'all gonna get up to tonight? I hear the Klines are throwing a barn party."

Aiden catches my eye and gives me a subtle head shake. I agree. I had something a little more intimate in mind. "I don't know. It's Scott's first time here and same with Olivia. Aiden and I want to show them around the property. Reckon we'll fill a cooler and take out the ATVs, if that's all right."

My dad nods. "Be safe."

"Where's Luis? Thought he'd be a part of the welcome band-wagon," I ask.

"He went home a little early. His little sister is going to be in a big play, and he wanted to be there for it," my dad says.

"Aw, man. I mean, glad he gets to see it, but I was hoping to hang out with him," I say.

"Next year," my dad says.

"All right, come on, y'all. Get in there and get settled," Uncle Ward says.

Aiden and Scott head to his room. I stand in the door and watch Scott move slowly through everything Aiden owns. I know Olivia will do the same. "Don't have too much fun in here," I say and continue down the hall to the next door on the right. My room. Everything is as I left it three months ago, but I feel like I'm a little different than I was three months ago. This room is my sanctuary, but something about it feels smaller now, and I know it has everything to do with the girl with the sleepy eyes. She made my world bigger.

My plants, my artwork, my awards, and family photos. I see everything through a different lens, knowing that Olivia will be here soon. What will she think of all this? Of the terrariums and propagation kit. Of my old worn-out bedding that used to be Uncle Ward's. Of every single little sign that points to me staying here forever, including my sketches of the cabin I want to build here. If I get the job running Hyde Hill Farm, my father has agreed to sell me a parcel of land to build on. My own space. I've already saved half the building cost. I wonder how that will make Olivia feel. If it will take us closer to being officially together or exasperate the already big differences in our post-college plans.

Sometimes, the fact that Olivia is leaving for God knows where next year—*next year*, not even just after graduation—hits me square in the chest, toppling me like a fainting goat. I'll be minding my own business, buying a coffee, and *boom*, I'm out. The deadline for her to submit her internship application to the university is in March, so I know she's been looking, but I've been too far in denial to ask her what's on the top of her list.

After making sure my room is exactly how I want it for Olivia, I join the rest of my family downstairs. The girls should be here in about twenty minutes, and I do my best to distract myself, the nerves and butterflies in my stomach in free fall.

Uncle Ward stirs his famous Ward War Stew. He named the stew—full of tender braised beef and packed full of savory spices, vegetables, and potatoes—Ward War Stew because he says it gives you all the energy you'd need to fight the Nazis. Nothing encapsulates my uncle quite like that little fact. Aiden checks the oven, revealing the yeast rolls puffing and shading to a delicious golden brown, and Scott watches him with adoration. My dad has my great-grandma's cookbook and uses the recipes whenever he can. Says it keeps the family alive. The rolls are one of the most coveted recipes.

I hear the gravel crunch outside, and my ears perk up like a watchdog's. Aiden drops the yeast rolls on the cooling rack and grins. "You look ridiculous right now, Mags. You look like you did in that home video. The one where you got the *Hannah Montana* singing doll for Christmas, and you peed your—"

"Aid, I swear to God, if you don't shut up, I'll tell Scott about the church incident of 2013."

"What's the church incident of 2013?" Scott asks, eyes hopping between Aiden and me.

Aiden wipes his hands in the kitchen towel and nods, his jaw tight. "Playing dirty, eh? All right, you're safe for now."

I drop my head back and groan. "Can you just be cool for once in your life?" I stand, and Aiden makes a show of looking me up and down.

"You really want to go there?" he asks, eyebrows raised in appraisal.

"Don't forget, the hottest guy in school asked *me* to the Klines' barn party my senior year, not you."

"That's bullshit. You're a lesbian. Doesn't count."

I open the front door and call over my shoulder. "So did the hottest girl, you little—"

"Wow. You guys are home for half an hour and are already at it," Tessa says. I almost walk square into her. She stands on the porch with Ashley and Olivia. Ashley holds a bottle of Buffalo Trace, and Olivia cradles a basket of baking ingredients and a Tupperware of something brown. She would've been better off bringing bourbon, but I don't tell her this. I'm so happy to see her. And oh my God, she looks stunning.

She wears tight dark jeans with black boots and a perfectly worn Levi's jacket.

"Hi. Sorry, Aiden was just—"

My dad brushes past me, gently pushing me out of the way as he joins us on the porch. "Move on over, Mags. My guests have arrived."

"Uncle Wyatt!" Ashley and Tessa call in unison as they bump shoulders and fight over who gets to hug my dad first.

Olivia peeks at me from behind the lovefest, her eyes wide in question. I shrug. There's no real explanation for how much they love my dad or for how much he loves them. It just is. Something about Tessa and Ashley brings out his goofy side. I think it's because most people he meets are either intimidated by him or treat him like he's the most serious person in the world. But Ashley and Tessa are always themselves around my dad and rib him like they would me or Aiden. They took to calling him Uncle Wyatt sophomore year because they "always wanted a crotchety old farmer uncle."

Apparently, that's the key to my dad's heart.

"I'm surprised to see y'all haven't dropped out to join a commune yet," my dad says.

Olivia grins, and I'm relieved that she sees this for what it is and not my dad being a giant asshole to two college-age girls.

Ashley pats his shoulder and shoves the Buffalo Trace into his chest. "We haven't completed our mediocre middle-age-man sacrifice. You know, they won't let us in until we do that."

My dad laughs hard. Hand over belly, chin over chest, rumbling kind of laughter. "Good to know I've been fattening myself up for a good cause." He holds up the bourbon. "Thank you for the Buffalo, girls. You know you don't have to bring anything."

I clap my hands and use this opportunity to pivot. "Okay. Enough of that. Dad, this is our friend Olivia. She's in Dr. Young's class with me."

He turns his attention to her. "Ah, yes. Olivia Cypress. Harold mentioned you during our last chat."

She steals a glance at me and clears her throat. "I did not bring whiskey, but I brought supplies to make an apple crisp for dessert. If you don't mind me picking a couple apples to use, of course," she says, holding up the basket.

"For a second, I thought maybe you were going to use someone else's apples, then we would have really had a problem." My dad smiles a wide, genuine smile and reaches for her basket. "I can take this off your hands, here." He scans the contents and raises a brow. "You know we're cooking dinner, right?"

Oh shit. I completely forgot that Olivia can't eat *anything* that we're making tonight. What kind of a potential girlfriend forgets that her almost partner is vegan and doesn't think to make a single thing she can eat?

Olivia smiles and points at the Tupperware in the basket. "It's lentil soup. I'm vegan, so I normally bring my own food with me. I know it can be hard to accommodate, and I didn't want to be a burden."

My dad turns to me, eyebrows raised. "First the hippie, then the Deadhead, now a vegan? Alder University sure has changed since I went there."

I clear my throat. "He's joking. He's bad at being funny, so you probably couldn't tell, but he is."

"Don't insult Olivia's wit, Maggie. I'm sure she could tell," my dad says. "Thank you, Olivia. I wish Maggie would have told us. We would have loved to cook a meal that you could enjoy with us. Forgive my daughter. She means well. You probably couldn't tell because she's bad at hosting, but she does."

"Wow. Can we please move past this comedy routine and let them inside?"

My dad takes a dramatic step out of the way and bows with an arm extended toward the door. Olivia follows Tessa and Ashley, ducking through the threshold, and thanks my dad on her way in. Then it's just me and him on the porch, looking at each other.

"You're here," I say, holding up my hand in measurement. "I need you to be here." I drop it a couple inches. "Tone it down a tiny bit. Your alter ego gives me weird anxiety, and I don't want Olivia to think you're like this all the time." I shake my head. "It's not how I described you at all."

My dad grins as if this entire weekend is one big joke, and I'm too dull to get the punchline. Everyone is having a grand old time, but I'm on edge. I realize I'm being a rigid ass as my dad keeps giving me that condescending smile. I think I'm nervous as hell to show Olivia this part of my life. It means literally everything to me. And it means everything for us. This is what I have to offer someone, and I'm offering it to her. It feels like make or break for us, and it's hitting me how much I want to make it with her.

"Maggie, people—"

I hold out a hand to stop him and whatever wise adage he was about to drop on me. He has a way of cutting right to my quick, and I need all the confidence I can get my hands on right now. I need to steady myself and loosen up at the same time. "I know. I'm the one who needs to adjust my attitude. I know."

He crosses his arms and nods, the descending sun bathing him in a golden light, highlighting the cut of his clean-shaven jaw, his black hair juxtaposed with the iridescent silver strands. I run my hands through my hair, wishing I could be as good a man as him. My dad sets the bar, and I try so hard to reach it, but I think I'm found wanting. Meanwhile, Aiden couldn't give less of a shit about the bar, yet he's blissfully happy, and my father adores him. I know he adores me, too, just...*argh*.

My dad ducks his head to capture my gaze. "You okay, Mags?"

I nod, trying to reset my attitude. Everything is perfect. "Yeah. Sorry, Dad."

He tilts his head toward the door and shrugs. I take a deep breath and nod. He drapes an arm over my shoulder as we walk inside together. "I like her. Olivia."

"Me, too," I say as we follow the raucous laughter into the kitchen.

Uncle Ward is either mid-story or mid-comedy act, and everyone is doubled over, dying. I swing around the island to Olivia, and she wraps her arm around my waist, wiping a tear of laughter from her eye. "They're something, huh?" I ask.

She can only nod, but she pulls me closer, and I feel much, much better.

"Ward War Stew in fifteen, y'all. Meet in the kitchen with your favorite Nazi-killing weapons, and we'll feast," my uncle announces.

Olivia looks up, rubbing my back. "Can I get a tour while we wait for our pre-battle provisions?"

She is impossibly beautiful, and I'm dying to kiss that beauty mark on the tip of her lips. "Of course. We'll go out on the ATVs after dinner and do a little night tour of the orchard."

"And your room? Is that where I can toss my bag? Or was I going to sleep somewhere else?" The mischievous twinkle in her eye makes my stomach growl. Or maybe it's the aroma of Ward War Stew. Either way, I'm excited.

"No. You'll be with me." I grab her hand and pull her down the hallway. "I'm giving Olivia a quick tour. Be back soon," I call to the rest of the group.

"A quick tour of your mouth," Aiden calls back.

I open the door to my room and pull it shut behind—

Olivia's mouth is on mine, only lingering for a second before she pulls back an inch. "Aiden promised a tour of…" Her breath is warm and sweet and rolls over my lips like the easy waves of the Gulf of Mexico.

I close the small gap with a little too much gusto. We stumble a few steps until her backside butts up against my desk. She lets out a sexy gasp, and I swing my chair out of our way. Olivia can't be more than five-foot-two, and it doesn't take much effort to grip her hips and lift her onto the edge of my desk, putting her right on level with me. Her chest heaves as she spreads her legs and pulls me into her.

"This is my room," I say through my heavy breathing. My entire body warms. My cheeks are bonfires.

After one last delicious kiss, she pushes me back and touches a finger to her lips. A deep blush runs from her nose and cheeks all the way down her chest, disappearing into her shirt. I want to find out how far south that blush has traveled.

"I think bunking with you will be just fine," she whispers from behind her shaky fingers.

"Good."

She takes a deep breath and hoists herself off the desk. "Now, for the tour of your room." She pushes past me and spins in a slow circle, taking in everything in one revolution before my art seems to catch her eye. "I love your drawings." She approaches the cross-sectional sketch of a cedar trunk, and next to it, the sketch of its root system. Her fingers hover over the paper, tracing the amorphous rings of past xylem growth.

"It's not a scientific sketch. The cambium isn't really that thick, but I like how it looks against the bark. Especially over that scar," I say.

She moves her pointer finger over the disrupted bark and wood. "What happened to it?"

I look at the scar I inflicted on the imaginary tree and shrug. "That one looks like a fire scar." I point to how the xylem rings crash over themselves like a wave. Not a calm Florida swell but a tight Pacific coil. "The tree grows new wood over its injury, so it looks like a big swoop."

"Yikes. Why did you want to draw that?" She turns her attention from the growth rings to me.

"It's cool. Minus the modern devastation and causes of wildfires, fires are a natural part of a forest ecosystem. Just like disease pressure and drought. Some conifers even require fire for their cones to germinate and produce new growth." I lean in and kiss her cheek, lingering close to her ear. "And don't get me started on cypress and fire," I whisper.

"Let me guess." She flips her hair over one shoulder and fans herself. "You think this cypress is on fire." She winks, biting a grin.

Her throat is still pink from our kissing, and I want to see it burn red again. I can't help it. This cypress *is* fire. I drag my teeth down the column of her throat like a paintbrush on canvas and pull back, enjoying the instant rush of blood under her skin. Her lips pop open, and she fingers the heated skin under her ear.

"Yes. It would appear, unlike your woody brethren, you are susceptible to burning," I say, my gaze following her blush centimeter by centimeter.

She straightens and clears her throat as if willing the coolness in her posture to relieve the heat in her blood. "You're saying cypress trees don't burn?"

"Mediterranean cypress hold so much water that they are seven times more fire-resistant than other trees," I say, a little breathless because this is one of *the coolest* tree facts I know. And it's about cypress.

She nods. *Nods.* Clearly, Olivia does not appreciate what my little statistic actually means.

"*Seven times* more resistant," I repeat.

She nods again. "That's pretty cool, Mags."

"No. No, no." I shake my head and grab her hand. "It's not just cool, it's extraordinary. In Spain, there was a fire over a plot of fifty thousand acres. It was the perfect combination of dry and windy, and the trees were basically a giant pile of kindling. The fire burned every tree to the ground. The fifty thousand acres were a charred patch of earth. Except for a bright green patch of Mediterranean cypress and the few plants that grew within them."

She blinks and cocks her head. "They didn't burn?"

"In a fire that raged over thousands of acres. They didn't burn." I suck my lip under my teeth and bob my head. "Cypress. You're a rarity."

She drops her gaze to her shoes before pointing to my sketch. "But this guy isn't a cypress tree."

I pat the wall next to my cedar. "He is not a cypress tree, you're right. But it's not sad. This guy is still a healthy, growing tree in my imaginary forest. I promise. He's just got a little more personality in his rings now. A story to tell."

"And these roots." She steps in front of the root system. "Is there a story in them as well?"

The heat in my cheeks blooms as I look at the drawing. My drawing. A drawing that I never anticipated a girl like Olivia seeing. Different types of cedar trees growing in different types of environments have great variation in their root systems, but I can guarantee that not one of them looks like my depiction. I took great artistic liberty with this one. A massive taproot shoots straight into the soil, fighting off the smaller roots that seem to squeeze around it. All of the gnarly, crooked roots carry a desperation in the way they curl and bend through the soil. Always searching.

As a whole, they form a rough similarity to a heart, the top roots arching from the center like shoulders, and the rest of the system tapering to the point of the taproot. I suppose, in my most poetic of selves, I'd say this heart-shaped mess of greedy roots could possibly— almost definitely—represent something inside me that needs *just a little more*. That's my taproot. And if pressed, I may admit that the devilish little roots trying to stop it represent the fears that hold me back from obtaining it. *It.*

"What is it?" Olivia asks as if reading my mind.

I stare at the sketch. "I don't know."

She points to all the open soil around the boundary of cedar roots. "Nothing is stopping them from spreading out and growing uninhibited, yet they tangle around each other and restrict themselves."

She squeezes my hand. "Nothing is stopping you, Maggie. What's that taproot reaching for?"

I scrape my bottom lip between my teeth and turn to her. "I want you to be mine."

She arches a brow and grins. "Oh yeah?"

"Yeah. Will you be my girlfriend?"

"I kinda thought I already was." She kisses me but ends it too fast for my liking. "While this is a sweet moment and everything, it's not lost on me that this was one big pivot away from having to answer my question. I've been yours since I ran into you in the doorway of Hyde Hall. And you know that, deep down. So, my Maggie"—she lays her palm flat over my chest under my clavicle—"what is it you feel like you can't truly have? What is *it*?"

"I'm only twenty." I'm shocked to hear myself say those words. I'm about to bare the weakest part of myself to this girl. To Olivia Cypress, the girl whose entire being is a painful underscore of how badly I want *it*. "What I want the most is this." I raise my hands to encompass our house and orchard. Of course, this is my deepest desire. "I want to run this place so badly. It's my heart and soul, but…"

She wraps her arms around my waist and tucks her hands under my shirt, rubbing the skin of my back above my belt. "It's okay. I got you."

I pull her against me, her head tucking under my chin. I'm a coward. I don't want to look anyone in the eye when I admit that this life isn't enough for me. That I feel stuck between the thing I want the most and the thing I want second most. That I'm the greedy roots in my sketch that crave more than the abundance they already have. "It's not enough. I want what you and Aiden have."

She squeezes my waist and stays quiet, tucked into the crook of my neck. I feel at peace with her listening to me. It feels like my first reconciliation. I was so scared to confess, but it feels so good. "Like I said, I'm only twenty, you know? I'm so lucky and have so much, which makes it hard to admit, but I want to be young and wild and free. I want to be able to drop everything on a whim and travel with you to see the world. I want to feel like I can mess up without the whole university keeping tabs on my career." I sigh. "And I want to yell at my mom."

She pulls back at the last part. "You want to yell at your mom?"

"Yeah. I never got to yell at her. Sometimes, I have dreams where she shows up at our front door acting like she never left. And I let her have it. I yell at her."

"Do you want to go to Nashville right now? It's Friday. We have plenty of time to be back before class on Monday."

I shake my head. "What? What about the festival and—"

"Your dad and Ward are clearly more than capable, and the softball team and AQF have it under control. Do you know where she lives?"

"Yeah. She writes me a couple times a year." I point to my desk drawer where I have a stack of her unanswered letters that haunt me every day. I know I should respond, but with every new letter I receive, the task feels even more insurmountable. Even more stressful. "But I want to be here for Fall Fest. It'll be fun, and I don't want to give that up for her."

She slides open my desk drawer and fingers the stack of envelopes. It's a thick stack, the bottom envelops beginning to yellow with age. She closes the drawer with her hip and hugs me again. "Okay. The offer stands."

"Maggie. Stew's ready," Uncle Ward calls.

I run my hands up her arms. "I'm so sorry about the stew. I can't believe I didn't think to make you something vegan."

"It's really okay, Mags. Par for the course. Every vegan knows to bring their own food."

"Well, don't get in the habit. This is the last time you'll have to do that here."

CHAPTER THIRTEEN

From where the fading sun sits above the western tree line, I'd guess we have about twenty minutes to make it to the ridge before it disappears below the horizon. I lift the cooler into Aiden's small tailgate and secure it with bungee cords. "All right. Careful, now. You have precious cargo," I say.

"I wouldn't call myself *precious*," Scott says through a smile. Aiden chuckles and cranks the four-wheeler to life.

"Oh my God, did Scott tell a joke?" Ashley asks as she climbs into the back of my four-wheeler next to Tessa.

"I didn't know you have jokes," I say.

"Ten out of ten, Scott," Olivia chimes in as she crouches into my shotgun seat.

"Leave my boyfriend alone. He's charming and funny, unlike you assholes," Aiden says. Scott grabs the "oh shit" bar as they peel out of the barn. "See ya at Rowdy Ridge," he yells as they disappear into the orchard. I cringe at his use of "Rowdy Ridge." We named it after it became our go-to place for hookups in high school. The ridge is western facing—hence the sunset we're about to catch—and is tucked behind a windbreak of Italian cypress. It's private and has an incredible view of the valley below.

"Ten bucks says Scott pisses his pants," Tessa says.

I start the engine and shift to reverse. "I'm too smart to take that bet. Aiden is wild on these things. Y'all ready?" Everyone nods and says some form of yes. I turn to Olivia, who sits next to me, a big smile spreading across her face. "It's pretty bumpy, but we do this all the time. I promise, it's safe."

She squeezes my thigh. "I'm so ready. Let's do this."

"Here we go," I shout, and we fly out of the barn. Not quite as recklessly as Aiden, but fast enough for the acceleration and inertia to throw our bodies around like rag dolls. Olivia's grip tightens on my thigh as I whip into a row of already harvested apples, the wheels bumping over rotting cores.

"I can smell the apples," Olivia yells into the rushing wind between us. She abandons my thigh to tighten her coat. It's cold as hell racing through the orchard on a late October night, but that's what the firepit is for. Aiden and I brought a bunch of leftover pavers that my dad didn't need and built a firepit on the ridge so we could fend off the cold of nights like these.

"Hold on," I shout and take a hard left to climb the makeshift trail we built on our side of Scout Mountain. Our butts catch air every time I drive over a big root or rock, and Olivia squeezes her eyes shut. This may be too fast, even for her. As the last bend in the path and Aiden's dust trail becomes visible, I slow to a peaceful crawl.

"Boo. Give us more of the adrenaline rush," Ashley calls from the back. But Olivia turns to me and winks, and that's all I care about.

"First part is for flying. Second part is for taking in the scenery," I say. And what a scene it is. The Blue Ridge Mountains are the second oldest mountains in the world. In the mornings, with the little bit of fog gathered about their valleys, the range looks like an ocean with rolling waves. They actually look blue like water. Not right now, though. Right now, they're backlit and black, topped off with a brilliant display of sorbet orange and dusty red.

I slow to a stop behind Aiden and park. Ashley and Tessa hop out of the ATV and help Aiden untie the cooler.

"This is gorgeous. Thank you for sharing this with me," Olivia says and takes in the sunset, the mountains, the trees, then turns back to me. "For sharing everything with me. Not just this."

I nod, and she shimmies out of her seat to help Scott start the fire. She hunches over the pile of kindling, tucking the hair that cascades in front of her face behind her ear. I know why I wanted to push her away when we first met. She lives the life I want, and seeing her happy and uninhibited made me sore and achy. But now, being close to her is like rubbing aloe over a burn. I don't know what my future holds beyond

Hyde Hill Farm—if it holds anything at all—but I know, right now, I have Olivia. And knowing that feels like I have the entire world.

Tessa pops open the lid of the cooler and fishes out a beer for everyone. Aiden fans the small fire with a piece of cardboard, and Scott lays another piece of wood over the top. Once the fire has hit a sustainable burn, we all settle and raise our beers.

"To Olivia and Scott," I say.

"Welcome to the family," Tessa adds. We toast our new additions and watch the flames jump and twist around each other. Olivia sits across from me, sandwiched between Aiden and Tessa, huddled into herself for warmth with a smile poking over the collar of her coat. She chuckles along with one of Aiden's stories of us getting into trouble when we were younger. I think it's the one about me biting into a wormy apple and crying. But I can't take my eyes off her. She meets my gaze over the tips of the flames. They burn in her pupils as she stares at me. Her eye contact isn't sweet or romantic. Not cute or playful.

It's hot.

Ashley knocks my knee, and I'm forced to break our connection. "Can you grab me another beer, Mags?"

I pop open the cooler. "Anyone else?"

"Yes, please," Olivia says.

"Me, too," Aiden agrees.

I pass around the cold cans and wipe the freezing condensation from my fingers on my thighs. "I also brought a little something else," Ashley says. She fishes inside her coat and slides out a split bottle of Buffalo Trace. "I know your dad doesn't like you guys drinking liquor, but I thought it was a special occasion, all of us here at Hyde Hill Farm together." She peels the foil from the stopper and uncorks it, taking a pull for herself and passing it to Olivia.

From my limited experience around Olivia and alcohol, she seems to enjoy it in moderation, but I'm curious how much she'll drink when the party isn't cut short by needing to drive a classmate home. We're in for the night, and Aiden and I are the only ones who have to worry about driving. I want her to have fun and enjoy, but I also hope she doesn't get wasted because there's a whole night ahead of us.

"Maybe after my beer," Olivia says. She passes the bottle to

Aiden, who then passes it to Scott. My brother and I know better than to drive down the mountain at night intoxicated.

Scott takes a big gulp of whiskey that surprises me. He clears his throat but holds in his cough. "Wow," I say.

"Scott is full of surprises tonight," Tessa says.

"Scott is fucking awesome." Aiden presses his lips to his boyfriend's.

Everyone smiles. They're adorable together. "Get a room," Ashley calls over the fire.

"We already got one," Aiden says, eyes still on Scott.

Olivia winks at me over the fire, and I cough on my sip of beer, dribbling the cool liquid down my chin onto my collar. I wipe it with the back of my hand, my cheeks burning under her gaze. She smothers a chuckle, no doubt enjoying her influence over me. "Don't mind her. It's Maggie's first time drinking a beer," Aiden heckles.

I scoff. "I just couldn't keep it down with the thought of you shacking up with someone. No offense, Scott."

"Reckon we'll all be shacking up with someone tonight," he says.

I crush my empty can and toss it at him. "Don't be gross, Aid. We might change our minds about letting you tag along with us all the time."

"Oh please, you'll be crying when I leave after graduation."

That was a fucking low blow. I stare at him over the flames highlighting every Hyde feature on his face, just like the sun did to my dad earlier. This is the first time he's actually said out loud that he plans to leave, and he does it as a jab in front of my friends. I'm speechless.

"I'll tell Sarah you say hi, though. Don't worry," he adds.

Rage boils over me. I bite my lip until the pain makes my eyes water, trying not to explode like a child. I'm the oldest. I'm responsible. I'm in control. He may have my dad's black hair and jawline. But he doesn't have his character.

I do.

"Shit, Aiden. A little uncalled for, don't you think?" Tessa says.

Olivia looks between us, her brows knitted with concern.

"Who's Sarah?" Scott asks.

Aiden pokes a log in the fire with a crooked stick, sending sparks into the air. "Relax, it's just a joke." I have never been more disappointed in my brother. He either knows me less than I thought or is crueler than I thought. "Sarah was Maggie's high school girlfriend," he adds.

"She wasn't my girlfriend," I finally say. I catch Aiden's eye and shake my head. "But thank you, Aiden, for being so compassionate."

Scott tilts his head and tries to ask again. "So who—"

Olivia stands and stretches her arms high above her head, releasing a long yawn and cutting off Scott's repeated question. "I am so exhausted," she says. "Maggie, do you mind taking me back? I want to get a good night's sleep for the festival tomorrow."

I nod. "Um. Sure. Of course."

Tessa stands, too, pulling Ashley with her. "That's code for Aiden is being an ass," she says. "Y'all put out the fire. We'll see you in the morning."

"Jesus. Sensitive much?" he asks.

Scott stays quiet as we pack away our empty cans, and Ashley plucks the bourbon from his hands. "We love you, Aid. But my girl is right, you're being mean. Totally uncalled for."

He shakes his head, hands raised in confusion.

"Y'all don't have to—" I start, but Tessa pulls me toward the ATV.

"We're ready to go, and you're the only one who can drive this thing."

We descend the mountain in silence. I drive slowly, my headlights only illuminating a few feet ahead of us before the trail hits a switchback or curve. Olivia's hand stays planted on my thigh. I feel protected and loved by my friends but also vulnerable and exposed. I don't want to need to be taken care of. I try to banish the thought that everyone was embarrassed for me. I focus on how they flanked me instead.

Fucking Aiden. We'll sort it out tomorrow. I want to push this out of my mind and make space for the rest of the night. Make space for me and Olivia.

CHAPTER FOURTEEN

G ood night," Tessa says as she and Ashley disappear into the guest room.

Olivia and I walk hand in hand down the hall to my door. I stop before I open it and look at her. "Are you sure you want to stay with me? There's no pressure. I can sleep on the couch and—"

"I've been looking forward to this all week, Maggie. Open the door."

I push open my door and light the candle Tessa gave me for my birthday last year. *Pure White Sage; A Candle for Your Inner Peace.* The three burning wicks illuminate my room in a soft dreamsicle glow.

Olivia drapes her coat over the back of my desk chair and drags her fingers over my back as she passes. "I'm going to change. Be right back." She disappears into my bathroom, and I use the opportunity to sneak to the kitchen and snag two whiskey glasses from the bar. I scribble a note on a napkin and leave it next to the bottle of Weller. I know better than to pour myself the E.H. Taylor:

Poured two drinks from the Weller. Olivia is twenty-one, and I'll replace it.

I sign my name and pour two generous servings before screwing the cap back on and placing the bottle on the corner of my note. He won't be mad. He'll appreciate the honesty. I snag the glasses and take a moment to appreciate the golden liquid coloring the monogramed *H* in the etched Waterford crystal. I love the weight of these glasses. They're solid. Something to really hold on to.

I knock once and open the door to find Olivia perched on the edge of my bed wearing navy blue pajama pants and an Alder U T-shirt, her hair pulled into a messy topknot like mine. "Oh, what do we have here?" she asks as I hand her a glass and sit next to her, feeling overdressed in my jeans.

"Now that I don't have to navigate down a mountain at night, I thought we could have a little nightcap. If you want to, of course."

She raises her glass, and I knock mine carefully against hers. "Cheers," she says and takes a small sip. "Wow. Yep"—she smacks her lips—"that's straight whiskey."

I chuckle and take a sip. "You don't have to drink it," I assure her.

She holds the glass to her nose and sniffs. "That first sip was an adjustment. What is it?"

"It's Weller. A wheated bourbon. It's my favorite. Not so intensely sweet and sour as the heavy corn and rye ones. A little more subtle and balanced."

She takes a smaller sip this time and lets it linger in her mouth before swallowing. "It's delicious. Like caramel and dried fruit. It's just a little strong."

"I'll grab you some ice." I take her glass. "Be right back."

"You're sweet." I pause in the door frame and stare at her, speechless. Taken by her simple compliment. "Go on. Be quick. I want to hang out with you," she says.

I return in a flash with her Weller on the rocks. "Here you are."

She takes a sip and sighs. "Oh, yeah. This is perfect. Thank you."

"No problem."

"How about you get changed? You're making me feel like you're about to run out the door all dressed up like that." She waves a finger over me.

"Yeah. Good call." I open my dresser and grab a pair of gray sweats and a FFA shirt that I've had since middle school.

"Oh my God," Olivia says when I walk out the bathroom.

I look at myself, a little alarmed. "What? Do I have something on me?"

"Is that FFA as in Future Farmers of America?" She eyes my shirt, her brows raised.

I take a nervous sip of my whiskey. "Yes?" I clear my throat. "Yeah. It is."

"Come here." Olivia pats the mattress next to her. Once I've sat, our thighs pressed together, she turns to me. "That is the cutest thing I've ever seen. My little future farmer."

I chuckle. "Current farmer, now." I wink.

"Yes. My *real* farmer."

Her possessive pronoun burrows into my chest, outwarming my whiskey. "Olivia—"

She holds up a hand to stop me. "You don't have to get into it tonight. But about what Aiden said by the fire…is Sarah someone you're hanging on to, or is she someone in your past? I just need to know before we go any further."

I take a moment to adjust to the one-eighty. Olivia knows me. She knows my hopes, my dreams, my fears. Sarah represents a fear. Nothing more. She doesn't represent a lost love or painful breakup. She represents what I'm afraid Olivia will do to me. What Aiden will definitely do to me. "I don't mind talking about it."

She nods. "So who was she? Who *is* she?"

"Sarah Freeman was my best friend through middle and high school. We were never officially in a relationship, but we were always intimate. Friends with benefits, I guess. But close as hell." I shake my head. "I don't know. Maybe we were in, like, an open relationship, technically. I don't think I was in love with her, but I really, really loved her. I thought we were going to Alder together. We had always talked about how we'd room together and live in East Sparrow together. I don't know if it would have been as lovers or friends, but I felt like we were meant to go through life side by side. She understood me." I wave at the window. "Understood all this. Her dad is a minister and the church outreach director here, and her family also has a farm. But it turned out that she never even applied to Alder."

"What? Did you know she wasn't going to?"

I shake my head. "I didn't know until she had already accepted her offer from Stanford. I can't blame her, and I don't. It's *Stanford*. I was so blindsided and hurt. She left for Palo Alto a month before classes started. I don't know why. I just knew that I was alone all of a sudden. She left me."

"That sounds like a big loss. Do you still talk?"

I squeeze her hand. "No. We tried to maintain a friendship freshman year, but we both knew there was no point. It's not like she was going to move back home. It fizzled out in the first semester." I blow out a deep breath. "Anyway, Sarah is a person from my past whom I loved once and no longer have feelings for. She didn't wrong me, but I can't help but chalk her up as another person who bailed on me and this place. My mom did, Sarah did, Aiden confirmed that he will, and you…" I look at her. A pang shoots through my chest like an expertly sharpened arrow. "I'm afraid to lose you."

"You won't lose me."

I give her a tight smile. "Won't I? Next year, you'll be gone for an internship. And after that, who knows? I don't want to be someone who holds you back from what you want, Olivia. You—"

"*You*," she interrupts. "I want you. I'm wicked good at prioritizing, and I'm telling you I want to prioritize us. I need you to trust me."

I nod.

"Do you trust me, Maggie?"

Do I? Do I trust the intoxicating girl who skips classes, loses her keys, travels on a whim, and refuses to bend to anything other than her own will? Do I trust that if I spend the small amount of time I have left at Alder with her, she won't make it worthless by ditching me? This feels like the one shot I have to meet my life partner. Sarah was the only queer person I knew in East Sparrow, besides Aiden. The odds are against me.

Olivia's eyes bore into me. She scares the shit out of me. She's like the Batman ride at Six Flags, scary as hell, but I trust I won't die when I lower the bar over my chest.

"I trust you."

"I know what you want out of your life, and I know what I want out of mine. I wouldn't drag us through a relationship if I didn't believe we could weave our dreams together. I know we can find a way."

I swallow panicked words and pose a calmer question. "But you are leaving next year, right?" I hate how it sounds. How my voice is a thin strand tugging each word from my mouth, about to break. She holds my gaze, and I can see something like pity in her eyes. "It's okay. I just…" I drop my gaze to my lap. "I'm running out of time before I have to come back here."

Her fingers skim my cheek and tuck a whisp of hair behind my ear. "I can't tell you where I'll be next year, Maggie. But I can tell you that

I've spoken to accounting and finance firms in the Northwest, one in London, two in New York, and one in Dublin. It's only one semester."

I've been avoiding this. The sour cherry pit in my stomach aches. *London? Dublin?* I won't see Olivia for an entire semester. I trace the *H* on my glass, struggling to respond, not wanting to put any of this negativity on her. She deserves to be exactly where she wants to be, even if it's on the opposite side of the world.

"I haven't picked any specific firm yet—I'm still in the gathering information phase—but I'm also going to apply to a few places in Atlanta. I could still attend some classes, then, and stay with you on the weekends."

I snap my head up and catch her eyes. The corner of her lips reaches for the beauty mark, a mark they'll never grasp. As doomed as Atlas. But her grin is golden.

"If you'll have me," she whispers.

"Wait. What? Of course I want you to stay with me, and of course I want you to stay close next year. But that isn't what *you* want. I thought you wanted to go international. London or Dublin. You..." I shake my head in disbelief of what I'm about to say. "You can't stay here, Olivia. You need to do what's best for you."

She bites her lip and fingers the bead of condensation dripping down her glass. I don't want her to actually leave, but maybe she needs to hear me say it and set her free. "There wasn't much I cared about leaving in Alder. Don't get me wrong, I love it here. But I can bring a photo of the mountains and the buildings wherever I go. I wasn't worried about missing part of my senior year of college." She takes a sip and pauses for a moment before meeting my eye again. "But now, I have you. And I'm not so sure I want to give up any of my senior year with you for an internship I can do here. I will always be working. I can always travel. But I'll never get my senior year back."

A warmth spreads through my chest. Maybe, just maybe, it's possible to have everything I've ever wanted. "Well"—I clear my throat—"sounds like you have some great options, and I'm excited for you no matter what you decide." I stand and take the glass from her, setting both on my desk. "It's getting chilly. Ready for bed?"

She pulls back the quilt, gesturing for me to get in first. I tug off my wool socks, tucking them in my dresser, and crawl into my childhood bed, thanking God that it's at least not a twin. A full-sized bed is plenty of space for us. She stares at me as I pull the covers over my legs. "You coming?" I ask.

She grins, the candlelight flickering over her mischievous eyes. "In a second." Before I can inquire further, she grips the bottom of her shirt and pulls it over her head. She is perfect. The candlelight contours her curves, shading under her bare chest and the sexy swell of her stomach over her waistband, and under her left breast is a pale birthmark that looks like South America. My lips twitch, aching to find out how it tastes. How she tastes.

I stare at her, unashamed of pacing her body, unable to stop mapping her. She gives me time to enjoy her display before she tucks her thumbs in her waistband and pushes her pajama pants to her ankles, stepping out of them toward my bed. My entire body is burning like that Spanish forest fire, and Olivia Cypress is my only saving grace. She slips under the covers next to me.

This feels nothing like Sarah Freeman.

"Yet again, Maggie, you're entirely overdressed," she whispers, her hand resting on the apex of my hip. It's growing chilly in my room, but Olivia's body under my covers is a furnace. I sit up and peel off my FFA shirt, tossing it across the room with my sweats. We don't pounce on each other, not yet. Our fingertips skim over each other as a thick heat saturates the air between us. Every inch of her body is soft, and when my fingers hit the curls between her thighs, a groan overflows my mouth.

I've only had a couple hookups that weren't Sarah. But sex has never felt like this, and I've barely touched her. She holds my gaze as she shifts and inches her thighs apart. I brush my fingers over her warmth, and her lips pluck apart, letting her soft breaths escape. Touching her feels like the warmest, safest home I could ever imagine. Warmer than nights spent playing cards and burning candles with my family. Warmer than knowing I'm exactly where I'm supposed to be in my life. And yet, at the same time, touching her feels like the most liberating adventure in the world. An excitement that clenches my teeth and makes me reach for something to hold on to because my feelings for her have grown into a juggernaut. I'm not sure there's any stopping them.

Wouldn't want to.

"This feels…" I begin to say, raising my hand to cup her cheek. I don't know how to articulate all the feelings that roar through me. I'm scared to tell her. For every assumption I've made about her, she's either shattered it or shown me why I was wrong. She's challenging and strong, and somehow, she picked me. I drop my eyes, trying to come up with words.

Olivia runs a thumb over my bottom lip. She grins at my miserably failing to tell her how I feel. "Everyone wants to wear Carhartt until it's time to do Carhartt shit," she says with a wink. "Do the Carhartt shit, Maggie. I promise, you won't be alone."

A single breath of a chuckle escapes my mouth, and I kiss her open palm. "I'm falling in love with you, Olivia. I'm falling hard." A glassy layer of wetness liquifies the cobalt of her eyes as she presses her hand over my heart. Now that I've started, I want to keep going. "Everything that scared me about you, every little thing that screamed at me to run away…those are the things I adore the most. I thought I knew exactly who I was down to the atoms that form me, but I had no idea how much of myself was missing. Until I met you."

I wait for her to respond beyond the tears in her eyes that are threatening to reach a critical mass and fall down her cheek. Beyond her fingertips digging into the skin below my clavicle and the twitch of her lips struggling to capture a word. Like in the threshold of Hyde Hall, I have Olivia flustered. I decide she deserves a little grace and a little more time to form her thoughts. I know it's not easy.

"Take your time. I'm just going to busy myself while I wait," I whisper against her neck and brush my tongue over her sweat-sheened skin. She shudders in my arms as I continue kissing her chest, following the blush trailing down her body. When I reach her breasts and tug one gently into my mouth, she groans and bucks underneath me, pushing me onto my back.

She swings on top of me, straddling my stomach, and I can feel her warmth and wetness on my skin. I almost lose it from the intense look in her eye. And from how her heated body smells like nothing, not one thing, except for *her*. She knows what she's doing to me as she sinks her weight into my upper pelvis and reaches behind her, discovering all of the desire I've gathered for her. Her gasp matches mine as she explores me, and I pulse around her fingers.

I've never felt more connected to another person. Not Sarah. Not anyone. Olivia's chest pumps with scattered breaths, and I tighten around her, refusing to let any more space between us. My whole brain is a jumbled mess of hormones and adrenaline and blood rushing in my ears until I'm lifted in a giant wave and crash all over her.

I don't give myself a moment to come down. I know she's on the edge, so I flip her underneath me and crawl down her body, spreading her thighs and stroking her until her entire body erupts into delicious convulsions. Our first time is quick as lightning and just as intense. It can be like that, I reckon. Sometimes, you build so much between each other that it's hard to contain once you strike the match. Tomorrow night, we'll go slower. Later tonight, we'll go slower.

I bury my face in her neck and breathe her in. Feel her frenzied heartbeat slowing against my lips. "I gave you some time to think," I say, smiling against her pulse. "Now it's time for you to do—"

"I love you," she says, the three words breathy and quick. I unbury my head from her neck and lean on my elbow to look at her. She cups my face with both hands, the scent of me and her mixing with her words and melting me. She gathers a deep breath. "I love you, Maggie. I want this for as long as you can give it to me, and I'm really hoping that's forever."

I smile against her hands and fall back into her, overwhelmed with delight and warmth. "Now that's some Carhartt shit," I say.

She scoffs and pinches me in the ribs. "Wow, Maggie. Wow."

"You know I love you, Olivia. Now come here." I pull her under me again, and we swim in the deep end of each other all night until we're nothing but puddles of spent muscle. I don't know what time we fall asleep, only that at some point, I drift off from one dream straight into another.

CHAPTER FIFTEEN

I wake to the sound of Ashley calling my name through the door. She knocks again. "Maggie? It's probably time to wake up. Bailey texted that they're leaving Alder now."

Oh shit. We've overslept, and today is Fall Fest. We have to shower, make breakfast, and get ready to welcome the softball team and all the AQF leadership in less than an hour. I nudge Olivia, who is still peacefully asleep next to me.

Ashley knocks once more and announces that she's opening the door. I pull the quilt over Olivia's bare back and hold up the sheet to cover myself. "Oh. My." Ashley looks between the two of us. "Okay, well, you're awake, so I will be going now."

Olivia stirs and startles awake at Ashley's voice. "Shit," she mumbles and pulls the quilt tight around herself. "Morning, Ash."

Ashley grins and raises an eyebrow. "It is indeed. Everyone's on their way. I suggest cracking a window. It smells like s—"

"*Okay*, thank you, Ashley." I cut her off, needing this wake-up call to end, oh I don't know, *yesterday*. She winks and closes the door behind her. Thank God.

Olivia slides down in bed, giggling and pulling me with her. I pull the quilt over our heads and consume us in a dark blanket fort. "I know we have to get going," she whispers. "But just know, I will be thinking about last night *all day*."

"Me, too." I kiss her and throw the blanket off. "I'm going to go shower in the guest bathroom. You can use mine." I shuffle around the room, gathering my things. She grabs my hand as I reach for the door.

"I love you," she says. And it hits me as intensely as it did last night.

I press one more kiss to her lips that still taste like us. "I love you, too."

❖

Uncle Ward flips the sizzling bacon in the cast-iron pan and hums along to his favorite Willie Nelson album, *Red Headed Stranger*. I pity the bastard who tries to tell him any different. The man is passionate about few things, but this Willie album is one of them. He is freshly showered and in a bright mood as usual.

"Morning, Uncle Ward. Thanks for cooking," I say, pouring myself a cup of coffee from the French press.

"Ain't no thang, chicken wang." He pads over to wrap an arm around my shoulder. I love him. And since I'm in practice from Olivia, I tell him.

"I love you," I say, squeezing him back.

I must not tell him often enough because he almost squeezes the coffee up my esophagus and says, "Dang, girl. I love you like hell." He returns to his cooking and cracks the oven to check on something that smells like cinnamon and clove. "I made a special vegan thingy for your girlfriend." He shrugs. "Might be shit, but it smells good."

I love not having to bat away "girlfriend" in a flurry of insecurity. She *is* my girlfriend. "I'm sure it's perfect. Thanks for thinking of it."

Olivia, Tessa, and Ashley walk into the kitchen together. I spotted Olivia tiptoeing into their room after she got dressed. I imagine they spent a couple minutes gossiping and talking about last night. Though I know most of last night is ours. I blush at the memories rushing back to me. Olivia stands next to me and wraps an arm around my waist as if reading my mind.

"Morning, girls," Ward says.

They reply in a chorus of greetings as my dad walks in from the back porch. "Howdy, howdy," he says. "Maggie, your brother and Scott aren't up yet, but I don't guess they have much to do with today. Let them keep sleeping?" He shrugs.

I shrug back. "Yeah, I don't care."

He nods and clears his throat. "Olivia?"

She steps out of my arms and straightens, looking at my dad. I'm not thirteen, so it's rare that I ever accidentally give a girl a hickey, but as I watch Olivia stand tall under the scrutiny of my father, I can see a pale, lip-shaped bruise peeking out from the collar of her sweater. It's faint enough that no one will notice, but it sends heat straight to my core.

"Yes, Mr. Hyde?" she replies.

His gaze passes over the rest of us and lands back on her. "Would you mind joining me for a walk in the orchard? It's cold. I recommend a coat."

She gives me a quick side glance, then answers, "Yes, of course. I'll grab my jacket and be right back."

"Excellent," he says.

I stare at him. "What are you up to?" I ask as he pours himself another cup of coffee.

"Relax. How does she take her coffee?"

"Black. She's vegan, and I doubt we have anything besides cream." I shake my head as he pours a cup for Olivia. This is so completely bizarre.

Olivia walks back into the kitchen, accepting the cup from my father. "All right, Mr. Hyde, I'm ready."

"Back in a flash," he says to me, and they disappear out the back door.

I turn to the rest of the family. "What the hell was that? Did Scott have to go on a private walk with Dad?"

Uncle Ward shrugs. "Don't think so, but maybe it's coming."

"He probably just wants to get to know her better since things are getting serious between you guys," Ashley says.

I shake my head and reach for a crispy bacon bit from the sizzling skillet. Ward smacks my hand before I can get any. "You crazy, girl? That's a quick way to get a flame licking." That's what he calls a burn, but regardless, I am an expert at picking bacon from the pan. "Here." He slides the plate of the cooled first batch in front of me, and I crunch on the crispiest one.

"I dunno. He had a hyper energy," I say. The most animated my dad gets is when he talks about Hyde Hill Farm or when Tessa and

Ashley come over, and he gets to play his favorite role of goofy old guy. Otherwise, he hovers within the equilibrium of subdued. But not this morning. He's after something. Has some end goal in sight.

"Well, you can ask her when she gets back," Ashley says.

It's unsettling to think about what my dad wants to talk to Olivia about. He's really not the type of guy to get over involved in our relationships, and my relationship being so fresh with Olivia makes me doubt he's having a "welcome to the family" talk. They just met, for crying out loud. I check the clock. Everyone should be arriving in about twenty minutes. Though I'm excited to welcome them and eager for Fall Fest, that doesn't leave much time to debrief Olivia about the conversation with my dad.

I startle at the feel of Uncle Ward's hand on my back. "Wouldn't worry yourself, Mags. When have you ever not trusted your daddy? Come on, now, and eat some breakfast." He turns to Ashley and Tessa. "All y'all. Get it while it's hot."

I pull out plates for everyone. When have I ever not trusted my dad? Never. But I haven't gotten the opportunity to talk to him about the cost per plant data for the peaches, and even though I trust him, it worries me. I serve myself a fried egg and biscuit. My dad and Olivia's walk has nothing to do with the data, though. So for now, I just need to eat and focus on the rest of the day.

"Morning." Aiden's voice fills me with warmth and familiarity, but I remember how much of an absolute dickhead he was to me last night, and I ignore him.

Ashley and Tessa greet him on my behalf.

"Breakfast is ready. Where's Scotty?" Uncle Ward asks.

Aiden yawns and wipes his mouth with the sleeve of his sweatshirt. "Shower." He ruffles his bedhead. "Um, Maggie?"

I chew my bite of biscuit in slow motion, refusing to swallow so I have an excuse to not speak to him. I look at him with raised brows. *Yes?*

"I was an asshole last night. I'm sorry. And about the post-graduation stuff, maybe we can talk more about that later?"

I cave whenever someone apologizes to me. Why wouldn't I? What more is there to be done? They say sorry, and I say it's okay. "It's okay." I sip my coffee to clear the biscuit cement in my throat. "And yeah. We can talk about the other thing whenever you want."

Twenty minutes later, I hear tires chewing through gravel. My stomach flutters with nerves, and Olivia and my dad aren't back yet. I dump my dishes in the sink, and Ashley, Tessa, and I walk out front to meet everyone.

I shield my eyes against the sun climbing the sky and thank God that the weather has cooperated. Car doors slam, and people flow toward our house.

"Is right here okay to park?" Bailey hollers from an old Jeep. Maya is already scoping out the space around the deck. I think I heard her say hi, but I can't be sure. Andy follows, giving my shoulder a squeeze and thanking me again for hosting.

"Yeah, that's great," I call to Bailey.

She and Noelle lock their car and meet us by the porch steps. We give each other hugs and share our excitement for the night to come.

Ashley wraps an arm around Bailey's shoulders. "Should we head inside for a cup of coffee and get our game plan together?" she asks.

Bailey tucks her sunglasses into the neck of her old sweater. It's the same old Eddie Bauer sweater she's always wearing. "I never turn down coffee."

We wrangle Andy and Maya, and I pour coffee for everyone while they settle in the living room. I'm anxious that Olivia hasn't returned, but she's not in a leadership position with AQF, so we begin to plan our setup without her.

We plan everything down to the minute. The day will be full of fun autumnal activities, starting with bobbing for apples and a pumpkin carving contest and ending with the Apple Wars as the finale. Between the games and pie eating, there will be speeches and Socratic seminars discussing the next steps for AQF. Our meeting lasts half an hour before we disband and wander outside to collect the culled apples for Maya and Kevin, the baseball team's star pitcher.

A rift formed between the softball and baseball teams last year, to the point where we weren't sure if they would be part of the Apple Wars or if it would just have to be between Maya and Daniella, another pitcher on the team. But according to the schedule in my hands, the baseball team is due to arrive at three, so I assume they have reached some form of agreement.

Noelle stops next to me on her way out to the orchard. "Hey. Where's Olivia? Thought she came with Tessa and Ashley last night."

I don't know Noelle or Bailey very well, but with every second I spend with them, my respect and love for them grows. It can be easy to forget that our small group of queer friends grows by the day, stringing connections across itself like a giant web. I forget that Ashley and Olivia go back to before we knew Ashley, and therefore, Olivia knows Noelle, Bailey, and the other AQF officers.

I don't know what to say. She's been on a walk with my father for almost an hour now, and I have no idea what they're talking about. That it must be serious because my dad wanted to be here to receive everyone, and he isn't. "She's taking a walk," I manage to say.

The back door cracks open, and my dad and Olivia walk in with the cold breeze. "Sorry. Lost track of time. Welcome, everyone. I had a quick chat with Bailey outside and am going to run an extension cord under the deck for her real quick," my dad says.

"Hey." Olivia walks to us and lays a hand on my lower back. Her cheeks are bright pink, and her grin is sincere, etching into the corner of her eyes. She wraps Noelle in a quick hug. Noelle's eyes widen in confusion. When she pulls away, Olivia offers an explanation. "Mr. Hyde was giving me the exclusive newcomer's tour."

Noelle beams. "Lucky. I'm going to head out and help gather apples. Catch you out there?"

"For sure," I say.

After the door shuts behind her, Olivia and I are the only two left in the living room. I grab her hand and pull her to my bedroom, which is now freezing from the window I cracked to air it out. I slide it shut and sit on my bed. Olivia joins me, and every touch and sensation from the night before barrels through my brain, stealing the curiosity I have about her conversation with my dad. I kiss her. And it's as hot and needy as I remember. She pushes her chest into me, and the feeling of her breasts against mine, even through layers of fabric, ratchets up my need. I reach for the button on her jeans, but she bats away my hand.

"We can't," she says, her words skipping through her teeth between kisses, her lips never leaving mine. "Everyone is outside." More kissing.

I hear some laughter and the unmistakable *thunk* and splatter of an apple against wood. My hand slips out of her warm shirt, and I pull away. "You're right. This day is going to be a blast, but if I'm honest, I just want it to end so we can go to bed," I say.

She plants one more kiss on me. "Me, too."

"So, uh, what was the walk about?" I smooth my shirt and unroll my sleeves, buttoning them at my wrists.

She licks her lips and nods. "Yeah. The walk was interesting." She meets my gaze and drops her hand in my lap to join mine. I interlace our fingers and wait for her to continue. "Maggie, we have a lot to talk about, but—"

"Oh God. What is it?"

"But," she continues, "now isn't the time. Everyone is here, and we have a party to throw. Everything is okay, I promise."

I shake my head. "I don't understand. What did you guys—"

She squeezes my hand and cuts off my question. "I want you to trust me. Everything is okay. Let's do today, and tonight, we'll talk all about what your dad wanted to discuss with me, okay? I'll tell you everything over that tasty bourbon you poured me last night. Deal?"

Of course, I'm bursting at the seams to know what they talked about, but more, I want to be the best partner to Olivia possible. I'm new at this, and I have a lot to prove to her. She doesn't want to get into it right now, and even though I do, I nod and kiss her cold cheek. "Okay. I trust that everything is okay, and we can talk about it tonight," I say.

She blows out a breath. "Great. And we can even do it naked."

CHAPTER SIXTEEN

"Ma-ya! Ma-ya!"

The entire—giant, I'm pleased to say—crowd that has swarmed our orchard all day has now gathered on the porch and overflows onto the grass next to the apple trees, chanting Maya's name with such heart and such fervor, we could be at the Women's College World Series at the bottom of the seventh in the championship game. I have no idea what happened between the softball and baseball team, but even though they showed up to participate, the tension between the two teams hangs in the apple sweet air.

It's palpable enough for me to be on high alert for any altercations, especially given the complete and utter beatdown Maya is serving this guy, Kevin. It's all fun and games until some dude's ego gets hurt, and we have to "escort" him off our property. Even though Kevin's competitive grin has morphed into a scowl, I'd be shocked if anyone crossed a line tonight. Coach Clayton and Coach Williams from the softball team cheer for Maya with the rest of the crowd. It would be a very, very bad decision for any of the baseball team to make a scene with the amount of faculty present.

I scan the energetic crowd. There's not just the coaches and Dr. Martin here; there are more professors and faculty than I can reasonably keep track of in my head. And because the club isn't recognized yet by the school, they are all taking a risk by being here. Especially in the wake of all the anti-LGBTQ+ legislation being pushed in the South right now. But their presence and this night speaks volumes against the current wave of hate.

The queer community of Alder and its allies are out at our farm celebrating and planning, and damn, there's something momentous brewing in this crowd. I can feel it in the rumble of my chest every time Maya hits a bull's-eye. Every time Bailey grabs the mic. And every time Olivia looks at me.

It's different tonight, the way she looks at me. Like she's a step further than I. A foot deeper. And she's waiting patiently for me to join her. *The water's great.* It's practically written on her face. I can't wait. I'm as hopeful for our conversation tonight as I am for AQF.

After Maya is declared the undefeated champion of the Apple Wars, the crowd begins to thin until it's just my crew and Bailey and Noelle, who we've convinced to stay for one drink. Bailey, as it turns out, is as into whiskey as I am, and my father pours us a celebratory glass of the Weller. With ice in Olivia's. Noelle opts for a beer.

"Well, y'all, I can't say I knew what to expect from this Fall Fest thing, but I am very proud to have been able to host it." My dad raises his glass. "Bailey, you've got yourself something special going on here, and as a proud ally of the queer community, I raise my glass to all of you making a difference." We clink our drinks and grin at one another. I'm pretty proud to be his daughter. "Anyway, Ward, let's you and I leave these future leaders of America to it." He convinces Ward to follow him out to the back porch with some cajoling. Uncle Ward has some serious FOMO.

Then it's the six of us in front of the fire, decompressing and chatting about the success of the evening. Aiden and Scott left an hour earlier for one of his high school buddies' Halloween parties. And though we've made up, it's nice to have the house alone with Bailey and Noelle.

"Y'all don't know how much of a difference having Fall Fest at your orchard made," Bailey says. "It just…" She sips her bourbon while seemingly struggling to match the right words to her feelings.

"It gave it the magic," Noelle supplies, and Bailey grins.

She squeezes Noelle's knee. "Exactly. It gave it the magic. And damn, it was magical."

I sink farther into the couch, further into the warmth of the whiskey and my friends. My heavier body pushes deeper into the cushions than Olivia's, and she caves into the divot with me, her entire right side flush against my left. There's no jealousy when I watch Bailey and Noelle be so perfect together; I know that kind of thing takes time. But I hope what I have with Olivia is mirrored by them. By their tranquil energy and adoration of one another.

"It totally did," Ashley says from her own warm cuddle puddle with Tessa. "I can feel it, Bails. This is our year."

"I just feel so brokenhearted, you know?" She shakes her head and stares into the amber abyss of her Weller. "Every pendulum swing against our momentum is deadly and painful and ferociously bigoted. I don't understand why folks put these people in office. We can talk about tax policy after we ensure our youth are safe." Her fingers whiten around her glass to the point where I'm wondering if she's about to need stitches. Her passion could be glass shattering.

Tessa hops into the conversation, and I sink into myself for a moment, struck by Bailey's conviction. I've white-knuckled over few things in my life. My mom, obviously. But that's not something I have control over. Olivia has white-knuckled me a couple of times. My fist tightening in her hair, in my sheets...I'm not trying to change that.

It's from our first argument in the dining hall. "We need a food labeling system that actually works," I whisper to Olivia.

The chatter continues around us in a white noise, and she leans away from me to meet my eyes. She looks startled, as if I just asked her to elope. "Well, yeah. What are you talking about? This is the first I've heard you talk about this. I mean, really talk about it beyond griping about organics and food deserts in a completely unhelpful way."

I shake my head and place a hand on her knee, hoping energy will somehow transfer into her, and she can understand what I'm trying to say because my words aren't coming.

"You are a badass, and I finally get it. You are going to make a huge difference, but I want to help. We need to build something that actually makes sense so consumers know what they're buying. We need to get *involved*. And access to fresh produce should be a right. Laura wants the same thing as us, but the problem shouldn't be solved by putting the burden on communities that lack access by telling them to plant a garden. That's just a Band-Aid. Everyone has the right to be able to go to their neighborhood store and buy fresh affordable food."

"Hell, yes." I snap my attention to Bailey, who stares at us with a mischievous grin. "That is exactly the kind of attitude that gets shit done. I know nothing about food deserts or agriculture but talk about being in a position of power." She snorts. "Well, Maggie Hyde, I'd say you're in a big one. And if you want to be in the business of changing the world, I don't think you could pick a better partner than Olivia."

I feel my cheeks burn from the attention, from hearing Olivia's name associated with me, from the need to get started on this project with my *partner*. But that's not what tonight is about. Changing the agricultural world is for tomorrow. Changing the sociopolitical world is for today.

"Sorry," I say, looking from Bailey to Noelle. I can feel Ashley and Tessa's eyes boring into me. "I got a little carried away. Listening to you talk about AQF and your goals got me thinking about my own passions and, well, Olivia's."

"She stormed out of our first breakfast date together because I brought up this very topic," Olivia says, a smile playing on her lips.

"In my defense, you were strictly on the side of organic food. I think we both want to see a system that actually works."

"Yeah. I think you're right. It's becoming clearer to me that some big changes need to happen," she says.

"Giant changes. We need a system that lifts up farmers who *actually* farm responsibly." I shake my head. "Sorry. Got carried away again. I want to stay focused on AQF tonight and how amazing your event was," I say to Bailey and Ashley.

"It's okay," Ashley says. "These things don't exist in a vacuum. They aren't exclusive of each other. Agriculture and civil liberties are connected in such vast and rooted intricacies. It's all about where the resources are funneled, and the fact that the people in power don't want to see under-resourced communities access them." She throws up her hands in frustration. "Because they're too fucking scared to see their fellow Americans rise in their own power."

Olivia nods and raises her glass. "Little do the fuckers know, they can't stop it. Here's to accessible food, civil liberties, and social justice."

We clink our glasses over the coffee table and drink to the principles that give us the label of "far left" liberals, but it all sounds very humanist to me. The bare minimum. It gives me hope to know these people. To know Bailey and Ashley will not stop fighting for our rights until their dying breaths. I'm ready to be that. I don't know how. I don't know what it will look like with the farm and my responsibilities here. But I know, now, I'm one of them.

CHAPTER SEVENTEEN

L ast night, I was too high from talking with Bailey and Noelle to get into whatever Olivia and my dad talked about on their walk. When Olivia and I went to bed, we put away their conversation and my outburst of support for her dreams and did what we'd been dying to do all day. Each other.

Our first time was fast and blistering, like a pot of water boiling over. But last night was different. I didn't need to rush into a conversation with her this morning because I know everything is okay. I could tell by the way she gripped my hips and pulled me into her the night before. I could feel that she was on my wavelength by the way she loved me slowly, laying plank by plank the scaffolding to take me higher and higher. She was deliberate and thorough, responding with care to every sigh and groan I emanated.

And with her, I was exultant. I lavished her with my fingers and tongue, pouring everything I feel for her into how I touched her. Bathing her in what I hoped she could tell was my admiration. I hope that when she raised her hips off my mattress to push firmer into my mouth, she knew what I knew.

And what I know is that we can help to change the world together. Olivia and I are meristematic cells, continuously growing and forming building blocks for each other and our passions.

When we get back to Alder, I drop off Aiden and Scott and rush to ditch my truck. I need to finish some homework for my Ag Econ class and edit an essay that's due on Tuesday. After I knock those two things off my to-do list, I'm meeting Olivia at her dorm to talk and work on our project. It's been about an hour since I've seen her, and I'm practically buzzing at the opportunity to see her again.

❖

Olivia yanks me into her room after my first knock. "Hey. I missed you," she says as she pulls me onto her bed.

"Already?" I ask, and she swats at me because she knows from my earlier texts that I've missed her just as much. "Should we dive into this?"

She takes a steadying breath and nods. "You ready?"

"Ready," I say and wipe my hands down my jeans.

"Okay. Here it goes. I feel like you've had time to absorb the initial shock of your dad's data, and he confirmed my suspicions on our walk."

"What? Holy shit," I say. I know I shouldn't be surprised. We knew. *We knew.* I think I'm more shocked that he divulged this information to her. And maybe a little hurt that he didn't tell *me*, his right-hand employee and daughter.

"I just wanted to get that fact out there." She sweeps an open palm in front of her chest. "There it is."

"Okay." I nod, waiting for her to continue.

"I'll start from the beginning. He looked into who I was before he decided to send you that data. Specifically, the CPP on the peaches," she explains. "Apparently, the Hyde family connections extend past the Department of Agriculture, and he was able to talk to some of my professors. He wanted to see if I was legit and skilled in finance." She flips her hair over her shoulder in a sexy show of confidence. "I am."

"Clearly."

"Yes. Before he told me this, he asked what I thought of the financial information he sent over. I got a little weird, but he assured me. He said, 'Go on. Tell me what you think about those peaches.' He nodded across the path at your peach trees, and we walked over to them."

I lean closer, completely intrigued. "You told him?"

She nods. "I told him his CPP was inflated beyond what's reasonable for labor, raw materials, and maintenance for a crop like that. Told him I thought it was reflective of the cost of a loan. He said 'Winner, winner.'"

I flop back on her mattress and groan. "Fuck. This is not good."

"Come on, it gets better." She pulls me by the wrist until I'm upright again, facing her. "Well, sort of gets better. He told me about how he knew deep down your mom was going to leave." I bristle at the words. Hurt by my mom leaving but more hurt that my dad felt like he could be so vulnerable with someone else and not me. "They were already behind on their finances. I guess your grandfather had some gambling debts when he died, which your father inherited."

"How…" I start, but I'm so overwhelmed I can't even come up with anything to say. I have this pristine image of my grandfather in my mind: a responsible, serious man. A man whose portrait hangs proudly in Hyde Hall. A man who carried on his father's legacy the way we carry on his. And this information took a fucking wrecking ball to all of that. He was irresponsible to the point of harming his own family. His own sons. And my dad lied about it. But not to Olivia. "I'm sorry. But what the actual fuck? Why did I not know this? Why wasn't I on that walk with you guys?"

She pulls my hand into her lap. "I don't think your dad has ever talked about this with anyone. I don't think your mom even knew. He took out a predatory loan to consolidate your grandfather's debt and plant the peaches and blueberries for her. He was stressed and made a bad choice. Then made another bad choice by refinancing your house and using that money to renovate instead of paying off his high-interest loan. He said he couldn't stand keeping the house the same as when your mom was there."

All of this information about *my* father, *my* family, crashes into my chest with such velocity, I feel like I may implode. But my hurt about being left in the dark is quickly replaced with worry for the situation my father has gotten himself into. I wipe my hands down my face and try to concentrate on what's important. "How bad is it, Liv?"

She plucks at my fingers, tugging on my knuckles like they're a fidget toy. "It's not great. But we can come back from it. He's still very on top of his finances, and even though he's underwater, he's not delinquent or anything like that. He's making his payments on time, but he's used most of the equity in the property already, so we'll have to make some structural changes to the business plan."

I stare at her. "You keep saying 'we.'"

She grins. "Yeah. Turns out, I won't be traveling far for my internship next year. Your dad offered me a job, and I said yes."

My world slows to a silent stop as a slurry of emotions crashes over me. I am too overwhelmed by this barrage of information to feel one specific way. I feel like someone smeared my rainbow into a muddy brown puddle of every color. There are colors I like and colors I don't like, but I can't see any of them.

"Hey, you okay? It's good, right? Means we don't have to be long-distance and—"

That's a color I know I love. It flashes in front of my face—a brilliant green—and I feel clearly happy for a moment. "Totally. Yes. I just need one minute to process all of this." I wave my hands in a chaotic circle that very much reflects my mixed-up feelings. I stand and take a couple of steps toward her bathroom. "I'm going to…pee."

She worries the silver ring on her pointer finger as I shut the door. My breathing is quick and shallow as I turn on the faucet and splash my face with water. I need to sort through these emotions one at a time before they use their combined force to strangle me.

I'm hesitant. Hesitant to accept Olivia into such an intimate space in my life. A space of professionalism between me and my father that has always felt fragile and precarious. I can barely maintain the delicate balance on my own, but throw in a brand-new girlfriend, and who knows what will happen? Not to mention Olivia's proclivity for losing keys, showing up late, not showing at all… I love her and think the world of her, but I do not want these things to reflect poorly on me. I may have more desires beyond running the orchard than I did before, but taking over Hyde Hill Farm is still my number one.

At the same time, my body buzzes with relief. This whole semester felt like a giant lead-up to losing her for good. Why would someone as special as Olivia stay with me long-distance while she travels to a cool new place to work her cool new job? I want her to enjoy her adventures, but I am so excited she's staying close next year. Though having Olivia involved in the family business will be a huge adjustment, I can't think of a more perfect test subject for her than the situation my family is in.

Lastly, I pray to God that Olivia Cypress can save us. Because it sounds like we're fucked.

I wipe my face with a hand towel that I hope is clean and hope is Olivia's. She waits for me in the same spot I left her in and watches me with careful amusement.

"I didn't hear a flush," she says.

I sit next to her. "Yeah. Didn't pee."

She fingers the wet strands of hair that edge my face. "I unloaded a lot of information on you. Tell me about what's going on in here." She plants her palm on my chest, and I inhale under it, drawing some much-needed calm from her.

"I'm relieved and worried. Relieved that you're staying. Worried that you're working on the farm." I shake my head as she nods. "Not because I don't think you'll be amazing and hopefully help us out of a hole, but because I'm already stressed about the work dynamic between me and my dad, and adding you to mix makes it even more tenuous. It's selfish, but I'm trying to be as honest as possible."

"I know, Maggie. I appreciate it," she says.

I stare, and her eyes search mine. "Can you save us?" I ask. I feel my eyes growing moist, how hers always look. But mine are moist with tears, not blue ice melt or electric summer storms.

She presses quick kisses to my cheek and whispers, "I don't know, baby." She rests her forehead against my temple and breathes deeply. "You hold a lot on those shoulders, Maggie Hyde. But you don't have to. Taking over the farm or not, fixing the finances or not, all of these things are not required of you. Do them or don't do them. The only thing you owe to the universe is to try to be happy. To give back the energy it's given you."

I shake my head. *The only thing I owe to the universe is to be happy.* A sardonic chuckle bubbles in my chest. "Easier said than done. I'm falling deeper and deeper into this life that I'm more and more unsure of every day. And now, it's not even a stable job I'm taking on. It's a mess." My voice cracks from the stress, but I refuse to cry. "I've spent my entire youth trying to prove my worth to my father. That I'm strong and dependable. That I would sacrifice it all for the Hyde Hill. Now, I'm not so sure I would, but I'm almost out of time."

She tucks a strand of my hair behind my ear, her fingers brushing my cheek. "I think," she starts, and her words are as delicate as her touch. She tucks a finger under my chin and gently guides me to look at her. "Maggie, I think that maybe, you are the only one forcing yourself to make a grand decision on running the farm. I bet, if you had a conversation with your dad, you'd find that it doesn't have to be so all or nothing." She squeezes my shoulder. "All of this pressure. All of the things you think you have to be. You're tormenting yourself. All you—"

"Owe to the universe is to try to be happy," I say. I know the score.

She smiles one of her sad smiles. Clipped and pruned. "I was going to say all you can be is who you are. Maybe you're a little different than you used to be. Maybe you're more than Hyde Hill, more than Alder, and more than your last name on a building. Maybe you're so stressed because what you thought was the truth about yourself no longer matches your heart."

I shake my head. "I can't…I can't do this right now."

She nods. "I understand."

"There's just too much. I want to help my dad, and I don't have space to question what I want." I take deep breaths as she waits for me to continue. "Can we talk about your ideas to help get the farm back in the green?"

"Yes. Of course." She squeezes my thigh. "I know from our conversations that you guys use minimum intervention when it comes to managing your crops."

"That's right. Yeah. We use plant spacing and pruning techniques to control yield. We use IPM as our approach to insect pressures." She cocks her head at my last sentence. "IPM is Integrated Pest Management. It's basically an approach to pest management that relies on the knowledge of your land, insects, and ecology. A plan is based off the specific pest's interactions with the environment and utilizes the most economic and least hazardous methods to control them. We use minimal pesticides. So the organic version of IPM would include organic pesticides, obviously."

Olivia grins and scribbles notes as I finish speaking. "Okay, great. So it sounds like Hyde Hill already implements environmentally conscious practices, except for maybe the pesticides you use?"

I suck in my lips and nod. "The pesticide we use isn't organic, but it's the most efficient and least detrimental one. And we use it sparingly. It's the most responsible choice."

"Is that the only thing that needs to change to be completely organic?"

"Yes, but I don't want to switch to organic, and neither will my dad. It goes against our core beliefs, Liv."

"I know, but there isn't another solution yet. Until there's a better system, going organic is the way to build equity back into your farm. So tell me more about how that would look."

Ugh. Going organic feels like giving in and giving up. But I don't know how else to fix this mess, and I trust her. I trust that this will be temporary. "It's not so simple. We need to figure out a combination of clay, oils, soaps, and other chemicals that will work for us. It will take time and money to switch from one pesticide to an organic solution that won't work as well."

She writes my words quickly. "How long?" she asks, eyes on her notebook.

"We can take a leap of faith and transition in the off-season. But we won't really know if we're successful until there's fruit on the trees."

"Okay." She finishes writing and closes her notebook. "We'll give ourselves a year to transition, then."

"So we're going to go organic, even though it's not the best way to farm the land?" I cringe at my whiney voice.

"For now, it's our best option."

Even a year feels fast. But I don't think it's the pace of transitioning to organic that has me nervous. It's the pace at which Olivia has earned influence in our family farm. Earned influence with me. It's not a bad thing, just a very new thing. "So what exactly is the plan?"

"Once you and your dad pick an organic solution to pest management, I'll run the numbers again to factor in the cost of transitioning, and we'll talk about raising the price of your crops. When you raise the price of your crops, you raise the value of your land. The goal would be to build equity in the farm through those higher prices."

I shake my head. "No."

"No?" Olivia stares, disbelief and question meet in a vee above her eyes.

"I don't want to pass our burden to the community. Especially not for a crop that's exactly the same as it was before," I say.

"I understand your concern, but you will be producing a—at least perceived—higher value crop that needs to be priced to reflect that. That's the whole point. And your pricing methods can account for distance. Sell higher to bougie grocery stores and cheaper in your own market, to your own community. You don't have to price in the same transportation cost to your local market."

I nod slowly, letting this idea settle in my brain. It makes sense and is probably our only option at this point. "Okay."

She grabs my thigh. "Yeah?"

"Yeah."

She blows out a long breath and drapes an arm over my shoulders. "How are you doing?"

I feel scattered. "I feel scattered."

"You should give your dad a call."

I'm again hit with an anger toward him. He should have been the one to tell me all of this. I shouldn't hear that our family farm is underwater from my girlfriend. I should be told that face-to-face. "I'm mad at him."

"I know. That's why you should call him."

CHAPTER EIGHTEEN

Aiden and I sit in the amphitheater enjoying dinner and watching the cold November air stir dead leaves. The amphitheater is one of the most beautiful places on campus. Its grassy stage is shrouded by two weeping willows, and the giant steps of seating are surrounded by towering pines. I bite into my carnitas burrito and watch two crows fight over a piece of soggy bread. Crows are cool and all, but they give me the creeps. As one pecks at the other's eye, I cringe and turn to Aiden. "You know I love you, and I want you to be happy."

He recoils as if he smells something sour and wipes guac from his mouth with the back of his hand. He sighs. "I love you, too." He takes another bite. "And I want you to be happy, too. What's your point?" he asks, his words gummy and wet.

"We never talked about what you said by the fire. Apart from you being an asshole while you were saying it, I want to know about your life. I want to know what your dreams are after Alder." I emotionally brace myself for the response I know is coming. Brace for my little brother to tell me he's going to leave. Brace for the pang of jealousy.

He wraps the last of his burrito in its foil and sets it next to him, then fishes a fresh napkin from his coat pocket and wipes his hands. "Well, you know Scott is Computer Engineering, and I'm Agricultural Business, so the West Coast—either California or Washington—would be ideal for us."

I nod as I wrap my leftovers. "You know, North Georgia—"

"I don't want to live in North Georgia for a fucking second longer than I have to," he says, sharp and angry. The gold flecks in his eyes hold the electricity of Olivia's but not from passion. From pain.

"Aid—"

"I can't stand it here, Maggie." He runs his hands through his perfect hair, and though it's short, its disrupted gel forces each strand straight up. He pats some of it down, but most of it remains in disarray, like him. "It's so heartbreaking and grating to live in a place where Confederate flags line our streets, our local politicians' campaign sign graphics are silhouettes of AR-15s, and I can't sit in an ag class without some alt-right dickhead muttering homophobic shit under his breath."

He takes a deep breath and lets his head fall back. A pine needle pokes out from the hair on the back of his head, and I reach for it. He flinches as if I'm throwing a punch. "Hey. It's okay." I show him the pine needle and throw it into the wind.

"I'm sorry I was an asshole, Maggie. I just...I can't stomach it. I know you have all this pride in our family and East Sparrow, but I don't. I can't live in a town where the entire population votes for a party whose literal platform on queer folks is that we shouldn't marry and are weakening society. How do you accept something like that? How do you let Mr. Benson casually wave at you and ask about your day when he has a Confederate flag bumper sticker and votes for the kind of people who want to ban gay books?"

"I don't know if Republicans actually—"

"They do," he says, shaking his head. "I was curious, so I downloaded their party platform from the RNC website. They're not lying when they shout on Fox News about what their party stands for. They hate us. They say in their platform that they don't believe in 'unnatural marriage,' and that the queer community is weakening family values. This is the kicker..." He smacks his lips. "They plainly say they form all their policies with this in mind. And we're shocked to see book bans and anti-LGBTQ+ legislation?" His voice flirts with shouting.

I stay quiet and let the cold breeze ease some of the fire Aiden is stoking in me. I didn't know he cared so much. I...I didn't know I cared so much, but with every word, my brother speaks, I feel my heart break. I feel an oppressive sadness. I feel angry. I think, since I grew up in East Sparrow, constantly surrounded by racist and homophobic imagery, it kind of felt like it was on me to deal with it. But *dealing with it* is really just enabling it.

"You think you're doing our family a favor by taking over the orchard after Dad, but no one cares, Maggie. Who the fuck cares if the second largest orchard in Georgia fails to pass on its generational privilege? You think our dead relatives care? Dad won't even care. It could not matter less. Don't trick yourself into thinking that land or that farm is ours. We didn't build it. It was handed to us by some guy who did. We're just stewards. And let me tell you, Mags, if you think only Hyde blood should run that place, then I reckon you're no better than they are." He finishes his speech by spitting on the ground between our boots.

Dirt gathers on his saliva, and it looks like one of those fancy chocolate truffles covered in cocoa powder. But a disgusting version. I clear my throat and hold up a hand in case he's about to launch into another intense tirade. "Just one second before you start again. I need a moment to digest all that."

I need more than a minute. He's right about East Sparrow. After Mr. Benson waves to us and exchanges forced pleasantries, I wonder what he says about us while he throws back beers at Valley Bar. No one has ever come after me or my brother, but how could they? If they're able, most of their children will go to Alder and graduate from the Department of Agriculture, which my great-grandfather helped establish. It's sickening, but have Aiden and I been protected from our community by our family's power? I don't know what being openly gay in East Sparrow would have looked like without being a member of the town's most respected family.

Maybe it would have looked closeted. Or unprotected.

"I want to tell you something, but I need you to promise not to tell Dad," I finally say.

He turns to me and searches my face. For a second, I wonder if he thinks of Mom when he looks at me. I drop my gaze back to his chocolate-truffle spit. What I'm about to admit is the same thing she had to admit to herself. She was so young—

"Of course. This is between us," he says, draping an arm over my shoulders and tugging me against his tan canvas coat.

"Lately, when I talk to you or Tessa, I feel…" I raise two upturned palms as if lifting an imaginary weight, and Aiden pushes them into my lap with his forearm.

"Pressure?"

I feel it. The bite of tears. I blow out a long breath and with it, any possibility of that stupid tear falling. "Yes. But that's not what I'm trying to say." The weeping willows toss their locks in the wind, and they tangle with each other before hanging still again. "When you guys talk about leaving after graduation, I feel jealous."

He squashes his spit with his boot and nods. "I know."

I snap my attention to him. "What? What do you mean? All I ever talk about is Hyde Hill Farm. It's the only thing I've ever wanted."

He shrugs and abandons my shoulders to tug his zipper the rest of the way up. "I don't know. Maybe you do want it, but when we were old enough to understand that one of us taking over was a possibility, you completely dimmed. You got all shadowy and intense."

I shake my head, taken completely off guard. "But—"

"It was obvious I wasn't interested, and I'm sorry if that made you feel pressured to be or do something you didn't want. But it isn't my fault. No one asked you to do this, Mags. And like I said, maybe you should reflect about why you place such a high value on a Hyde running the place."

I stay quiet as I sort through my emotions. Apparently, I'm a self-contained pressure cooker, and no one asked me to be.

Aiden clears his throat. "That land isn't even ours. It's native land. Cherokee land. I think it's pointless to feel so much pride in owning land that was stolen and parceled out to white men."

I chuckle. Not because it's funny, but because it's sad I didn't come to these realizations on my own. I'm supposed to be the smart, reasonable sibling, but I couldn't pull my head out of my ass long enough to see past all of my misplaced pride and self-induced stress. "I'm such a dumbass."

A smile stretches across Aiden's face. "You're just now realizing that?"

I shove him in the shoulder. "Shut up." Our chuckles quiet, and the cold wind picks up. "I wish you would have shared these feelings with me earlier."

He presses against my side for warmth. "Didn't think it was anything you wanted to hear until now."

"Reckon you're right." I shiver and tuck my chin into my coat. "One more thing before we go because it's fucking cold."

He nods for me to continue.

"That alt-right dickhead in your Ag class who you mentioned, is he real?"

He sighs. "Unfortunately, yes."

"We should tell Dad. Get him kicked out."

Aiden leans away from me and looks me up and down. "Are you joking? His little cronies would beat the shit out of me. It's fine for now. I promise."

As we walk back to the quad, I think about Aiden's bully. Think about the anti-LGBTQ+ bills being passed and books being banned and how every right-wing politician has bolstered the bigot who is bullying my little brother. I drop Aiden at Grayson Hall and wrap him in a quick, tight hug before going home.

Ashley's house is dank with humidity from all her plants respiring and all her party guests perspiring. She finally gave into the pressure and is throwing her first house party of the year. It couldn't have come at a better time for me. I desperately need to focus on anything that doesn't have "Hyde" in the name. I've texted my dad a couple times this week, and we agreed to call each other tomorrow to talk about Olivia joining our team, but that's tomorrow. Tonight, I'm partying like there is no tomorrow.

The gray couch where the guy covered in tattoos makes out with the girl in the leather jacket? That's the couch I'm going to sleep on tonight. I'm not driving. And neither is Tessa, Ashley, Olivia, Aiden, or Scott. We're crashing here.

"You…" Olivia starts, then takes a sip of beer. I labeled her Solo cup with her name and dotted the i's with hearts. "You are so cute when you try to dance. What is this little jig you're doing?" She sets her cup on a plant stand and steadies my hips, guiding them into a slower sway. "So rhythm is something you did *not* inherit."

My hips hit each beat with the help of her hands. "That's what I have you for."

"And us," Ashley shouts over the music as she and Tessa sidestep a particularly sweaty guy in cutoffs who drops it low like it's his job.

The party is packed. Almost the entire AQF student body is here, along with a handful of girls from the softball and basketball teams. Robert and his partner, Jules, DJ in the corner of the living room and set the upbeat tone by playing hit after hit. Everyone almost explodes when Jules plays "Dancing On My Own." Tessa yanks me between her and Ashley, and Olivia closes the tiny circle with me in the middle.

I swear the walls are shaking with all of us shouting the lyrics into the sweat-saturated air and testing the strength of Ashley's floor as we jump against each other, shoulders bumping into shoulders, walls, and drinks. With Ashley, Tessa, and Olivia enveloping me, I dance in a cozy cocoon, sandwiched by the people I love most in this world. A feeling of euphoria builds in me. It starts as a tickle in my toes and buzzes up my legs to pool and warm in my chest before prickling the roots of my hair.

The song comes to an end, but I am just so *into it* that I keep dancing, hoping Jules will replay it, until a soft hand cups my cheek, and a slower beat fills the house. I smile into Olivia's warm touch. I'd like to curl into her palm like a little hamster and sleep there tonight. She grins as she watches me try to melt. "You guys got my girlfriend stoned," she says between chuckles.

Tessa drops a hand on my shoulder, and I buzz under that plane of contact, too. I think physical touch may be my love language. And, yes, I may have eaten a gummy. A delicious little blue gummy bear with superpowers. "How you feeling, Mags? You good?"

Talking feels like a lot of work, but I am *good*. "So go-od. Good party. Good music. Good folks. You're good folks. All of you," I say as I point at the three of them.

"Maggie," Ashley says, tugging my hand to spin me toward her. "I gave you *half* of a gummy. Right?"

I nod. "Yes. Half."

"Good. Because for someone who rarely gets high, a whole one is a lot," she says.

"But I opened the drawer and took the other half when you left," I shout. "Two halves." I hold up bunny ears, and everyone busts into laughter.

"Well, that makes sense," Tessa says.

"Let's go outside and get some fresh air," Olivia says as she tugs me away from Tessa and Ashley and through the damp crowd.

The cold air shocks my heated skin. In a nice way. A few people mill around the keg, and I spot Andy laughing with a girl from the basketball team. Emma, I think her name is. Emma touches Andy's shoulder. She must bend to Andy how I bend to Olivia. They have phototropism; Andy looks like Emma's light.

"Oh, good. I finally found you guys. How's it going, Emma?" Maya asks as she joins their conversation. I watch Andy's entire body angle toward Maya. How she watches Maya's lips as she speaks. Maya is clearly Andy's light.

Emma clears her throat and seems to force a smile. "Hey, Maya. It's been good. Congratulations on that marketing scholarship." She holds up her Solo cup, and Maya knocks it with hers.

"Thanks. I appreciate that."

"Well," Emma says, "I'm going to go find Rachel. See you guys later."

I sip my beer as I watch Emma walk away. It's not hard to see what's going on there, even for a stoned person. Emma likes Andy, and Andy loves Maya. I shrug.

"What are you thinking about over there?" Olivia lays a hand on my wrist, and I turn to her.

"I was just watching something." Olivia chuckles and wraps her arm around my waist, tugging me against her. I feel bad for Emma. I wish for everyone to find their Maya, their Olivia, their Tessa or Ashley. I can't believe how lucky I am to have found Olivia. I pull her against my chest and kiss the top of her head. "Sorry I got a little high. Lately, everything has felt like..." I tighten her up, squeezing until she laughs and pushes away.

"Like a lot of pressure?" she asks, smoothing her shirt.

I grin, my eyes squeezing almost shut. "Exactly."

"I know, love. I know. Hey, do you want to go home? I know you've been talking all night about how you get to sleep on the couch, but we could go back to my dorm. My roommate went home for the weekend."

I lean in and whisper in her ear, my hands on her hips for balance. "Does a beaver build dams?"

She laughs into my neck, all warm and breathy and lovely. "Does a beaver build dams?" she repeats, wiping laughter from her eyes. "Oh my gosh. I'm putting that one in my pocket for later." She leads me back inside by my hand. "Come on, Mags. Let's go say good-bye."

❖

I've sobered up for the most part by the time the cab drops us off, and when we walk into her room and I'm hit with the overwhelming scent of her, she's the only drug I feel. I pause by the door and watch as she slides open the dresser and pulls two T-shirts and two pairs of shorts from the second drawer. She looks at me in the dim light of her lamp and motions for me to join her. "Come here, you."

I cross the small room and present myself to her. She looks beautiful in her tight sweater dress and Docs, her hair falling over her shoulders. She pushes my coat off my shoulders and hangs it over the back of a chair with care, then works on unbuttoning my shirt. She folds it into a perfect square and lays it on her desk. My jeans are next. She slides the tail of my belt from the loop and yanks me into her, kissing me as she works it loose. I pull her deeper into the kiss as she unbuttons my jeans and pushes them over my hips. I kick off my shoes and pull my pants off.

"I've got them." Olivia pulls away to fold my jeans as neatly as my shirt and adds them to my pile. I'm left standing in my bra and underwear. Her gaze falls down my body before she turns away and pulls her hair over her shoulder, exposing the zipper at the nape of her neck. I pull the metal tongue and reveal her back, inch by inch, until there is a delicious triangle of skin on display. Like she did with my coat, I push the dress off her shoulders and watch it fall, getting caught on the generous curve of her hips. She doesn't waste any time pushing it all the way down. With none of the care she showed my clothing, she kicks it to the corner of the room.

I kiss the knobby bones of her spine to her neck, where I nibble her sweet skin to her ear before she looks back at me and captures my lips. The more her tongue presses against mine, the harder she pushes back into me. I run my hands up her sides to her bra and work on unhooking the clasp. The tight elastic around her ribs goes slack, and her breasts tumble from the lace that held them. Her bra falls to the floor, and I cup her breasts, each of them barely overflowing my hands.

She groans into my mouth and breaks away, handing me the shorts and T-shirt she picked out for me. "Put these on, and let's go to bed," she says, a little breathy. Her chest is blush pink as she pulls on a shirt.

She slides off her underwear and tugs on her shorts. I change into my matching outfit and scoot into bed next to her, molding my body against the side of hers. She places a warm hand on my cheek and kisses me. "I can't have sex with you. You're too high," she whispers.

My hand finds her hip and squeezes. "I'm not high."

She chuckles against my lips and pushes some hair behind my ear. "You were walking in the clouds at Ashley's house not too long ago. Let's just cuddle and chat tonight. We can do whatever we want in the morning, okay?"

I don't like to argue with Olivia...anymore. I cuddle into her side and imagine her sliding all the stress I've been feeling off my shoulders as easily as she did my coat. I feel lighter with my head on her shoulder and her fingers stroking my arm. I feel more at home than on the farm. More right than when I'm pruning or harvesting. More loved than I know what to do with.

She reaches over me to turn off her lamp and kisses me. "Sleep tight, my Maggie," she whispers against my lips, and it's the sweetest lullaby I've ever heard.

My head goes a little fuzzy in the dark, and I whisper back, "I'm a little high. You're right."

I don't know what time it is when I wake up, but judging from the inky black of Olivia's room, I'd guess it's around two or three in the morning. Olivia's deep, slow breathing tells me she's peacefully asleep. I take a few moments to enjoy the sound of her sleeping next to me and the feel of her back pressed against my arm. I blink against the dark as the memory of her undressing me replays in my mind. She stirs and pushes the backs of her thighs against me. The desire from last night rekindles as the warmth of her body surrounds me.

Without waking her, I roll onto my side and rest my hand on her hip. Her hair smells subtly delicious, like the rest of her body, just slightly different. A different shade of her. I breathe against her neck, bathing myself in her warmth as I inch my hand under the hem of her shirt. Her breathing is still deep and steady as I drag my fingers over the soft skin of her stomach. I stop at the base of her breast when I feel her swallow, and the cadence of her breath changes. A little shallower. A little more of this world.

I move my hand to her breast, my thumb brushing over her soft nipple and lingering as her flesh tightens under my touch. Her lips pluck apart, and she releases a quiet moan into the dark. I squeeze and send my hand down her thighs, which she spreads for me as she pretends to sleep and switches positions to her back.

She doesn't say a word and neither do I as I feel up her body under the covers, and the familiar heat of us builds in her sheets. When I run my hand from her curls to her breasts again, she catches my wrist and pushes it back down between her legs. I run my fingers up the loose fabric of her shorts until they brush against the damp center of her. Another small sigh escapes her lips, and I slip down her body.

As I make love to Olivia in the middle of the night, in her dark dorm room with her corkboard of Polaroids and her quilt tangled around my right ankle, I feel whole in a way that I've never felt before. At a time in my life when my watertight ten-year plan feels as likely to happen as heads or tails, I feel this contentment filling me. Like I'm bellied up to a Thanksgiving feast, and the homemade apple pie has just been served.

Olivia's breath is fast as she tightens her grip on the back of my neck and pulls me harder against her until she spills into my mouth. It's more satiating to me than anything I've ever tasted.

CHAPTER NINETEEN

The weekend is the kind of exhausting that leaves me feeling spent in the best way. My eyelids feel heavy, and my focus skitters from daydreams to replaying my favorite scenes with Olivia, to attempting to make a mental to-do list for the upcoming week. I feel a little guilty that I'm fading in and out of Father Kyle's homily, but at least I'm here. I had to force myself to leave breakfast with the crew and walk my tired butt to Mass.

"Go, Maggie," Olivia said when I was considering skipping. "You'll enjoy the rest of your day more if you do."

Aiden was looking a little guilty as I gathered my things. I told him to walk me out, and as we stood in front of the dining hall, I said, "I'm proud of you. If Mass isn't you, then I don't want to see you trying to be something you're not." He wrapped me in a tight hug and planted a rare kiss on my cheek, which I immediately wiped off.

But here I am, sitting in my usual pew because even though I may not be *exactly* who I thought I was, Mass is still me. And even though I may not be paying the most attention to Father Kyle, every Catholic knows it's all about the Eucharist. Because my brain is already frolicking in literally every field that isn't Mass, I quietly leave after Communion, before the final blessing. It's rare I leave early. Normally, I consider it cheating. But I also have a phone call with my father to attend.

I gather my coat around myself and sit on a bench outside of the Ag building. I don't know why I walked here. I just kind of ended up here. The metal of the bench freezes my ass through my jeans, but the feeling is so separate from my brain right now that it doesn't bother me.

I dial my dad's number and wait for him to answer, not sure which dad will pick up: boss or father. Not sure which Maggie will speak.

"Hey there, sweetheart. How are you?"

The warmth of his voice dulls the sharp edges of the anger I have for him, leaving me momentarily speechless.

"I know, I know," he says. "Maggie, I'm so sorry I didn't share that information with you first."

"Yeah." My voice startles me as the anger returns. "Why didn't you tell me first, but also, why didn't you tell me *ever*? Do you not trust me? Have I not earned the right to know about the health of our own business? You know, the business that has been my dream to take over since I could walk?"

"I understand why you're upset."

I laugh into the phone. Never have I acted out so much in my entire life. "Upset? I'm not upset. I'm angry, Dad. I'm angry that I've done literally everything you've ever asked me to, and you confide in a complete stranger over me."

"I—"

"I can't believe you." I'm hot all of a sudden, uncomfortable in my sweater and jacket. I unzip my coat to let in some cool air, hoping it will ease some of the fire consuming me.

"May I speak?"

I nod, knowing damn well he can't see me.

He clears his throat. "I am so very sorry. If I could have it back to do differently, I wouldn't hesitate to tell you. Though it was clearly the wrong decision to withhold that information from you, I didn't want to burden you with it. It was my stress to carry. I didn't want you to have to live under the pressure of someone else's financial problems."

"So you gave us some cryptic spreadsheets and let us figure it out without talking to me? What kind of bullshit is that?" I cover my mouth when I hear myself curse at my father.

"Maggie Hyde—"

"I'm sorry, Dad. I didn't mean—"

"This is still *my* business, and you are still *my* daughter. Understood?"

"Yes, sir."

His sigh is heavy and tired sounding. "I needed some help, and I don't trust these financial advisors for one second. They're snakes and salesmen just trying to sell me on this fund or that consolidation program. When Dr. Young was telling me about your project and your new partner, it gave me an idea."

I shift my weight from one butt cheek to the other. "An idea?"

"Yes. Your project to increase production is perfect. I need to build back equity into the farm, and when I learned that Olivia is a finance major, I got in touch with a couple of her professors to vet her."

"What, uh…what'd they say?"

"They said she'll forget her pencil and lock herself out of the building, but she never misses a decimal point. That she has an eye for numbers and a passion for ag finance. So I took a leap of faith."

I smile against my phone and realize my jaw has been clenched until now. That description is so perfect. I wouldn't trust Olivia to remember her keys, but I'd trust her with my life. Hands down.

"Maggie?"

"I'm processing."

"I just needed to talk to her first to make sure she understood. You know?"

I shake my head. "No."

"You were working *together*. I wanted to know she was solid and trustworthy before I confirmed the truth behind that data. I wanted to know you had a true partner to help you—us—through it all. And, well…you sure as hell do."

The wind nips at my neck, and I tug my zipper up, frustrated with the hot and cold of this conversation. What he's saying makes only half sense. I am so over this right now. So burned out. "When does she start?"

"She's coming on Tuesday to walk me through what she has in mind."

"Right. Well, Dad, I honestly need some time to sit with all of this. I don't really have anything else to say."

"Everything's going to be okay, sweetheart."

I laugh again. This time sharp and sardonic. I want him to feel the uncomfortable edges against his skin. "When you put the future of our business in the hands of a twenty-one-year-old college student, that's really hard to believe. I gotta go."

"Maggie—"

I hang up before he can say anything more.

And I won't be speaking to him for a while, until he hopefully forgets that I hung up on him. I slink into the bench, the bar across the back holding my head as I look at the dusty blue sky. I'm not mad at Olivia. In fact, my dad is probably right. She may be our best chance to right our financial situation, but I feel so betrayed by him that it annoys me Olivia will be shoulder to shoulder with my father on Tuesday, trying to save the farm.

I guess that position, that responsibility, is what I've always wanted from him. And he so easily gave it to someone else. I groan to the sky. I don't know finance the way she does. *Buck up.* What's more pressing is our project due this Wednesday and finals the week after that. Though I'm good at the course content, thanks to my work, I haven't even started preparing.

I push myself up and walk back to Magnolia. Most deciduous trees have crisped and dropped their leaves for the winter, and the chill in the air is constant. Alder in the winter is beautiful. It doesn't snow too often, but I can just tell the gray stone's natural habitat is the cold. It feels out of place in the humidity and heat of summer. Like a polar bear in Florida. Well, sadly, like a polar bear probably anywhere at this point.

I push open my door to find everyone crowded into our room, drinking Three Taverns, a brewery from Atlanta.

"Maggatron is back," Tessa yells.

I slide to the floor next to Olivia, and she hands me a beer. The label reads "Prince of Pilsen." Sounds tasty. I crack open the can and take a sip.

"What do you think?" Scott asks, nodding to the beer.

"Delicious. I've only had their Night on Ponce. Where'd we come across these?"

"I picked them up after lunch. Figured it's a good weekend to enjoy a couple brews before our busy week starts," Olivia says.

"We have to finish our project tomorrow," I half whisper. I feel a little guilty when I say it because the truth is, Olivia has done eighty percent of the work. Most of what I've done has been confirming chemicals, processes, and prices. She's done all of the grunt work of planning and putting together a pitch. All we have left is to transcribe it to PowerPoint.

Ashley skips the Grateful Dead song that is currently playing, and a Killers song fills the room.

Olivia squeezes my knee and smiles. "Are you worried?" I shake my head and drop my gaze to my beer. "Good. Because you know I got this. It's basically done. Okay?"

I nod. "Are you ready for Tuesday?" I ask.

She studies me for a moment before quirking an eyebrow. "What*ever* are you talking about?" she asks, mocking me.

This is what stresses me out, not our project. What stresses me out is Olivia's first day working with my dad. She doesn't know how hard he is to please. I want to make sure she has a full tank of gas and knows where her car keys are. I want to ask her to leave fifteen minutes earlier than planned because we never know what can happen on the roads. I want to reiterate that my father is of the "yes, sir" generation, and that he expects perfection.

"Just..." She raises her brows and waits, daring me to say something. Telling me that to say something would be to say I don't trust her. "Good luck, is all. You'll do great."

"Nice save, love." She winks and sips her beer.

I swallow all of my warnings. Maybe tomorrow, while we finish our project, I can broach the subject again. I kick off my boots and tuck them under my bed, trying to lean into this night with my favorite people. Trying to let go of all the things that are truly not mine to carry. The farm is my father's business, and Olivia is her own person. I'm just an employee. Just a student. Just a girlfriend. Maybe I can manifest simplicity.

"That dickhead in my class, Mags. The one I was telling you about at the amphitheater?" Aiden says, and Scott tightens his grip on Aiden's knee at the mention of said dickhead.

I cross my legs and straighten. "What happened? Are you okay?"

He sets his beer on my desk and nods. "Yeah. I'm okay, but he wrapped caution tape around my desk chair on Friday."

"What?" Scott hops off my bed and paces around our small room. "What did your professor say?"

Aiden tugs his wrist to get him to sit, and he perches on the edge of my mattress, fidgeting in all of his anger. "He asked if I needed scissors, and I said no. I used my knife and threw it all in the garbage. That was that."

"He needs to be reported," Scott says between gritted teeth.

I stay quiet as I take in this new information. Someone is fucking with my little brother, and it is blinding me with anger. But this is Aiden's life, and I want to respect what he wants to do in the situation.

"Scott may be right, Aiden. How do you feel about reporting this guy?" Olivia asks.

"Yeah, report his ass," Tessa adds.

"I don't know. I'm going to give it a little bit and see what happens." He shrugs. "He hasn't *really* done anything yet, and I feel like reporting him would only make things worse for me."

"You gotta do what feels right for you, Aid. We have your back no matter what," I say.

He snags his beer and fingers the tab, taking a deep breath. "I'm going to wait for now. I just wanted to let you guys know what's up."

"Fuck the bully," Ashley says and raises her beer.

"Fuck the bully," we all shout and knock our cans together.

"All right," Aiden says. "Enough of that. Let's crush some beers and listen to Taylor Swift."

"No," Tessa whines. "Come on. Really?"

"Excuse me. T Swift is a legend and will not be disrespected," Olivia says.

Ashley pulls Tessa in for a tight hug. "Sorry, babe. I think Aiden gets to choose tonight." She kisses Tessa and takes the phone from her hands.

We spend the rest of the evening laughing and listening to Taylor's latest album. The smile stays glued to Aiden's face, and I realize I want him to leave. I want him to go to California. I want him to be as happy as when he listens to Taylor Swift.

CHAPTER TWENTY

Olivia leans over me and covers my hands with hers, stopping me from adding the most epic transition that PowerPoint has to offer. Sound effects included. "Oh. Oh no." She slides her laptop out of my hands and taps away at the keyboard. "Maggie, I'm sorry, but I have to revoke your styling privileges. This"—she plays my "fly through" sound transition between slides—"this is horrid. I cannot, in good conscience, present this to Dr. Young."

"Oh, come on. It's fun. Spices up the presentation a bit. Don't you think?"

She chuckles and continues to strip our presentation of all my flare. "Dr. Young already thinks I'm a complete space cadet with nothing to offer. I want him to take me seriously."

I scoot my chair closer and nibble her neck as she works. The basement of Magnolia is empty except for a guy baking muffins in the kitchen, but he's out of sight around the corner.

"Mm. Don't get me carried away, or we won't finish tonight," she says, closing her eyes and dropping her head back.

I continue to kiss down her throat. "Or will we?"

She straightens and swats at me. "No more funny business until we finish this project, okay? I'm gone all of tomorrow, and then it's due."

I sigh and take a sip of water. "Fine. But can we at least keep my cool design? It kind of looks like roots."

"How about we keep it for a couple slides and use actual photos of Hyde Hill Farm for the others? It's a presentation on Hyde Hill, after all. Deal?"

"Deal."

She kisses me on the cheek as a reward. "Good."

I dropped the conversation of her first day of work before, but I've been waiting for the right moment to bring it back up. We're just putting the finishing touches on our presentation, and it's almost nine. It feels like my last opportunity to talk about it.

"What time do you start tomorrow?"

She continues to work on the graphics, fading a photo of the orchard into the background. "Eight."

"That's pretty early."

"It's fine. I'm used to early mornings from my classes," she says, drawing out her syllables. She's on to me.

"Sometimes, in the valley, you can get stuck behind a tractor. Especially in the morning." She turns to me, and though it feels like I should stop talking, I keep going. "You might want to leave extra early. 'Cause it's your first day, and you never know what might happen." She continues to stare. "Do you, uh, have enough gas?"

She scoffs. "Maggie, what the hell?"

I lean on my knees and lick my lips. "You don't know what he's like. He can be intense and hard to please. If you're even a second late—"

"Then that's my business. I'm an adult, and I'm sorry if this situation is hard or weird for you, but from my perspective, I'm meeting with my first client tomorrow morning, not your dad. I can handle myself, okay?"

I nod.

Her cheeks are rose pink from her anger, and her eyes hold that familiar charge. "Look, I know this stresses you out, but it bothers me that you don't trust me. If it were up to you, we'd be turning in a project that looks like a fifth grader did it. I'm professional, okay? I've been working on your father's pitch since we got back from Fall Fest. It's impeccable, and it's going to work." She takes a breath and rubs her hands over her thighs. "And I won't be late. I promise."

I fish my hand into her lap. "Okay," I say.

"Okay."

I squeeze her hand and smile. "I'm excited to hear how it goes."

Her lips break into a grin, and her eyes cool into glacial lakes instead of summer storms. "Yeah. It's going to be great."

"Just make sure you know where your keys are before you go to sleep."

She swats me hard in the shoulder with her notebook. "You are definitely not getting any now."

"Ouch. Come on." I rub my shoulder and pout.

"Nope. No way." She turns her attention back to our project and finishes uploading the photos of Hyde Hill throughout the slides. "Okay," she says. "I think we're finished here. Take a look."

I slide her laptop in front of me and scroll through our presentation. Though the airplane noise transition was awesome, she's right. The PowerPoint is crisp and professional-looking, with minimal distracting elements and detailed analysis of growth for our orchard. She faded our photos to be used as backgrounds and highlighted them to be used as visual aids. Everything looks perfect.

"Wow. You're very good at what you do," I say, pushing the laptop away.

"I know." She saves the presentation one more time. "Is there anything you want to change or add before I send this to Dr. Young?"

"Nope. It's perfect."

She emails a copy to Dr. Young and closes her computer. Though I know she's not mad at me anymore, I can tell our energy is a little off after my warnings for tomorrow. "I'm going to get going," she says.

"You sure?"

She leans in and gives me a sweet kiss that takes away some of the sting. "Yeah. I want to go over a couple more things before tomorrow and get a good rest. Love you."

I walk her to the door. "I love you. Good luck tomorrow. Call me if you need anything, and don't let Uncle Ward distract you too much."

She turns back and waves. "Promise."

We all have later starts on Tuesday, so we meet for brunch in the dining hall before our classes. Everyone except Olivia, of course, who notified her professors that she would be absent today due to school-related activities, and Ashley, who has a meeting with AQF. Not so shockingly, none of Olivia's ag or finance professors cared. They were excited for her.

The students of Alder have begun their pre-finals stressing. I can see it in how they push half-eaten meals out of the way to make space for textbooks and notes. In how they don't even take off their coats to enjoy breakfast because they'll only sit for a second. Everyone is a little grumpy and a lot tired. Now that our project is finished, I reckon I should join the rest of the student body and dive into the world of finals prep. Tonight. That gives me almost an entire week of studying.

I hand Mr. Rick my lion card to pay for my soup and sandwich. "Any holiday plans, Mr. Rick?" He's my favorite person who works in the dining hall. Something about his caterpillar eyebrows and boyish grin reminds me of Uncle Ward.

"Working most of the holidays for winter semester, but I have Christmas Eve and Christmas off. Spending it with my nephews in Hiawassee." He hovers my card over the reader and drops his voice. "You know, between you and me, soup isn't all that good today. Sure you want it?"

I peek at my bowl of minestrone and shrug. "It's mostly for sandwich dipping anyhow. I'll stick with it." He nods and swipes my card. "Glad you at least get a couple days off to see family."

He hands me my receipt. "Me, too, Maggie. Enjoy. And don't forget to study hard."

I smile. He ends every conversation with "don't forget to study hard." He is definitely Uncle Ward's long-lost twin. "You got it, Mr. Rick." I take my tray and walk to the table where Tessa, Scott, and Aiden sit eating and chatting.

There are a few moments each semester that stop me in my tracks like an open palm against my chest. It's an overwhelming feeling of warmth and joy and gratitude. It demands every ounce of my attention. The university—stone and people—requests my adoration. I take a breath and give in, looking over my shoulder and taking in the cozy beauty of the dining hall. The cavernous earthiness of it. The sound of stressed students and the smell of home-cooked—

"Oh shit, Maggie," Scott calls.

Soup burns through my shirt before I pluck the hot wet fabric from my body. My wrist aches from breaking my fall but not more than the searing embarrassment of the spectacle I just made of myself. Turns out, I didn't *completely* stop in my tracks.

"Maggatron is *down*," Tessa says between laughing fits.

Aiden is at my side in a second, helping me up as I slip around like a newborn doe in my minestrone. A crew member approaches with a mop. "You okay there, dear?"

I hold my soaked shirt away from my body and nod. "I'm so sorry for the mess. I can—"

"It's my job. Not a problem. Go get cleaned up, now."

Aiden walks me over to the table and peels off his sweater. "Here. Change into this. I'll grab you another meal."

I take his sweater. "Thanks, Aid."

When I return, a new soup and sandwich wait for me at our table. "Sweater okay?" he asks.

"Fits like a glove. Nice and warm, too. I owe you one." He smiles and tugs me in for a quick hug.

"I don't think I've ever seen you fall. Sorry for laughing. The minestrone really got me going," Tessa says, wiping mayo from the corner of her mouth.

I chuckle and shake out my wrist. "You're forgiven. I'm sure it was quite the scene."

"Your wrist okay?" Scott asks.

I nod. "Yeah. It's just not used to catching my entire body. It'll be fine." He raises a blond brow as if he doesn't believe me. "I promise," I say and take a cautious bite of my soup, not wanting to get it all over Aiden's wool sweater, too. It's soothing and warm but bland. There's not enough acid, and every flavor falls flat into a pile of mush. "Mr. Rick was right." I drop my spoon next to the bowl. "This soup was not worth the effort."

"I know," Scott says, "a rare miss from the kitchen crew."

"So how's your girl's first day going?" Tessa asks.

I shrug. "I don't know. I already pissed her off by being overbearing last night, so I didn't want to bother her this morning."

Aiden clears his throat and wipes his hands. "I texted Uncle Ward to see how everything was going, and she, uh, didn't show."

"What?" I shout. I don't mean to, but the word barrels out of my mouth like a cannonball. "What do you mean she didn't show? Did she call? Is she okay?"

He winces, his shoulders pinched to his ears. "I don't know. This is secondhand from Ward. You know how he is. I assumed you knew what was up. Sorry, Mags."

I look around at my friends, trying to pull out individual emotions or coherent thoughts. Worry. That one hits me right between the eyes. I fish out my phone and text her: *Heard you didn't make it to the farm this morning. Are you okay?*

"I need to go check on her." Everyone nods as I stand and gather my things. "Aid, do you mind?" I nod toward my barely touched meal.

"I got it. No worries."

"Thanks. I'll catch y'all later."

I rush to Olivia's dorm, feeling a little panicky, but no one is around to let me in. I sit on the stoop and wait, plucking at the pilling on my socks and hoping someone will show soon. Is the creep of annoyance right behind the wall of worry? Yes. But I can't think that way right now. I'm just worried about Olivia's well-being. Not about if she couldn't handle the responsibility and bailed.

"Need a swipe?" a tall guy in a charcoal peacoat asks.

I stand and nod. "Yeah. That'd be great. Thanks."

He holds open the door for me, and I half walk, half jog to Olivia's room. I knock and wait as someone shuffles around inside. The door cracks open, and it's a girl I've never seen before.

"Hey. I'm Maggie."

It looks like I've woken her from a nap or a very late sleep-in. She wipes her eyes and tugs at the hem of her sweatshirt. "Hi?"

Right. She has no idea who I am. "I'm looking for Olivia. Have you seen her lately?"

She yawns, and her sleep breath tickles my nostrils. I try not to flinch. "Yeah. This morning. She was headed to Asheville to visit a friend for the night."

I grip the door frame. "Asheville? She was supposed to be somewhere else this morning. And we have a presentation tomorrow."

The girl shrugs. "I dunno. You know Olivia. She'll be back when she's back."

"What? I don't—"

"Look…" She looks me up and down, seemingly struggling to recall my name.

"Maggie," I supply.

"Right. Maggie. This is not unusual for Olivia, okay? Nothing to worry about. Her best friend lives in Asheville, and I'm sure she'll make it back for your presentation."

"But—"

"Listen, I've been up half the night studying, and I really need to eke out as much sleep as I can before my next class. So do you mind?" She inches the door closed as she speaks, and I take the not-so-subtle hint.

"Yeah, sure. Of course."

The door shuts, and I'm left alone in the hallway, wondering what the hell is going on. I walk through the mostly empty halls back to the exit and send another quick text to Olivia: *Hi. Your roommate just told me you're in Asheville. What's going on?*

Back at Magnolia, I grab my things for class. As I walk through campus to Hyde Hall, I feel a twinge in my jaw and realize I've been clenching it. I'm sure I look like another stressed student the week before finals, but I'm not thinking about finals at all. I'm wondering why my girlfriend bailed on her first day of work with my father. Olivia can be forgetful, sure. Mishaps are magnetized to her, somehow. But none of that explains why she bailed on us for Asheville.

I fall into my seat in my Pest Management in Horticulture class and pull out my phone. I'm still too angry at my dad to ask him what happened, so I text the next best person: Ward. *Hey, Uncle Ward. Aiden told me Olivia didn't show this morning. What happened? Did she at least call?*

It takes him half the class to respond. *Hello, Ms. Magtastic. Your dad said she texted that she couldn't make it.*

What? That's it? No reason for bailing?

Just that something came up.

I shove my phone in my pocket and try to avoid snapping my pen in half. She didn't even text me. She didn't even give me a heads-up that she wasn't going to show. Even after I expressed how anxious I was, she just…ran. I imagine her laughing with Riley and having a grand time doing whatever hip things they do together in Asheville. Probably snapping more Polaroids. All smiles while I sit here with my head and my heart in complete chaos. How am I supposed to feel about this other than gutted clean? Now that I know she's with Riley, I'm left reeling.

My professor is drowned out by the hum of white noise in my head, and I'm feeling like I've pulled three all-nighters studying for finals, but I haven't even cracked a book. I thrum my fingers over my thighs in exasperation. *Fuck it.* I pull out my phone and open my conversation with Olivia. It may not be the best idea, but I need a place to put all of my frustration. I choose to put it on her: *Well, have fun in Asheville, I guess. Would appreciate if you're back for our presentation tomorrow.*

I cross my arms and wait for class to end so I can go be pissed off in private.

❖

The next day in sustainable production, I avoid chatting with Dr. Young, who's busy sorting the presentation order and making sure he has everyone's projects, and I stew alone in my seat because Olivia hasn't shown yet. Class starts in three minutes, and as I've learned with Olivia, she could show up anywhere in the next fifteen or not at all. I don't even know if she's in the state.

Given that she bailed on my dad, it wouldn't surprise me if she bails on me, too. What's a dumb PowerPoint compared to your first professional client and your girlfriend's dad? I don't know our project as thoroughly as Olivia, but I know it. And I can rely on Dr. Young's love for all things Hyde to get a good enough grade on the presenting portion. As he finishes rummaging around his desk, I realize my foot hasn't stopped tapping the linoleum since I sat. I guess I'm nervous to present alone. One more text. *Not that this will make a difference, but please come to class. It's just selfish at this point.*

Send.

It only takes a minute for the anger to morph to regret. So much regret that I hope she doesn't show so I don't have to face her.

"Okay, class..."

Olivia cracks open the door and slips past Dr. Young.

"Right, Ms. Cypress. Nice of you to join us."

She nods an apology and sits next to me, her energy muted and tired. She doesn't have any class materials except the clear presentation folder with the printout of our project. She shoves her car keys in her pocket without looking at me.

"As I was saying," Dr. Young continues, "we will start the presentations with Laura and Molly."

They shuffle around their desk and gather their presentation supplies while I gather the courage to speak to my girlfriend.

I open my mouth and hope something good falls out. "Olivia—"

She snaps her attention to me. "Nice text." I can see from the intensity in her stare, from the sharpness of her normally earthy angles, that I'm in deep shit.

"What was I supposed—"

"Listen." She closes her eyes for a moment as if gathering the energy to speak. "I don't want to talk to you right now. I'm here for my grade, not for you. I'm going back to Asheville for the weekend after classes on Friday. Maybe we'll talk after finals." She turns her attention to the printout in front of her.

"What? I can't..."

She raises an eyebrow as she stares. "You can't what? Think the best of me? Trust me?" She bites her lip, her eyes beginning to water. "It's always the same boring story with you. And I can't be with someone who looks for the worst in—"

"Quiet, please. Ms. Cypress, you're already late, and now you're whispering while we're trying to begin presentations. We're cutting it close with time, and I'd appreciate it if you showed some respect to your classmates," Dr. Young almost shouts.

"Sorry," she says.

"Dr. Young," I say. Olivia shakes her head, eyes glued to our table. "It was me. I asked her—"

"Maggie, please. Enough. It doesn't matter," Dr. Young says as he dims the lights. "Take it away, Molly and Laura."

I swallow every word Olivia said to me, my body imploding from...*what was that? A breakup?* I don't hear anything my classmates say as they flow through their presentation. And through the next presentation, an ache forms in my joints. A hollowness gathers in my chest. And Olivia looks anywhere but at me. I have no idea what's going on with her. But I guess I blew it.

Then it hits me. *Ashley.* Ashley has to know what's going on. Why she's going to Asheville. They're basically best friends. Instead of going to her roommate, I should have asked Ash.

"Maggie and Olivia, you're next," Dr. Young announces.

Olivia grabs the presentation and stands. I follow a few steps behind, empty-handed until Dr. Young gives me the PowerPoint clicker. Our introduction slide with a picture of Hyde Hill Farm glows on the screen, and Olivia begins to speak. She sounds confident and professional, and I get lost in her voice and the horrifying realization that I've probably blown it with her. My one shot. Gone.

She clears her throat. "Maggie."

But there has to be a chance left for me to get her back. I can't—

"Maggie." Olivia elbows me, and I snap back into focus. "Next slide, please."

I click to the next slide. The muffled laughter coming from the darkened room doesn't faze me in the slightest. I couldn't care less about them or my grade on this stupid project. All I care about is Olivia. All I care about is having her in my life.

After a few minutes, I wake from my daze when Olivia announces, "The end," and asks for any questions. I expect Dr. Young to pounce on her with some condescending question about her methods or some complaint about the detailing on the slides, but even he seems taken by her work. Two of our classmates ask questions about the finance side of our project that Olivia has no problem answering. They take note of her responses.

"All right. Well done, you two." Dr. Young refers to his clip board. "Nate and William, you're next."

I fall into my chair while the next presenters prepare. "I kinda thought you might hop in and say *something* up there," she says. She crosses her arms and stares forward.

Did I not say a single word? "I…I'm sorry."

She nods and remains quiet through the rest of class. When Dr. Young dismisses us, she's the first one out the door.

When my classes are done for the day, I walk home to Magnolia, hoping Ashley will be where she always is: my dorm room. I open the door to find her lounging on Tessa's bed with her laptop balanced on her stomach, DJing while Tessa examines a slide through her microscope.

"Hey, Mags," Ashley says.

I slide out of my coat and kick off my boots. "Hey."

Tessa pulls back from the eyepiece and examines me. "Why so melancholy?"

I sigh as I tug on a ratty sweatshirt. I need some comfort. "Because I may have completely obliterated what I had with Olivia."

Ashley slowly closes her laptop. Music stops. She sits up and waits for me to keep talking.

"She didn't show up to work and never let me know what was going on. Not one text." I sigh and rub my eyes. "So I may have texted her. Nothing that bad...until I *still* hadn't heard from her, and I got frustrated. Then I might have sent some questionable messages."

Tessa leans on her knees and watches me. "Questionable how?"

"I called her selfish." I wince.

"Shit, Mags." She blows out a breath and scratches through her long locks. "That's not very cool."

I hold up my hands in exasperation. "Well..." I look at Ashley. "I don't know what the hell is going on. Care to shed some light, Ash?"

She glances at Tessa. "Um," she starts. "I don't love being in the middle of this."

I groan. "Please. You don't have to get into what Olivia has confided in you or whatever. Just...why was she in Asheville? Why did she skip out on my dad? Was it too much pressure, or did—"

"Look, I assumed you knew everything that's going on. She hasn't mentioned you guys are in a fight or anything." She takes a deep breath. "Riley's mom died. She was his only parent, and she named him the executor of her will." She looks at a Tessa, sadness gathering in her eyes, and back to me. "He's only twenty-three and doesn't have any siblings. Olivia is his best friend, and he needed her support. Not only her emotional support, but he needs help sorting through the will. He's completely shattered and lost. So she called your dad and told him what was going on."

I shake my head. "What? Uncle Ward said she didn't say anything."

Ashley crosses the room to sit next to me and squeezes my knee. "And what did your dad say?" I stay quiet. "I'm sure he was protecting her privacy when Ward asked. He's her employer. And isn't he, like, super professional?"

I nod. "Yeah, that makes sense. But why didn't she let me know what was going on? This whole thing could have been avoided."

Tessa switches off the light on her microscope and chuckles. "Your girl was born in retrograde."

I shake my head. "What? What does that have to do with anything?"

"It means, I can almost guarantee that if she was on the phone, texting, using GPS in the middle of the night, that her phone *definitely* died. And with everything she was managing with Riley, I bet she either forgot her charger or just didn't think to plug it in." She points at me. "And when she did, you had probably already sent some lame, accusatory—"

"Insecure," Ashley adds. I raise my brow and stare at her. "Sorry."

"Yep. Insecure texts. And—"

"And she didn't respond because I assumed the worst of her instead of the best," I say, Olivia's words ringing in my head.

"Case closed," Tessa says.

I groan and flop back on my bed. "What do I do? She's so angry, and she's leaving for Asheville after class on Friday."

Ashley lies down next to me. "I would give her some space. She has enough on her plate with helping Riley and managing finals prep without having to deal with you."

"Agreed," Tessa says. "Send her a nice apology text and say you hope to reconnect after finals."

Hearing an explanation illuminates the fact that Olivia was right. *She always is.* After everything we've been through, in a moment of uncertainty, I looked for the worst in her. I was looking for the worst in her before this even happened. When I was bugging her about making sure she knew where her keys were and if she had gas in her car, I should have been supporting her and telling her how much I love her, how proud I am of her, and that I have every confidence in her. But clearly, I don't. Or I didn't. How many times did she have to prove herself to me?

"Yeah," I say. "I guess that's all I can do."

"Don't worry. It's going to work out," Tessa says.

"Yeah. Something tells me you two just...*are*," Ashley says.

I really hope they're right.

CHAPTER TWENTY-ONE

It's not often that it snows in early December. Most of our snow is well after the holidays, but on this Saturday before finals, a modest dusting covers campus, and flurries continue to fall from the sky in lazy spirals. I hop over snow-obscured bits of the uneven stone paths to avoid another fall.

Even after the week from hell, I can't help but smile as I walk to the dining hall with my hands shoved deep in my coat pockets and my nose so cold, it feels like I dipped it in IcyHot. My mom used to tell us that magic only happens if it's snowing. When we watched Christmas movies and the first flakes fell on set, she would gasp and whisper, "There's the snow, baby. Don't worry, it's all about to happen." And she was always right. Though I think *she* might have been the magic, the zip, the whipped cream I didn't order but that showed up on my French toast anyway.

A warmth forms in my chest as I walk through the plumes of my own breath. And it must condense against the cold because I feel moisture gather in my eyes, but the memory of my mom isn't chased by the usual sadness or ache of loss. It stays with me, as if she's whispering to me now. *Don't worry, it's all about to happen.*

This strange feeling is a much-needed relief after last week. I sent Olivia one text, like Tessa told me to, but haven't heard from her since our presentation because Dr. Young canceled our last class to give us an extra day to prepare for finals. In an attempt to distract myself from the sharp pain of fucking up my relationship, I've been studying nonstop for two and a half days. But now, I get a break from studying—and from my exhausting sadness—to have brunch with Aiden.

I hop off the stone path onto the concourse. A small gathering has formed at the mouth of the dining hall, and there seems to be some kind of commotion in the middle of it. I can feel cortisol pump into my blood as I approach. Something feels off.

"Excuse me. Can I just…" I push through the few students to find my brother face-to-face with some farm boy I've never seen before. He must be Ag Business if we haven't shared any classes, but his whole vibe screams backcountry. His boots are as heavy and cumbersome looking as his *Don't Tread on Me* belt buckle, and a tattoo of a skull with the American flag flowing in the eye sockets covers his forearm. The crowd and the lack of a coat on this guy tells me I've walked up on a "let's take this outside" moment.

"Aid," I say as I sidestep one more person to get to him. "What's going on?"

The other guy laughs. It's as performative as his entire being. "Is this the other one?" he asks. "The other flaming Hyde? It really does spread, doesn't it?"

I turn to Aiden, who looks more annoyed than scared. He sighs and holds out an open palm. "This is Jesse. He was kind enough to come outside when he saw me to let me know that my coat looks gay."

I laugh. "Ah. Very astute, Jesse. You're smarter than you look. Don't let anyone tell you differently." I wink and earn a few chuckles from our minimal audience.

He licks his cracked lips and shakes his head, taking a step toward us. "Y'all don't belong here. Not at Alder. Not in our classrooms. It's just a matter of time before they start banning gay kids, too," Jesse says. He's so dumb, it's almost unbelievable. *Almost.*

Aiden nudges me. "Well, I think I found out who my secret admirer is."

I grin. I like where he's going with this. If gay is the worst thing to be in Jesse's mind… "Oh, this is the guy who likes to sneak a peek at the urinal?" I point at Jesse.

Aiden erupts in laughter with the rest of the students watching us.

"Fucking…" Jesse takes three long strides and shoves Aiden hard in the chest. He stumbles backward before righting himself and grinning.

"I think you hit his sensitive spot, Mags," he says. He looks at Jesse, and his eyes have the same wild ember as Uncle Ward's. "Shove me again, big boy. I know you're dying to touch me." As Jesse gears up to shove him again, I see Aiden reach for his waistband, the same place where my Zancudo is pressed into my skin. The place where I know his Benchmade is pressed into his. When Aiden stumbles back, I launch into Jesse with my shoulder, putting enough space between us to land a solid punch square on his nose.

He hits the concrete, the bright red blood gushing from his face looking particularly gruesome as the heat of it melts through the thin layer of snow. I stare at him as he groans and holds his nose. The crowd around us has grown, and a flurry of chatter, clapping, and shouting builds among it, but it's all muted and otherworldly. The melted snow and blood runs in a small stream, just like the wet, elongated "F…uck" that flows through Jesse's bloodied mouth and hands. I resist the urge to cradle my fist as I watch him suffer.

"Maggie." Aiden's voice is the only clear thing I hear. He grabs the arm of my coat and drags me away from the gruesome scene I painted. "We need to get out of here. Now."

It's okay, baby. It's all about to happen.

"Give 'em to me," Aiden demands as we walk through the top level of the parking deck to my truck. I toss him my beloved keys and slide onto the bench next to him.

We're silent as he drives us off campus and into town. He turns into the small shopping center that has a pet supply store and the Greasy Grouse, a cozy local diner. He parks and says, "Let's get something to eat." As we walk to the front door of the wooden building, I notice Ashley's Camry on the other side of the parking lot.

"Tessa and Ash are here?" I ask.

He holds open the door for me. "Yeah. I invited them."

If Nan's interior is like being inside a blood vessel, the Greasy Grouse's interior is like being in the bark of an oak tree. Every surface is wood. The wooden booths sit on wooden floors, which flow almost seamlessly into the wood paneling of the walls, which are covered in black and white family photos and antique gas station and Coke signs. The tables are preset with fraying plastic flowers, maple syrup and butter, and a one-sided menu, each item containing some variation of only five things: eggs, sausage and bacon, biscuits and gravy, waffles and pancakes, or chicken fried steak. I don't know if the owner, Mr. Burnette, has ever even heard of eggs benedict.

We walk past the long bar that separates the wood from the white of the kitchen and steel of the pans. Ashley and Tessa sit together in a booth, sharing coffee and a biscuit with whipped honey butter, one of the few variations of condiments.

Their hushed conversation stops as Aiden and I slide into the booth. "Hey, guys," Tessa says.

"Maggie," Ashley says, grabbing my hands as I reach for the menu. "Are you okay? Aiden texted us what happened."

I slowly pull my hands into my lap and look from her to Tessa. Bags have begun to shade their eyes from constant late-night finals prep. They look stressed. Concerned. "Yeah." I grab one of the single-serving creamers and shake it. I can feel everyone staring at me. It feels like someone told a joke, and I didn't get the punchline. "What? My hand is sore from punching him, but I'm fine."

Tessa leans on her elbows, the ends of her long curls pooling into heaps on the tabletop. "Why did you, uh, punch him?" She braces after she asks me, as if she thinks I may reach over the table and punch her, too. Aiden watches me, and I see guilt in his eyes. I punched Jesse because it was the only thing I could think of to avoid the alternative: Aiden pulling out that pretty Benchmade and mucking it up in Jesse's flesh. In a human. And I couldn't let that happen.

So everyone is staring like I'm unstable and harboring a hidden penchant for violence. But I was trying to protect Aiden from making the worst decision of his life. He would have been expelled. Gone to prison. *Wait...*

"What do you think the consequences are for hitting someone at Alder?" I ask, completely ignoring Tessa's question to avoid exposing Aiden's almost catastrophe.

A server appears at the end of our booth, his eager smile like a giant Carnival cruise floating up on our battleships. He asks us if we want to order drinks, and Aiden orders coffees.

After he disappears, he turns to me. "Maggie. You didn't just *hit* him." He winces as he speaks. "You broke his fucking nose in front of, like, twenty witnesses. I think we should take a minute to collect ourselves. Have a cup of coffee and some food. Then call Dad."

The realization of what I've done—the consequences of what I've done—squeeze themselves around me like itchy, drying mud. My stomach is in free fall. I go to a university that refuses to even allow a gay club. They will have no sympathy for the homophobic violence we were experiencing in that moment. I'm totally fucked. *I* could be expelled.

"I need to get out." I nudge Aiden.

"What?"

"Let me out. I need to call her," I say.

He grabs my shoulder to stop me from shoving him off the end of the booth. "Stop. Call who?"

"Olivia. Obviously."

"Maggie," Ashley starts, "I don't think—"

"Right now, she's still my girlfriend. And I…I need to talk to her. I don't know what to do." I resign and drop my head against the back of the booth. I know I can't call her. She can't help me, and to call her because I'm panicking would be selfish. I can't expect her to just drop everything and come running back to me because I'm having a crisis. Everyone watches me, and I sigh. "Okay. Fine."

Mr. Royal Caribbean returns with two coffees. "Anyone ready to order?"

"No. Thanks," I say. I'm ready to eject anything and everything that's in my stomach, which is nothing at this point. I guess I can eject my intestines and run, sea cucumber style.

Aiden orders biscuits and gravy, scrambled eggs and bacon, and a waffle. "You need to eat *something*," he says after the server leaves.

"Don't come at me all patronizing when you're the one who almost stabbed the guy." I'm slightly horrified I said it out loud, but I'm annoyed for catching all the heat. Does he not remember reaching for his knife?

"Excuse me, what the hell is she talking about?" Tessa asks. She and Ashley stare at Aiden.

His brows rise to his hairline. "Almost stabbed him? What *are* you talking about?"

"When he shoved you the second time, you reached for your knife. I saw you. I saw you almost make the biggest mistake of your life, so I thought I'd put the guy on his back so you wouldn't do anything stupid."

He closes his eyes and shakes his head. "I was never going to"—he drops his voice and does a quick scan of our surroundings—"stab the guy. Jesus, Mags. I was reaching for my phone. I wanted to get him on video. Once someone is already acting wild like that, if you start filming, they lose their damn minds." He sighs. "He was the one who was supposed to shoulder all the consequences from the university. Not us."

"Oh no," Ashley whispers. A quick tear splashes next to her plate of biscuits and butter. She wipes her cheek. "None of this is your fault. Either of you." Her look of concern skips from me to Aiden. "You were faced with emotional and physical violence. That guy should bear the responsibility of *his* actions." She shifts her weight to pull her phone out of her back pocket. "I'm texting Bailey and Robert."

I grab her wrist. "Please don't. Not yet. I haven't told my dad. I don't even know if Jesse is going to go to the university or press charges or what."

"Okay. But the issue is *him*."

I nod, allowing her words to comfort me. For a second, I was feeling a bit like a monster. "Yeah," I say. "Not sure how much good that will do me, but yeah."

Our food arrives, and we eat quietly, one of us occasionally floating an idea between bites of bacon and waffles. As we work through the plates of savory and sweet, I run through a million possible outcomes in my head. My favorite being the one where Jesse reflects on his hateful actions and decides to do nothing except write Aiden an apology letter. The odds are low for that outcome, so I think about what to tell my dad when I call him after breakfast. The sticky feeling of doom never leaves me, but damn, those biscuits and gravy are fire.

After breakfast, I take myself on a walk through the snowy campus. The slow snowfall has been constant, and what was a dusting before "the incident" has become a thick blanket of white. For some reason, the cold cuts right through my coat, straight to my bones. My teeth chatter as I pass my original destination: the arboretum. I pass the physics building and walk to my safe spot. A spot I know will be warm. The greenhouses.

I fumble with the keys, my fingers clumsy from the numbing cold, and let myself into the hothouse at the end of the row. The humid warmth instantly eases me.

I sit behind the small workbench in the back corner and push the empty seed trays and pruners out of the way. Dust some dried potting soil to the ground and lean on my elbows. I'm momentarily flooded with the memory of Olivia on this bench. On my flannel shirt. I shake my head and focus. I know I have to call my dad, and I will. I just need a minute to be alone and process. Even after "the incident," even after the realization that I could be expelled, the most pressing thing on my heart is still *her*. I would be stronger right now if she was here. She would know exactly what to do.

When warm blood pumps to my fingers again, and I gain enough dexterity to navigate the tiny keyboard on my phone, I text her. I text her because I can't help it. *Things are weird here without you. I've had the strangest weekend, and if I'm honest, life is tugging that loose thread. The one to my favorite sweater. You're gone, and I—*

A tear splashes against the dusty worktable and startles me. *You're gone, and I'm scared* is what I want to write. *You're gone, and I'm about to lose everything* is what I want to write. *You're gone, and I pick you over everything* is what I want to write. The short time I had left of college—the time I was already trying to grasp and keep forever—could be gone. Could be *gone*. I could be done here, forever. The time to be confused about what I want is over. If I'm expelled, I'll go back to East Sparrow and settle into my new life there. My old life there. Another tear splashes next to second, and the thought of going back to Hyde Hill Farm breaks my heart. The thought of losing her shatters it.

You're gone, and I'm naked without you. Send.

When I lay my phone facedown on the tabletop, it vibrates violently against the wood, flooding me with hope. I fling my hand to it like the tongue of a spring peeper to an unsuspecting insect, but it's not her. It's my dad. I take a deep breath and answer.

"Maggie."

I clear the hesitation from my throat and will myself to sound strong and confident. "Yes, sir?"

"I just got off the phone with Dr. Young," he says. This wouldn't concern me if Dr. Young wasn't also my academic advisor.

"Dad, I can explain—"

"Come home now." His words are blunt, the kind of tone I don't argue with. Normally.

"But, Dad, finals are next week, and I have to study."

"Now." And that tone, I *definitely* don't argue with.

"Yes, sir."

I take a moment in my greenhouse. A moment more of not knowing. Right now, I'm still a student. I avoid my Alder email account and enjoy sitting in the greenhouse as an official Alder undergraduate while I still can. Then I head for the parking deck.

❖

When I realized there was a possibility of being suspended or expelled, I thought I would explode with fear and pain, and I am. But I've also never felt more alive. This is the first time in my life where I don't know what next week will bring. Well, not the first time. I've had this feeling before. Olivia makes me feel this way. She makes me feel like anything could happen on any given day. With her, life is a favorite-sweater kind of joyful.

I will get her back. I just need to do this first.

I park in my usual spot by the back barn and walk across the gravel to the front porch. There isn't as much snow here as there was on campus, but there's enough to catch the moonlight and fracture it into a shimmering dust. It kinda takes my breath away. Bolsters me. I turn my attention to our house. It glows in the darkening night, like always. When I start walking again, the front door flies open, and my dad launches from the threshold.

I lose all of my courage and resolve as he barrels toward me. "Here," he says and pushes a heavy bag into my arms. It's the picnic bag that also acts as a cooler and has compartments for cutlery and glassware. It's comically out of place in my shaking arms as I follow my father to what feels like my execution. "Come on, Maggie. Get in."

He starts an ATV, and I wonder if this actually *is* my execution. I stare at the shotgun seat, stuck in my spiral of silly, terrifying thoughts.

"Maggie."

I get in and buckle up, clutching the bag to my chest as he drives into the orchard. He cuts through the Pink Lady and the peaches to the property line. We follow the edge of the farm and climb in elevation until he turns left back into the orchard. It's row forty-three of the Honeycrisp. I know this row. And I know what it means to him.

If you hit the timing right, row HC-43 hosts the most beautiful view on the property. It's the highest elevation row, and the trees on either side frame the moon as it soaks the rest of the orchard in silver. He parks and walks to the end of HC-43. "Come on, now. Don't wanna miss it, and it's rising fast," he calls over his shoulder. The sun is long gone. He's talking about the moon.

He sits on the little stone step at the end, the feature of HC-43 that is the cherry on top, the thing that makes it *too* perfect. It's not a real step, but there's a square stone embedded in the ground that's about a foot high, forming a natural seat for admiring the stunning view. I sit and hand him the picnic bag, tugging my coat tighter, grateful this spot isn't covered in snow. My butt is cold enough without my jeans being soaked.

He unzips it. "This is where I proposed to your mother. To Delaney." I stay quiet as he rummages through the bag. "I timed it perfectly. Just like tonight. But the moon was fat when I proposed. Fat and dusty orange like a circus peanut, I'll never forget."

My chest rises with excitement when he pulls out a bottle of Weller Full Proof, an allocated bottle that costs three hundred dollars. A bottle I didn't even know he had. He pours two glasses and hands me one. "Happy birthday, Maggie."

"What...it's not—"

He looks at me for the first time this evening. "Tomorrow, December fifth, you turn twenty-one."

I blink into the night. *Holy shit.* Tomorrow is my twenty-first birthday, the birthday I've been obsessing over for the last five years, and I've been so consumed by everything that I didn't even see it coming. The birthday plans conversation simmered out when Olivia left for Asheville, then finals prep, then the fight...

"I got this bottle for you a couple years ago for your twenty-first. I hope you don't mind sharing."

I stare at him under the moonlight. For the first time, he looks a little weathered. The gray in his beard sparkles against the glow of the moon, but the grooves framing his eyes are deeper. His usual sun-kissed skin is dulled. "This...this is mine?"

He grins and releases me from all of my fears. "Sure is." His chuckles warm me. "Are you going to sit there staring at my wrinkles all night, or are we gonna drink this bourbon?" He raises his glass, and I clink mine against it. "Happy birthday, sweetheart." We both take a sip.

The Full Proof hits my tongue with cinnamon hazelnut toffee and chocolate-covered black cherries. I sigh. How can I not? This is the most delicious thing I've ever tasted. "Fuck, that's good," I say, and cover my mouth the second I hear it. "Sorry."

My dad laughs and wraps an arm around my shoulder. "You know, you're just like her."

I shake my head and raise my brow. "What?"

"I know it's not what you want to hear, but you're just like your mom. And let me tell you something, Delaney is amazing."

I don't understand. This is the opposite of what I thought. Of what I thought I wanted to be. "Aiden's like mom."

"No. Aiden is Aiden. Since he was a little boy, I knew he was gone." He holds his glass against the sky. "His heart isn't one for East Sparrow or working on this farm, and he's always known that about himself."

I tap my boot against the grass and rock and struggle to understand what he's saying. "Mom wasn't one for here, either, but I am."

"We fell in love so young and got married when we thought being married was the same as being in love. I knew from the moment I put that ring on her finger that I was what she wanted, but this"—he nods to the orchard—"this wasn't. She wasn't one to be contained by me or this farm, and I was a fool for trying to make it work. I thought after we had kids, the dullness in her eyes would brighten back up."

He shakes his head, and I watch as his eyes water. I can't remember ever seeing my father cry. "Foolish," he says. "I thought putting another weight on her would help her feel more at home, but adding another lock on a cell only makes someone feel more trapped." He wipes his eyes and looks at me. "No offense, kid. You and Aiden are the greatest things to have ever happened to me, but it's not fair to assume motherhood would be the be-all and end-all of her happiness. I wanted her to stay mine so badly, I convinced her to do something I knew deep down she didn't want. To settle here and be a housewife. She is so much more than that. And you, Maggie, are so much more than Hyde Hill." I soak in his words as he takes another sip. "I worry that, over the years, I've put you in the same position."

"I—" My voice cracks as I prepare to tell him my deepest fears. My deepest desires. "I love our farm, and I want to work here, but I don't want to give up everything else, you know? I'm scared that if I take over, it will be the only thing I ever do. The only place I'll ever be." I clutch my glass to my chest. "I want to be free."

"Who says you can't have it all?"

I've watched him obsess over our farm. I watched him spend every minute of his life in the orchard. Watching him made me feel like there was only one way to run this place. "If I run the business, I want to be as dedicated as you are. You literally never leave the farm, except for conferences and to get supplies. I'd want to be rooted here the way you are. Hyde Hill is who I am. It's in our blood."

He sighs. "I was more adventurous with Delaney, but after she left, I poured all of my energy into the farm. Used it to avoid dealing with my broken heart. Don't use that as an example of what this job should be. It should be just that, a job. You are vast and wild like her. Sure, you grew up here, and working the orchard helped mold you, but no matter what you choose to do or where you end up, you have strong roots. And roots are—"

"Roots are advantageous," I say.

He smacks me on the back and laughs. "That's exactly right. You could travel to the ends of the earth and carry that power with you, always. As for the job...if you want it, it's yours. I'd be a fool not to offer it to you. And you can manage this property however you want. Being a good boss means knowing how to delegate and trusting your team. Hire a GM, hire a team, give yourself the freedom you need. Or don't. It's up to you, and there is no rush. Okay? I've got a lot of years left in me."

I feel warm tears on my cheek, and I bury my face in his shoulder. "I love you, Dad."

He wraps me up and kisses my head. "I love you so much, sweetheart." I pull away and wipe my eyes, catching my breath. "So you broke someone's nose, huh?"

I nod, wiping my nose with my coat sleeve. "So you took out a bad loan, huh?"

His laughter is loud and carefree as his head falls back, and he bellows his hiccupping chortle to the moon. "Sure did, kiddo. Sure did. Let's talk about your fuckup first. I talked with the dean after Dr. Young called. You've been suspended for next semester."

I take a sip of my drink and let it sink in. *Better than being expelled.* "Could've been worse, I guess. I'm sorry, Dad."

"What happened?"

I fill him in on Jesse and the history he and Aiden have from class. How Jesse was accosting us, and I thought Aiden was reaching for his knife when he was actually reaching for his phone. And how I punched Jesse in the face.

He sets down his glass. "And now, we're here," he says.

"And now, we're here."

"Sometimes, things happen out of nowhere that we can't control. I'm sorry you and Aiden had to put up with that punk, and I'm sorry you have to shoulder the consequences. I'm going to the university tomorrow to talk with the board of trustees about what happened. I don't know if I can get them to change their minds about your suspension, but this Jesse kid needs some consequences, too."

"You don't have to—"

"Yes, I do." He sighs and rubs the back of his head. "I'm sorry again for not telling you about the finances."

I wave in front of my face. "I think I've learned recently that life isn't so black and white."

"Oh yeah?"

I shrug. "Yeah. It's okay. We're all just trying to do our best, and sometimes, you break someone's nose or tell your daughter's girlfriend all our family business. It happens."

He laughs again. "You got yourself a good one in Olivia. How's her friend doing? Such a heartbreaking situation."

I stare over the tops of countless apple trees, and run my finger over the lip of my glass. "I wish I could give you an update, but punching someone in the face isn't the only bad thing I've done this week, and Olivia isn't currently speaking to me."

"Hmm. Care to enlighten your old man?"

"When I heard she didn't show, I asked Uncle Ward why, and he didn't give me a reason. And she didn't respond to my texts for a while, confirming in my head that she'd ditched you. I assumed the worst, but she's the best." I shake my head at my stupidity. "I don't know if she's still mine."

He grabs me by the scruff and gives me a little shake. "You've always been bright, Mags. I'm sure you'll figure it out." He stands and holds out a hand. "Come on. You need to head back."

I tug myself up and pack my Weller into the bag. "You're kicking me out?"

"You've got some studying to do and a girl to win over. My only advice: let her get through finals before you start begging for her back. Respect that she's dealing with more important things right now, okay?"

"Okay."

After my dad drives us back to the house, I sit in my truck and process our conversation as my windshield defogs. In my head, I had a father who wanted me to keep my nose to the grindstone. To stay focused every minute of my life and take Hyde Hill Farm as seriously as he does. I thought I had to be exactly that. Thought I had to force all of my funny fractures and wonky angles into the management role he'd carved. But I don't.

I'm—almost—twenty-one. Who knows what I'll do? I could go back to school and get my master's in public policy. I could travel the world. I could come home and take over the farm. And I could take over the farm and still get my master's, do research, and travel the world. I can figure all that out later.

There's one thing I need to figure out now.

CHAPTER TWENTY-TWO

O kay. So you're saying you want it to look bad and stupid?" Tessa asks. She and Ashley navigate the PowerPoint I'm trying to put together for Olivia. I've given her the space she needs, and it's been as easy as pulling on a wet, sandy bathing suit. But how am I supposed to get her back if, through trying to get her back, I give her another reason to not be with me? To ruin her finals week with a giant distraction would be like hand delivering a red flag.

"It's not bad and stupid. It's cute and stupid. I want every silly font and every epic transition." I lean over their shoulders and point. "Oh. There. Definitely a bunch of clip art, please."

Tessa selects a throbbing red heart and drops it on the slide titled "Ten-Year Plans Are for Suckers."

"Okay, that slide is golden," Ashley says. She clicks to the slide titled "My Life Was Upended. I Got Suspended." She scrolls through the cartoonish clippings. "This one needs something funny so she knows you're kidding."

"How am I kidding? It's the truth," I say.

Ashley turns. "I just think that you've never been happier. Even in this position, where you're fighting to get a girl back, you're at peace. I don't think you and Olivia would have ever worked if you didn't get to where you are now. Where your happiness doesn't hang on someone else, but is created here"—she pokes me softly in the chest—"in you."

I cover her hand with mine, pinning it against my heart. "Thank you," I say.

She grins and pulls her hand back. "Yeah. Of course."

"I think I should add one more slide." I close my eyes and think. "Choose your own adventure."

"What? No. Come on, Mags. What if she doesn't choose the answer you want? We're not making slideshow offshoots for every option," Tessa says.

"The reason I lost her in the first place is because I didn't trust her. We don't need a backup. I know what she'll pick."

Tessa and Ashley spend another half hour finishing my slideshow with me. After I make them show me three times how to access it and navigate all its features, we head upstairs to my room so I can grab my bag. I have to be off campus by five tonight because my suspension officially starts after today's last final.

It was a whirlwind of a week. I refused to have any birthday celebration on Sunday because everyone was cramming for exams. I was lucky to be so prepared, or my grades surely would have suffered from me being so scattered. And sad. I've been chest-achingly sad all week. Olivia made it very clear that she wasn't ready to talk by not speaking to me and sitting next to Laura for our final. But I can't let those feelings drown me because even though I'm exhaustingly depressed, I'm also hopeful. I feel like a brand-new person, a better and more complete version of myself. A version of myself who gets the girl. A version of myself who will be okay if I don't.

"You're sure you have everything?" Ashley asks.

I double-check my bag for my phone charger and laptop. "Yep. I think I'm good to go." Ashley gave me some insider information that Olivia will be driving to Asheville after her finals today. She should be leaving in about an hour.

"I can't believe you're missing half our junior year," Tessa says, her long curls bouncing from shoulder to shoulder as she shakes her head.

"Nothing's set in stone. I can appeal my suspension, and I will. But I'm going to focus on Olivia today. Then I'll figure out the rest."

"Okay. Call us if you need anything," Ashley says.

"I will."

❖

Hesitation and doubt swarm my brain as I raise my fist to knock on Olivia's door. A lot has happened since that Tuesday, and I hope she can see I'm not the same person I was last week. I hope she can see me.

"What are you doing here?"

I drop my fist, swallow, and gather the courage to turn and face her. My duffel bag cuts into my shoulder, and I drop it at my feet. I take one more awkward second, then I turn. Olivia stands in the hall with a cup of coffee and a bag of Chex Mix. Her hair is in a messy bun, and she wears the clear plastic glasses she only wears when she's tired or her contacts are hurting her. She's wrapped in a gray Hudson High sweatshirt and her coat.

I point to the Chex Mix. "The, uh…the rye chips are the best," I say.

She stares at me and pushes her glasses up her nose, looking annoyed. After a second, she says, "Obviously."

The fact that she said anything at all gives me a sliver of hope. "Road snacks, huh?"

She sighs and looks to the ceiling, seemingly gathering something. Then she looks at me, and I notice the dullness in her eyes. They're bloodshot-pink and bleary. She scratches her forehead, careful not to whack herself with the bag. "What do you want? I'm on my way out."

I take a step toward her, and she raises her brows, stopping me in my tracks. "I want twenty minutes of your time. That's it."

She shakes her head. "I can't do this, Maggie. I have to go."

She brushes my shoulder as she walks past me to her dorm. When she's about to open the door, I blurt, "I didn't deserve you when I had you." She pauses, gripping the doorknob. I swallow. *Now or never.* "We would have never worked out if the last week and a half didn't happen. I needed to mess everything up to grow into who I'm supposed to be. And the person that I've become…*that person* finally gets it. That person is someone who could date Olivia Cypress," I say.

Her hand falls to her hip, and she turns.

"Let me show you," I say. "Twenty minutes. That's it."

She groans. "Fine. Twenty minutes. That's it."

I can't help but grin. "Okay. But the timer doesn't start until we get there."

"Get where?"

"The greenhouses, of course."

❖

My suspension was pretty clear about my access being revoked from the entire university until my senior year, but Dr. Petrova hasn't asked for my key to the greenhouses back, so I'm going to pretend it's okay. I snuck in last night to make sure the projector was still here. It's the perfect spot for my PowerPoint. We have a memory here, it's warm, and a bunch of beautiful plants can't hurt. I pull down the white screen behind the workbench. It seems weird to have a projector setup in a greenhouse, but we have classes in here sometimes and use it to play videos of grafting techniques or to display class notes.

I plug in my laptop, just like Tessa and Ashley told me, and fire up the projector.

Olivia takes a sip of coffee and watches me with an amused smirk. "What is going on? Last I checked, you're terrible at this stuff."

I slide a chair from behind the workbench and position it in front of the screen. Perfectly square. I dust it off and pat the seat. "Come sit." She rolls her eyes and takes another sip of coffee. "Oh, come on. It's the best seat in the house, and it's a sold-out show."

She finally sits in the plastic chair, her legs crossed and brow raised. She looks like a sexy strict librarian as she watches me open my presentation. My nerves prickle, and I take a few deep breaths before I enter full screen and begin.

I grab my little clicker and stand tall next to the screen. Clear my throat. "Thank you, Miss Cypress, for attending my presentation tonight. As you can see from my first slide, this presentation is titled 'Maggie Effed Up but Is Better Now.' Enjoy."

I glance at Olivia and see a hint of a smile as I click to the next slide. My signature transition fills the greenhouse with the sound of an airplane zooming by. I read the title. "'I Failed to Trust, Now You Are Disgust.' This slide details the horrible mistake I made when I berated you about being prepared to meet with my father. Then being an asshole when I thought you bailed. But what I've learned is that was just a sign that I wasn't ready to accept something else…"

I click. The next slide is the one titled "Ten-Year Plans Are for Suckers." She chuckles against the plastic lid of her coffee. "I see you like the title of this one," I say. She looks at me and smiles, nodding for me to continue. My heart swells. "Right. As the last slide stated, I came to realize that my dumb actions weren't the root of the problem. My fear of letting go of the life I thought I wanted for the life I know I want—the life you opened my eyes to—possessed me and turned me into a terrible person." I click, and the clip art of a ghost zooms in from the side. She chuckles again, and I know I'm nailing it.

Before I move on, I look at her. "I'm really sorry, Olivia. I hope you understand what I'm trying to say. I wasn't afraid of being with you or of you being late to work. I was afraid of what I truly wanted. Freedom."

She stays silent but nods again, her foot bouncing casually.

"The next slides are more of an update on my life," I say and switch to the next. "'My Life Was Upended, I Got Suspended.'"

Olivia chokes on her coffee and plants both feet on the ground. "What? You got suspended? What happened?"

I nod to the PowerPoint, which has a bulleted list of the events of the fight, but her eyes are on me. "Aiden's bully was instigating a fight outside the dining hall. He shoved Aiden twice. And the second time, I thought Aiden was reaching for his knife." Her jaw drops into her lap, and I wave in front of my face. "He wasn't, but I thought he was. So to avoid letting Aiden make a huge mistake, I punched the guy in the face and broke his nose."

She covers her mouth with her hand, her eyes wide. "What? Oh my God. How long?"

"Well, it only took a second, I reckon."

She squeezes her eyes shut and shakes her head. "No. How long are you suspended?"

"Oh. One semester."

She stands and walks to me. I hold my breath as she reaches for me and squeezes my arm. "Are you okay?" she asks.

I nod. "Yeah. It was actually a very liberating experience. The fight and the suspension." She lingers and smiles. "Excuse me, ma'am. We're on a schedule." I nod to her seat.

She drops her hand and walks back to her chair. "I'm glad you broke it," she says over her shoulder.

"Broke it?"

"His nose."

I laugh and suck in a deep breath. "Yep." I shake my head at the memory. "It was a gusher, too."

"*Ugh.*"

"Yeah. Okay, stop distracting me. Now, for the final part." I click through another awesome transition to my "Choose Your Own Adventure" slide.

"Oh, geez. What now?" she asks.

"Now you get to play a little game. You get to…choose your own adventure," I announce in my best game-show-host voice. I click and read her first question. "Miss Cypress, would you prefer to see the slide labeled 'She Accepted Maggie's Apology,' or the slide labeled 'Maggie Is a Dickface'?"

She throws her head back and laughs. "I really want to pick 'Maggie Is a Dickface,' but…I'm going to have to choose 'She Accepted Maggie's Apology' for two hundred, please."

I bite my lip to stop myself from completely cheesing out. "Lovely choice. Lovely choice, Olivia," I say, and it takes a metric ton of willpower not to run to her and kiss her. I click and read, "'Maggie is in eternal gratitude for your forgiveness.'"

She chuckles, her eyes wide. "Wow. Cocky much?"

I point my clicker at her. "Ashley warned me you'd think that. But it was my attempt to show you that I trust you."

"Oh. I—"

"One more slide." I click to the next. "Two, actually. If you pick the right adventure." I wink. "Okay. Would you rather tell Maggie to kick rocks or give her a chance to show you how much she's grown?" I pause and look at her. I've felt pretty confident up until this moment. Olivia stares at me, her fingers lightly drumming her coffee lid. Then a mischievous grin spreads over her lips.

"What are you doing right now? Are you free, or do you have somewhere you need to be?" she asks, her eyes superglued to mine.

"What? I, uh…no?"

She bites her lip and stands. "All of this growth and you still haven't learned the difference between a choice question and a yes or no question. I'm disappointed, love," she says as she steps into my space.

"Free. I'm free," I sputter.

"Feel like going for a ride?" She jangles her keys. "Could use some company and I want you to meet Riley. He could use the distraction of friends."

It worked. *It totally worked.* "I'm in. But I want some road snacks, too. Peanut M&M's."

She stands on her tiptoes and leans in, only an inch from my mouth. My grip on the clicker is so tight, I may crack the damn thing. Her warm breath tickles my lips, and I shut my eyes, hoping she'll close the small space.

"Deal," she whispers. Her lips are dry, and her mouth tastes like coffee. The kiss is delicious and comfortable and sexy. It's *perfect.* She slides the clicker out of my grip and hits the button.

The last slide zooms into frame. It reads, "I missed you so fucking much" with the cheesiest clip art heart I could find.

She drapes her arms around my neck. "I missed you, too," she says. "It's been a really hard week without you."

"You can tell me all about it in the car." I pull her into a tight hug, reveling in the feel of her in my arms again. It felt like years I was without her.

She kisses my neck and pulls back to look at me. "We need to make one quick stop first."

❖

Olivia starts her car. Not any old junker like the rest of us have; she drives a new-looking Toyota RAV4 hybrid. I knew she was fancy. I wiggle my butt into the creamy leather seat and flip on the seat heater. "Wait. Are these real leather?"

"Not a chance. Buckle up."

I do as commanded, and she drives us down the university's driveway. I can tell she's a good driver. She must take extra care to not let her calamities follow her behind the wheel. "Where are we going?"

She grins and squeezes my knee. "You'll see."

The car slows as the road levels out into the valley, and she flips on her blinker. "The Greasy Grouse?"

She parks in a spot far from the entrance, and I wonder if it's so no one scratches her car. Didn't peg her for the type. "Is that okay? I could use something more substantial than Chex Mix."

"Yeah, but…" I try to give her a serious look.

She laughs and says, "We'll still get M&M's. Don't worry."

"Peanut."

"The only kind worth getting. Obviously." She leans over the console and gives me a quick kiss. "But first, real food."

I nod, ready to replace the memory of the last time I was here, last week. They hadn't decorated for Christmas then, but when I open the door for Olivia, we're blitzed with lights and every crafty Christmas decoration imaginable, including an upsettingly lifelike and life-sized Santa standing next to the host stand and a giant tree decorated in green and red lights and handmade ornaments in the far corner. The merriment is contagious.

"Wow," I hear myself say. I turn to Olivia, whose eyes are bright as she scans the diner.

She slips her hand in mine. "They're over there. Come on." She guides me through the glowing diner to a big booth close to the Christmas tree. In that booth are my best friends: Tessa, Ashley, Aiden, and Scott. My entire chest is molten with warmth and gratitude as Olivia and I slide in the ends of the booth.

I'm muttering a confused hello and about to ask how the hell everyone is here when the server presents me with a colossal lava cake topped with whipped cream—surprise whipped cream—and a single candle. "Happy birthday, sweetheart," the lady says and disappears into Santa's workshop again.

My eyes sting with tears, my emotions raw from all the highs and lows of the last couple of weeks. "Guys," I say, my voice cracking.

Tessa grips my shoulder and gives me a gentle shake. "You didn't think we were going to let you get away without a celebration, did you?"

"I…I don't know." I blink a few times, my brain trying to absorb everything as my friends begin to sing.

Olivia's foot taps my ankle, and she smiles a smile that steals the glory from every Christmas light in this joint. "Make a wish," she says.

I take a moment and blow out the candle.

Aiden swipes a finger through the whipped cream and pops it in his mouth. "Thought you might not be able to blow 'em all out."

I laugh. "It was tricky, but I managed." Everyone grabs a spoon and dives into the absurdly large lava cake. Hot chocolate pours out of the brownie and mixes with melting ice cream and whipped cream in a delicious mess. I wipe my mouth, my teeth aching from the onslaught of sugar. "Can someone explain how you're all here?"

Aiden sips his Coke and grins. "It was a pretty complicated plan, so try to stay with me, okay?"

I nod. "Okay."

"I talked to Olivia. Case closed."

"What? How did you know she'd be willing to come? How did you know I'd come?"

Olivia clears her throat and interjects. "Aid, your explanation was great and all, but do you mind if I hop in and clear up the rest?"

He points his spoon at her. "All yours, Liv."

She pushes the chocolate massacre to the end of the table and leans on her elbows. "Aiden came over the night before you made your slideshow and told me what you were up to."

"Aid, what the hell?" I say. He shrugs.

Olivia squeezes my wrist. "He didn't get into details—I didn't know about the fight—but he told me you talked to your dad and had reevaluated everything. That I should give you a chance to show me. He told me your plans to try to win me over and that everyone was going to have dinner here tonight as a birthday surprise before break. I tried to speak, but he just said I was your ride and left before I could answer."

I blink in surprise. Aiden made this all happen. "Aid—"

"I love you, Mags. Happy birthday," he says.

I can't control them anymore. The tears escape my eyes, and Tessa pulls me into her chest. "Damn, dude. You made her cry."

The booth fills with soft chuckles.

"You're a Sagittarius, right?" Scott says from across the table.

I wipe my eyes with my sleeve and nod.

"She is now," Ashley says through a big smile.

"Yeah. She finally accepted her true, adventuring, Sagittarius self," Tessa says.

"Congratulations, Maggie." Aiden grabs the menu. "Okay. We're ordering real food, right? I'm starving."

My stomach growls, and I snag myself a menu, too. "Yes, please. I could eat everything in the kitchen."

"Hey." Olivia's foot rubs the inside of my ankle. "How's that ten-year plan going these days?" The smirk on her face is every bit as condescending as it is sexy. I deserve it.

I crack into a grin. "I'd say it's about as intact as Jesse's nose."

Everyone erupts into laughter, and Scott asks, "What'd you wish for?"

I take a moment to come up with something. "World peace, obviously," I say, and everyone chuckles at my *Miss Congeniality* reference.

I don't tell anyone—not even Olivia—that I didn't make a wish before I blew out the candle. Wishes are for suckers, and I just want to live my life minute by minute, one day at a time, with the people I love.

EPILOGUE

Olivia cuddles into me as we walk with my family through our small Christmas tree plot on the edge of the orchard. It's tradition to plant one tree every spring and saw one down every winter for the holidays. After our trip to Asheville, I convinced Olivia to spend a couple days at the farm before she goes back home to her mom's for Christmas.

Aiden points to a medium-size tree with some bare patches. "No way. It ain't full enough yet," Uncle Ward says.

We stroll past them to the other side of the plot. "Oh. I think that's the one," Olivia whispers. The snow-covered fir stands tall and fat among the other trees, making it known that it is *the one*. My dad, Ward, and Aiden gather around.

"That's it. Good eye, Liv," my dad says and drops to his knees with the saw. Ward steadies the tree as he cuts through the trunk.

Back at the house, we sip spiked hot chocolate and decorate the tree by the fire. My dad plays Elvis's *Christmas Album*—the best Christmas album in the world—on the record player, and Olivia sits next to me on the couch, taking a break from decorating.

"I was thinking," she whispers.

I take a sip of my hot chocolate and lick the whipped cream from my upper lip. "Oh yeah? What about?"

"I think I know the first place we should explore together in the new year. If you're up for it, of course."

"Reckon I'd go anywhere with you."

She smiles and kisses my cheek. "We'll see about that." She swallows. "I was thinking maybe Nashville…"

"Oh." I rub her thigh and run my tongue over my sugarcoated teeth. I think about how I've felt my mom with me the last month. In the snow, in the whipped cream, in my dad's support, and in the new strength I feel. The letters in my desk drawer hold so many pleas to see me. So many apologies. Desperate explanations. Ten-dollar bills. And a shit ton of love. I think I'm finally at a place to accept that love. And to accept my mom.

"Yeah." I clear my throat. "I can think of someone we may be able to stay with."

She gasps. "Really?"

I squeeze her hand and smile. "Yeah. It's about time." She lies her head against my shoulder as we watch Uncle Ward use the stepladder to perch the angel on top of the tree.

"It's perfect," my dad says.

Everything is as it should be. My family is together with Olivia; we helped get Riley situated in Asheville; and the appeal for my suspension was denied, but it was for the best. AQF has supercharged their efforts thanks to my suspension and complete lack of punishment for Jesse by the university. And Olivia talked with her professors to switch her work internship to next semester instead of senior year. So we get to travel around in the spring while she works with my dad to get the orchard back on track. Her plan seems like it's going to work. My dad checked his Hyde pride at the door and set up a meeting with Olivia and her finance supervisor, just to make sure it was a viable solution.

It is.

As for me? All I can say is this evening is lovely. I'm sure tomorrow will be, too.

About the Author

Ana is an award-winning author of sapphic romance. She worked in the Pacific Northwest wine industry for eight years and now lives in her hometown of Atlanta, Georgia, with her wife, their fluffy German shepherd, and a mildly evil cat. She loves all things fermented or distilled, walking the local trails, and eating pastries. So many pastries. She is currently working on her next book and dreaming of a beach trip.

Books Available From Bold Strokes Books

Before She Was Mine by Emma L McGeown. When Dani and Lucy are thrust together to sort out their children's playground squabble, sparks fly, leaving both of them willing to risk it all for each other. (978-1-63679-315-3)

Chasing Cypress by Ana Hartnett Reichardt. Maggie Hyde wants to find a partner to settle down with and help her run the family farm, but instead she ends up chasing Cypress. Olivia Cypress. (978-1-63679-323-8)

Dark Truths by Sandra Barett. When Jade's ex-girlfriend and vampire maker barges back into her life, can Jade satisfy her ex's demands, keep Beth safe, and keep everyone's secrets…secret? (978-1-63679-369-6)

Desires Unleashed by Renee Roman. Kell Murphy and Taylor Simpson didn't go looking for love, but as they explore their desires unleashed, their hearts lead them on an unexpected journey. (978-1-63679-327-6)

Here For You by D. Jackson Leigh. A horse trainer must make a difficult business decision that could save her father's ranch from foreclosure but destroy her chance to win the heart of a feisty barrel racer vying for a spot in the National Rodeo Finals. (978-1-63679-299-6)

Maybe, Probably by Amanda Radley. Set against the backdrop of a viral pandemic, Gina and Eleanor are about to discover that loving another person is complicated when you're desperately searching for yourself. (978-1-63679-284-2)

The One by C.A. Popovich. Jody Acosta doesn't know what makes her more furious, that the wealthy Bergeron family refuses to be held accountable for her father's wrongful death, or that she can't ignore her knee-weakening attraction to Nicole Bergeron. (978-1-63679-318-4)

Tides of Love by Kimberly Cooper Griffin. Falling in love is the last thing on either of their minds, but when Mikayla and Gem meet, sparks of possibility begin to shine, revealing a future neither expected. (978-1-63679-319-1)

Catch by Kris Bryant. Convincing the wife of the star quarterback to walk away from her family was never in offensive coordinator Sutton McCoy's game plan. But standing on the sidelines when a second chance at true love comes her way proves all but impossible. (978-1-63679-276-7)

Hearts in the Wind by MJ Williamz. Beth and Evelyn seem destined to remain mortal enemies but are about to discover that in matters of the heart, sometimes you must cast your fortunes to the wind. (978-1-63679-288-0)

Hero Complex by Jesse J. Thoma. Bronte, Athena, and their unlikely friends must work together to defeat Bronte's archnemesis. The fate of love, humanity, and the world might depend on it. No pressure. (978-1-63679-280-4)

Hotel Fantasy by Piper Jordan. Molly Taylor has a fantasy in mind that only Lexi can fulfill. However, convincing her to participate could prove challenging. (978-1-63679-207-1)

Last New Beginning by Krystina Rivers. Can commercial broker Skye Kohl and contractor Bailey Kaczmarek overcome their pride and work together while the tension between them boils over into a love that could soothe both of their hearts? (978-1-63679-261-3)

Love and Lattes by Karis Walsh. Cat café owner Bonnie and wedding planner Taryn join forces to get rescue cats into forever homes— discovering their own forever along the way. (978-1-63679-290-3)

Repatriate by Jaime Maddox. Ally Hamilton's new job as a home health aide takes an unexpected twist when she discovers a fortune in stolen artwork and must repatriate the masterpieces and avoid the wrath of the violent man who stole them. (978-1-63679-303-0)

The Hues of Me and You by Morgan Lee Miller. Arlette Adair and Brooke Dawson almost fell in love in college. Years later, they unexpectedly run into each other and come face-to-face with their unresolved past. (978-1-63679-229-3)